PROTECTED HEART

QUEENS OF KINGS (BOOK 3)

LAQUETTE

PROTECTED HEART

QUEENS OF KINGS (BOOK 3)

LAQUETTE

DEDICATION

To Doris D. (Grandma) for teaching me that, "Old Man Can't has been dead a long time."

ACKNOWLEDGMENTS

To God, from whom all blessings flow, thank you for the gift, the desire, the support, and the opportunity. To Damon, this does not happen without you. Love you forever. To Sterling and Semaj, my heartbeats, the best parts of me. To my family and friends, thank you for putting up with my craziness. To Sarah and Hot Ink Press, thank you for the opportunity and the support. To Shyla Colt, thank you for treating me with such kindness and for always opening your door to my many crazy questions. To Piper Kay, I will never be able to thank you for making me, "Push the fucking button." To Elizabeth, thank you for making my crazy sound amazing. To Lexie Craig, thank you for supplying me with my new motto, "Hustle until you don't have to introduce yourself" (unknown). To all of my JMC and LIJ people, your love strengthens me. To Samantha, thank you for doing what you do. To my Loungers, you guys hold me down and keep me going. Thank you so much for the loyalty and encouragement. To the readers, you will never know how much I have loved writing the Queens of Kings series. Thank you for taking this journey with me.

Keep it sexy,
LaQuette

COPYRIGHT ACKNOWLEDGEMENTS

Protected Heart
Queens of Kings (Book 3)

When trust becomes a matter of life or death...

Heart Searlington, captain of the seventy-fourth precinct in Brooklyn, New York, has everything she could ever want. The sexy as sin husband, the perfect house, and the perfect addition to their family, four-month-old Amare.

But when a senseless act of violence threatens the lives of two people she loves, Heart does what comes natural to her...she protects what's hers.

Kenneth Searlington, billionaire real estate tycoon, is living the ultimate dream—family, friends, and wealth. Life couldn't be more perfect, until trusting the wrong friend puts his life on the line.

When he can't trust friends or family, Kenneth takes matters into his own hands. Who should Kenneth trust? The wife who lied, or the friend and family who betrayed him? Maybe the only person he can trust is himself?

When protecting the heart she loves forces Heart to omit certain truths about herself and those she loves, can Kenneth see past her betrayal long enough for her to keep him alive?

PROLOGUE

*K*enneth felt the blessed warmth of wet suction around the length of his cock. There was only one thing that brought this specific kind of pleasure and just the thought of it had him ready to spill this magnificent morning nut before consciousness had fully taken over his mind.

"Fuck," he growled out and opened his eyes just enough to witness the portrait of his wonderful wife looking up at him with a mouthful of his cock.

She continued the quick downward slide of those full cider-colored lips, winked good morning to him, taking a painfully slow glide back to the tip. She circled that angry crown with a light flick of her tongue, forcing him to clamp his fist at the base, just to keep the moment from ending prematurely.

He wove tight fingers into the wayward strands of hair falling all around her face, pulling her head back and painting her lips with his sensitive tip. "If you want this to last more than five minutes I'd suggest you keep that sweet mouth of yours to yourself," he hissed through clenched teeth.

She lashed out her agile tongue and passed it through his now-dripping slit, collecting the clear pearl that sat so perfectly at his tip.

"Who says I need more than five minutes?" she asked, the sexy curve of her lips bending into an alluring smile. "I've got a busy schedule today; let's make this happen, rich boy."

He quickly snaked strong hands beneath her arms and pulled her up the length of his body. Loving the human blanket splayed all over him, he closed his eyes and reveled in the feel of her skin against his. He grabbed a handful of her ass and pushed her down on him, her folds wrapping perfectly around the tight skin of his shaft pulling a synchronous moan of pleasure from both of them.

He didn't need to check and see if she was ready, the way she was dripping down his length, bathing his balls, there was no question she was just as eager as he to get this particular session of bumping and grinding started. Without opening his eyes, he pulled her up until she straddled his waist and moved a hand between them to steady himself as she rolled her hips in that perfect way that made his fucking toes curl and his eyes roll back inside his head.

She went to cant her hips forward and he locked steel fingers around her hips to keep from moving. He pulled her down to him and held her mouth in the perfect position for him to drink from her.

Tongue, teeth, lips clashing against one another made his blood spit with passion. When he was done, he brought down a firm hand across her ass and listened for the little hitch in her breath that let him know it was just this side of painful mixed in with a whole lot of pleasure.

"Work that shit, Mrs. Searlington," he growled, his voice sodden with heat. He felt her walls clamp down on him. It was their little code, their reminder of who they were when they each stripped away the world and stepped into this room. Here, she was his wife, and he was her husband and no other title mattered.

He grabbed her hips and urged her to pick up the pace. He wasn't lying when he'd said this was going to be quick. Heart's hot mouth on him was like elementary school math, one plus the other meant ragingly quick orgasm. A lesser man would be embarrassed by that. Kenneth knew that shit had nothing to do with his stamina and everything to do with the fact that his woman gave the best blow jobs ever.

There wasn't a trick in his past that had ever brought him this much pleasure. Once this woman walked into his life, all others ceased to exist.

He pushed up, meeting her movements with as much force and fire as she gave him resulting in that distinct smacking sound that only came from fucking. Her walls began that familiar locking motion that signaled her end. Her muscles frozen as she peaked and fought against the powerful spasms rocking through her. He kept up a steady rhythm; he could feel his climax ascending the length of his spine. He wrapped a firm arm around her waist and pulled her down onto the bed leaving her a little bit stunned.

He pulled out and let his legs fall over the side of the bed. He stood at the end, gave her a knowing look and watched as she cat-crawled across the bed. When she reached him, she turned over on her back and let her head hang over the edge of the bed. She licked her lips once, and opened her mouth as wide as her jaws would allow.

He stood still as she slowly swallowed him, and waited for that glorious moment when the very tip of his cock was wedged inside her throat. He was so ready, and she knew it. He pumped once inside of her mouth and he felt the fire edging him closer to his peak.

"Shit woman," was all he was able to say before she swallowed around him and set off the familiar chain reaction. His balls pulled up and he felt the first spurt fill her mouth. The sight of the graceful curve of her neck moving in a swallowing motion taking all of him down made for an irresistibly erotic image that he never tired of seeing.

When he was finally able to control the movement of his own body, he pulled out of her mouth and collapsed onto the bed with her. His eyelids too tired to open; he felt her moving around the bed. Soon her head was resting against his chest and her arm was secured around his waist. He found the strength to smile and snuggled deeper under the arm currently holding him hostage, the contact of their sweat-slicked skin sizzling with a satisfying after burn.

"Baby," he wheezed in a noisy puff of air. "You can wake me up like that anytime you want."

"Is that so," she answered.

Breathing was just too difficult and air just too precious for him to
waste either on words.

He simply nodded his answer instead.

"Well, then maybe we should arrange things so we can play hooky
and spend the day in bed?"

He turned over and looked down at her. She wasn't slick, and he
knew exactly what she was doing.

"So that's what this little morning seduction was all about? You're
trying to deter me from my plan?"

She rolled her eyes. "Don't make it sound so sinister."

"Heart, you know I have to do this."

"Kenneth, the only thing I know is that I have a bad feeling about
this. Just stay here with me and forget about all that's supposed to
go on."

He leaned down pressing a firm kiss to her mouth. It made something inside him break a little to see the first signs of disappointment
pulling at her face.

"Heart, I have to do this. Please, I don't need resistance from you, I
need your support. Please," he asked. "I need you with me on this."

She pulled her bottom lip in and nodded her head. "Fine," she
conceded. "I'll be there, but for the record, I'm not happy about this at
all, Kenneth. Not one bit."

She pulled out of his embrace and soon he heard the spray of the
shower heads running. It was never a good day when his wife didn't
welcome him into her shower. Shower time always mean an extra few
minutes of marital fun before they began their individual days.

"Let's just hope this isn't a precursor for the rest of my day."

CHAPTER 1

*C*aptain Heart Searlington shifted her eyes across the expanse of the buzzing crowd from her vantage point in the van. On the outside they looked like every other news vehicle parked in the area. On the inside, there was state of the art surveillance equipment mounted to all of the van's walls to help them stay in contact with their team and monitor the scene from all possible angles. She and her second were hiding in plain sight monitoring the changing landscape.

After more than a decade on the job, and more than a few in command, her trained sight looked for chinks in the protective armor she and her precinct had put in place to protect everyone in attendance today. Sure, it was supposed to be a regular news opportunity, no vetted threat of danger that she and her people knew of, but in a situation like this, something that could go from mild and innocuous to crazy and deadly in a heartbeat, she wasn't inclined to take that chance with their lives. The people that were gathered in the streets, the officers that were under her command, and the husband that was sitting on the raised platform, waiting to take his place behind the podium to address the crowd. No, these lives were too precious for her not to prepare for the worst while praying for the best.

She passed her eyes again across what was fast becoming a large gathering of people. The inhabitants of the East New York neighborhood were eager to see what all the buzz was about. Some peeking out of their windows, curtains shifting to the side were the only clue that someone was actually watching. Others, those more brave and curious, were flocking to fill the empty block of Autumn Avenue between the South Conduit Boulevard and Pitkin Avenue to see why the news vans were lined up on their streets. One side of the block taken up by the massive mega-church that served the community, the other side of the block filled by Mac's Place, the community outreach center overseen by a partnership between her beloved Seventy-fourth precinct, The Greater Mount Zion Baptist Church, and the East New York community that she was sworn to protect.

These were her streets and her people. She'd grown up here, taken her initial post here as an officer in order to give back to the neighborhood that had raised her. East New York was rough, brutal, and violent at times, but it was also home and she'd decided a long time ago that it and the people who inhabited it were worth her protection and her respect.

She knew these people, and they knew her. Through the years she'd built a solid reputation in this community as a tough but fair cop. Although most of the resident thugs kept their distance from the lady cop that didn't play, there were some that would still try her if given the chance. Those were the fuckers she was looking for this morning. Those that would put her will and her command to the test and endanger the people of her beloved community and the husband that she loved more than her own life.

Her eyes backtracked to find the subject of her thoughts. Kenneth Searlington, the man who'd plowed into her life four and a half years ago and nearly smothered her with love was smiling and talking with his attorney, A.J. Tenetti, seemingly unbothered by the buzzing of the assembling throng of people and news crews. He was wearing his usual smooth business veneer. Posture confident, smile welcoming, and eyes bright with intelligence, he was too damn sexy for his own good and definitely for hers too.

She tore her gaze from Kenneth's polished form and it landed hard on his attorney's. The sight of Alexis-Jeovonni—A.J.—Tenetti always made Heart roll her eyes, sometimes with just her mind, most times in front of the woman's face. Friend and confidant to Kenneth, he viewed A.J. and the rest of the Tenettis as family. Heart saw them more as an annoyance and A.J. as problematic. She didn't really know what it was, hadn't put her finger on it in the last four and a half years, but there was something off about that young woman and her family that her husband either chose to ignore or was actually blind to. Either way, Heart always kept an eye on her to make certain whatever bullshit that woman had going on didn't bury her husband.

Heart heard the voice of her second in command pull her out of her thoughts. "Looks like this shindig is about to start," Bryan Smyth's calm tone flowed through the van. "Is everyone in position? Sound off."

She listened one by one as team members announced their positions. There were uniformed officers on the streets, setting up barricades and mixing in with the crowds, but with her husband out there, she wouldn't leave his safety to just anyone. There, but unseen, Bryan's team of detectives were placed strategically all with the same goal in mind. Keep anything from out there from hurting her husband.

Smyth took his hand off the button that controlled the microphone and turned to her. "You figured out what we're looking for, if anything at all?"

She shook her head. She didn't have anything concrete, nothing more than concern, or what

Kenneth had termed a wife's paranoia. But her skin was tight and itchy with worry. Something was off, and she wanted to be prepared for it.

"I've been trying ever since Kenneth decided to get this project underway for him to take a more behind the scenes position. But he won't listen. It has to be him publicly fundraising for this venture, has to be him doing the press junkets to get public interest and support. I just don't feel so good about people connecting his face to this project."

"Mac, you gotta know why he's so determined to do this himself, why he won't just pass it off to some anonymous face to represent his interests."

She took a deep breath. Yeah, she knew why, but damn if that made her feel better.

"I know why, and I understand it, but it bothers me that he's still so affected by the past.

Guilt like that is dangerous, it's going to lead him somewhere neither of us wants him to go."

The silence took over again; nothing new when they were on the job. She and Smyth had spent years sitting on stakeouts like this, sometimes hours passing before either of them mumbled a word. They each watched and waited, for what exactly, only time would determine that, but she and her team would be ready. They were always ready, that's just how they rolled.

Tired of the silence, Smyth opened the door and stepped outside.

"I'm gonna make my rounds, you stay put and monitor things. If something pops off, we're gonna need eyes on all angles."

She nodded, not really liking the plan, but agreeing to it. In her role as Captain she'd tried to learn to take a step back from the action —tried being the operative word—which still kind of pissed her off, by the way. Her role of captain was to guide and supervise now, not to be in the middle of the action. That was Bryan's bag now.

She ran the house, he managed command. Yeah, she knew that, but that didn't mean she was dancing a jig about not being the one to set up the plan for today. It wasn't what she wanted, especially where her husband's safety was in question. Her natural instinct was to be out there, gun in hand; daring anyone to fuck with what was hers. But that wasn't her job any longer, that was Bryan's and she had to swallow that fucking huge pill on a daily basis since she'd accepted her promotion to captain.

She was captain and they both knew that she had the final say about everything concerning the precinct and the personnel, but if she undermined her second's authority with their subordinates, there would be anarchy in the house. And that shit she just couldn't have. So she stomped down on the beast that wanted to jump in and control everything and sat back in the van while the rest of their team took a more active role in their operation.

A quick glare of red light bounced off of the podium area and snatched her attention.

"Smyth, did you see that?"

"Yeah," Bryan answered. "Everyone in position, find the source. It's coming from the roof of one of the adjacent buildings."

The steady dancing red light that was bouncing off of her husband's jacket lapel validated the uneasy feeling she'd been carrying around the moment she'd found out this event would be taking place.

"On my way," she spat into the air. Not waiting for further communication from her team, she hopped out of the van and headed for the podium.

~

"You're certain you still want to do this? Once you put this information out there, you'll never be able to take it back."

Kenneth Searlington sat next to his lawyer and childhood friend, A.J. Tenetti and smiled at her. She was the pain-in-the-ass kid sister of his best friend growing up. She annoyed and made them both miserable as children, usually by tattling to her parents about whatever secret plans he and John were attempting to execute. She'd thrown them under the bus countless times, and danced a jig when she'd done it, but as much as she loved seeing the two of them in trouble, she would always come to their rescue, ready to do battle with anyone that tried to do them harm.

That protective streak and her brilliance with law made her the only candidate when he sought legal representation for matters both personal and business-related. She fought for him harder than any of his own biological family members, and when he'd decided to take on this project, she'd been the one whose help he knew would be vital to his success. And even though there were more than a few years between them in age, she was still determined to protect him and his peace of mind, even if that meant protecting him against himself.

"I have to do this, A.J."

She shook her head. "No you don't. You can walk away at any moment. You can repay all the money you've raised, and completely walk away from this unscathed. You don't have to wear the guilt of the past like a cloak, Kenneth. Just say the word and I'll shut this shit down. I know that cop wife of yours would agree with me. Hell, it would be the only thing the two of us will ever agree on."

Kenneth laughed. She was right, his wife, and his surrogate sister weren't besties. The truth, they hardly tolerated each other's presence. They smiled politely and exchanged pleasantries, but as soon as that was over they each moved to their respective corners and stayed in them until the party was over.

Kenneth ran his finger in a circular pattern around his temple and blew out a long breath. This shit was getting old really quickly and it needed to stop. He was beyond caring why they didn't like each other, although he knew absolutely why, he just wanted the two women he was closest to, the two women he loved, to get along and play nice. It was more important now than ever.

"This is essential to me, A. J., I need to do this. I couldn't do it for her while she was living;

I have to at least give her this in death."

A.J. shook her head and threw up her hands in submission.

"Whatever you say, Kenneth, it's time to get started. I have other business to deal with today besides this sideshow circus."

He reached a friendly hand across the armrest and gave her hand a gentle squeeze.

"Thank you," he whispered.

"For what? Helping you make a mockery of your family's name?" she answered letting her irritation color the air around them.

"For being my friend, and helping me do what I needed to do to put my sister's memory to rest, even when you didn't agree with it."

"Yeah well…don't be surprised when my bill is heftier than usual. There's a surcharge for getting on my nerves and not doing as I say."

Kenneth laughed. She said it with a smile, but he was damn sure she wasn't joking. Her time and her skills weren't cheap, but he'd never regretted paying her lofty fees because she'd always come through without fail.

"Send the paper work to Abby and I'll have your money wired to you by the end of business."

She clucked her tongue and let her siren red lips spread into a wide and contagious grin.

"Now that, my friend, is what I like to hear, a man that's about paying me my money."

Kenneth shook his head and stood up and buttoned the navy blue suit jacket hanging perfectly from his broad shoulders. He looked out over the crowd that filled the streets and looked for any familiar faces. He knew his wife and her team were around, exactly where, he wasn't certain. He knew she was close, he could feel her. He always felt her when she was near.

He'd wanted his wife by his side, it was only proper for the type of announcement he was about to make, but being caught on camera was still a little tricky for her. As a police captain she rarely if ever worked undercover anymore, but a few years ago she and her team had uncovered a prostitution ring that had called for her to play a key role in an undercover operation. Since then, brass wanted her out of the spotlight and so public news conferences held by her wealthy husband were strictly forbidden at this time.

Kenneth walked up to the podium and held on tightly to its edges. It wasn't that he was afraid of public speaking, no, in his line of work of commercial real estate; he made his living by waxing poetic about the properties held by his company. But this was different, this was about something real, someone who was real, and his emotions were bubbling just enough underneath the surface of his skin that he was a little off his usual confident center.

He ran his thumb over the thick platinum band on his wedding finger. It was a habit, one that always soothed him when he wanted to be near his wife. He took a breath and calmed himself, and cleared his throat before speaking.

"Good morning, everyone," he said as he smiled into the crowd. "For those of you that don't know me, my name is Kenneth Searlington and I'm a volunteer at Mac's Place. Over the years

I've come to realize that Mac's Place is much more than a recreational center for this community, for some, it's home. It's where they receive help, validation, and most of all, love.

The only problem is as wonderful as Mac's Place is, it can't meet all of the needs of some of the people that frequent it.

I know some of you are looking at me and wondering how I would know anything about the needs of this community. I'm not from East New York, and I've certainly never had to deal with any of the problems that arise when one is faced with all of the demons that plague those who live below the poverty line. But trust me when I tell you, money doesn't make you happy, and money doesn't mean that demons can't come into your home and destroy those you love either."

He dropped his head for a second, attempting to gather the composure he felt slipping away from him. A familiar squeeze of his arm had him looking into the familiar hazel eyes of his friend, A.J. She smiled at him, and that gave him just enough strength to push forward with his speech.

"My sister grew up in the same house as me, with the same parentage and same opportunities. None of that mattered in the end. In the end, she still died a violent death due to activities related to her drug addiction."

He stopped there, and took another breath. There, he'd said, freed that secret and hopefully pulled that heavy monkey off of his back.

"My twin sister, Karolyn Searlington Grant died because she was addicted to drugs and she couldn't overcome her addiction. Working here at Mac's Place and seeing how many of the lives of those of you that frequent it have been affected by this plague, I've decided that I need to do my part.

"You see, I was so blind and uninvolved in my sister's life that I didn't see the struggle she was going through, I didn't get involved. By the time I became aware, it was too late, and I was burying my sister. I decided then that I never wanted another person to know that pain, and so

I've decided to open up a counseling facility that will fall under the jurisdiction of Mac's Place.

It will provide counseling for all who seek help here, whether it's due to addiction or just needing someone to help guide you through the darkness. Karolyn's House will be a place of refuge and redemption for any who seek it."

Kenneth took the scissors that A.J. handed him and cut the ceremonial ribbon that was tied across the doors to the new facility. He turned back around to a sea of cheering faces and nodding heads. They were happy, and he'd finally done something to help, even if his sister would never benefit from that help, someone's sister in this neighborhood would.

His smile began on the inside and beamed through to his face. He clapped along with the people and barely noticed the ripple of disruption coming from his left. His eye caught sight of

Bryan, his friend, his wife's second charging toward him, yelling, "Get down, get down!"

Kenneth unsure looked down and saw a small red dot of light zeroed in on his tie. He followed the line of it and saw someone on a rooftop with what looked like some sort of lasertipped light pointed at him. It still didn't compute until he saw a second matching light join the first, this one coming from a side angle. He turned just in time to have Bryan tackle him to the ground and fall in a hard thump on the concrete.

Stunned, not certain of what exactly was happening, Kenneth looked up at Bryan who was now slumped over him in dead weight.

He tried to lift his arm and move him to the side, but sharp pain lanced up from his abdomen halting his motion.

He laid there, chest heavy from nearly two hundred pounds of muscled cop lying on top of him. He struggled to take a deep breath through his nose to calm the panic that was threatening to take over when he smelled the familiar metallic scent of blood. Whose, he couldn't tell, but either he or Bryan was bleeding and by the overpowering scent of it, there was lots of blood spilling from one or both of them.

Kenneth's heart began to pound in his ears, the loud drum beat corresponding with the ache in his gut. He tried to stay focused, but the sound of his heart was drowning out all of the noise around him, he struggled to keep his eyes open, he was very tired all of a sudden. The only thing his mind could grab hold of as darkness bled into the sides of his eyes, spilling into his line of sight and clouding it inch by inch was the only thing that had ever mattered to him.

"Heart, I love you."

CHAPTER 2

*H*eart sat in the hard plastic chair in a rigid tripod position. Her back hunched over, her arms bracing the weight of her torso, the muscles in her chest working so hard to force air in and out of her lungs. She'd almost swear it was her that had been shot instead of Kenneth and Bryan.

Just the thought of associating that condition with the two men she trusted and cared most for in this world, it made the dull pain that had been resting in the center of her chest explode, the force of the ache pulling her spine straight and lifting her out of the chair.

"Arggh," she screamed and slammed flat palms against the hard tiled walls. "What the fuck is going on, someone needs to tell me something." She turned to walk toward the nurse's station and was impeded by a tall, dark figure that had stood between her and trouble too many times for her not to recognize who it belonged to. "Porter, out of my way."

Her former boss held up a hand, stopping her where she stood. The fact that he still had that kind of power over her adding to the delightful mood she was already in just added to her rage.

When was she going to be able to tell this nosy old man to kiss her ass?

Never. That old fucker is gonna have you by the balls until his last breath. That's the way he trained you, the way you've trained your subordinates. Heel and listen to him.

She took a deep breath and closed her eyes. Her own mind was turning against her. No surprise there, everything else about this day was down the crapper, why shouldn't she add getting into a battle with her mentor and former boss to round things off nicely?

"Captain," she heard the authority and emphasis he placed around the word. She opened her eyes ready to let some slick shit slip past her lips when she saw a flash of concern in his. He stepped into her personal space, something only allowed for those closest to her. He bent down placing his mouth next to her ear and spoke so only she could hear his words. "I know you're worried, but you are the head of your house. One of your brothers is down, and the rest of your house is going to be looking at you to figure out what the hell they should be doing."

She allowed her eyes to pass around the room and realized the entire surgical waiting area was painted with a dark blue wall of her brothers and sisters. How had she not seen them? They were there, pressed with their backs against the wall, all turned toward her, all waiting, all expecting. What, she couldn't really say, but she knew whatever it was, they needed it to come from her.

Fuck if the old man wasn't right yet again. God, when was she going to get that omniscient secret super power that Porter always seemed to possess throughout his entire career? She could sure use some of that shit right now. Her people were looking to her, and at this very moment she knew she didn't really have shit to give them.

She felt a chill shake through her core, fighting to lock down every muscle to keep even the slightest shiver at bay. "But Kenneth," was all she could whisper.

"I know," he whispered in return. "That boy is as much my son as my own flesh and blood, but he needs you to hold him down out here. You can't fall apart, MacKenzie. You don't have that luxury right now. Too many people need you."

He wasn't wrong, everything was on her shoulders. The house, her husband, and Bryan, she was responsible for all of them. She could almost hear the steel inside her locking into place. She damn sure felt it. Her shoulders pulled back as she stood to her full five-nine height. She scoped the room, making contact with each officer there letting them know they would be strong because she was strong and she would expect nothing less from them.

"I know you're all worried, and I know you're all scared. I know because I'm feeling it too. My husband and my brother in blue are being cut open because some fool decided to lick off shots into a crowd. Now I don't know who the hell is responsible for this, but I know that fool just wrought hell onto himself, because we are going to run this son of a bitch to ground and unleash hell on his ass.

"I know it hurts that our brother is in danger. We each know that every morning we suit up and walk out on to those streets there's a chance we could end up in the same predicament that Smyth is in right now. So I need you to do for Lieutenant Smyth what he can't do for himself. I need you to fight and pray. You fight for your brother's justice, and pray for the bastard that put him in harm's way. But most importantly, you find that motherfucker and bring him to me."

The room was eerily quiet, but all their eyes were alive with fire. It was a bright and living thing that she could almost feel in that room, bouncing off of them onto all the surfaces surrounding them. They nodded and filed out of the room one by one, leaving just her and Porter alone in the middle of the four walls.

And when the last one had walked away and closed the door with a quiet click behind them, she fell into the waiting arms of not just her mentor and former commanding officer, but a father who was afraid of losing two sons. One he'd raised through circumstance, and one he'd groomed professionally for almost a decade.

The moment his arms closed around her, the fight left her and she collapsed against his wide chest, letting the pain spill from her eyes and mouth in fat tears and loud wails. Her heart was torn in two resting in the rooms with her men and the only thing she could do now was hope to God it would one day be whole again.

She pulled back from Porter and wiped the wetness on her face with her sleeve. She could give a fuck about how nasty that was, or how jacked up she looked right now. The only things that were on her mind were speedy recoveries for Kenneth and Bryan, and their shooter being brought to justice.

"Shit," she moaned as she realized what she'd just said. *Justice.* She needed to call her cousin. She needed to find Justice. Jussy couldn't find out from anyone else that Bryan had been shot. Not to mention Heart knew for a fact that Bryan still had Jussy listed as his next of kin and emergency contact. They might have spent the last few years apart, but Heart knew better than most how much love Bryan still held for her cousin. She pulled out her cell and pressed the speed dial number reserved for her cousin and waited for the phone to ring.

"Hey cuzo, what's going on?"

That voice, Jussy was always so full of laughter and fun, and Heart knew that once she left her message, all of that light and cheer would crumble into something dark and sullen.

"Justice, you need to come home now. Bryan's been hurt."

~

*J*ustice was restless. That wasn't the newsflash of the century. Jussy was always the kid labeled 'busy' out of the Amare children. It was true, Justice wasn't known for having an abundance of patience, instead, there was always a steady to-do list to keep anxiousness that usually crept up inside Jussy every time that familiar twitch began to manifest after sitting too long.

"What the hell is going on? Why the hell can't I rest?"

Justice thought about the rest of the Amare siblings and thought back to morning roll call. Each morning no matter where they were in the world, or how far out they were spread across the globe, they always synchronized and checked in with each other. True would call their oldest brother Law and Justice on three-way, then Law would call Free, and whoever had a line left open would call their father Hunter, and their cousin Heart.

It was their ritual, their way of checking in. With most of the family still being active military and Heart working in law enforcement, they had to touch base as regularly as they could in order to make sure everyone was safe.

They all took roll call seriously and on pain of death, they knew you didn't miss roll call if you knew what was good for you. Justice had been at peace after this morning's raucous call with the family. They'd all checked in and everyone was doing fine. So why was Justice feeling like something was terribly off?

The sounds of Sister Sledge's "We Are Family," chimed through the air. They all had that circa 1979 ringtone assigned to the members of the Amare tribe in their contact list. Justice looked at the face of the screen to see the tiny thumbnail of Heart's face illuminated by the light on the screen.

"Hey cuzo, what's going on?"

There was a beat of silence that alerted Justice that something wasn't quite right. Then Heart's shaky voice filled the line.

"Justice, you need to come home now. Bryan's been hurt."

The familiar spark of dread leapt to life inside Justice. Justice understood fear. At seventeen years old, Justice had signed up for the Marine Corps, following in the Amare tradition to serve in the armed forces. From birth, the Amare kids were taught that there was no greater privilege than to serve one's country in honesty and truth. The Amares didn't just believe that, they lived it.

Everyone from mother to father, and all four children had served in the varying branches of the armed forces. Growing up like that, always wondering if Daddy was going to make it home from his latest deployment or if your brothers and sister were going to make it home with all their working parts accounted for, that was real fear. That was something Justice and his family lived with every day. Yet standing here now with Heart on the phone, Justice could only recognize that this strange emotion threatening to cut off the air necessary for breathing was far beyond fear, no this was panic.

"I'm on my way."

Justice grabbed a charger for the phone, wallet, a jacket, and keys and headed for the car. Never slowing down long enough to worry about packing a bag or a change of clothes, Justice headed for the car. If the go-bag in the trunk of the car wasn't enough, Justice would buy whatever was missing once New York was in view. The only thing that mattered right now was getting to Bryan, making sure he was all right.

~

"*H*ere you go, baby girl." Big Willie held a steaming cup of coffee in front of Heart.

She shook her head, not sure if the churning in her stomach would bring the black liquid back or not.

"Take it," he urged as he shoved his meaty paw in her face again.

Her nerves raw from waiting for news about Kenneth and Bryan, she didn't have much fight left in her to go up against her former lieutenant, William Seyah.

"Any updates?" he asked.

"No," she sighed. "Seems like they've been in there for hours and no one has come to tell me anything."

"Don't worry," Porter said, "they'll tell us something as soon as they can."

Both she and Willie looked at Porter and then shared a knowing look together. They were always a lot less optimistic than their former captain, but they nodded anyway, hoping that magic all-knowing thing he always had going on was working even now.

The click of the waiting room door pulled her attention and made her stand in expectation.

She watched as each of Bryan's team members walked in the door. All five looked like she felt, tired, frustrated, angry, and scared as hell.

Barret Jenson, Adam Thomas, Ada Ramirez, Sage Santini, and Timothy Grazzo met her in the center of the waiting room. They each acknowledged Porter and Seyah, giving them the respect due to the former guard, then they all settled their gazes on Heart and she realized, she didn't have to default to the two men at her side, these were her people now.

30

"Captain," Grazzo spoke with just a hint of hesitancy in his voice. "Has there been any news about Mr. Searlington and the lieutenant?"

"No, not yet," she answered. "We're still waiting. Do we have any idea what happened out there today?"

"We know that there was only one shooter, we're just going through footage and canvassing the area to try to get a fix on where he was," Ramirez answered.

"The shot came from the roof across the street from the treatment center. Smyth and I saw the laser sight locked on Kenneth. That's what pushed us into action."

Grazzo shook his head. "No, the shot didn't come from across the street. When we looked at the footage, there was someone on the roof with a laser, pointing it at Kenneth, but the shot actually came from somewhere off to Kenneth's left."

Heart thought about that. Something didn't make sense. "Did we have anyone positioned over there? Did anyone see anything?"

They all looked to each other; all seeming to know something that none of them appeared to want to share with their captain.

"Who the hell was positioned there and why don't any of you want to tell me?"

Grazzo was the only one that seemed to gather up the confidence to lock eyes with her. He was young, but he'd spent the last few years showing her that he'd earned his new sergeant's shield. She was looking at a future captain, of that she had no doubt.

"Sergeant, who was positioned there?" she bellowed.

He steadied his gaze before speaking again. "You, Captain. The shooter came from the opposite corner of where the van was positioned. Looking at the tapes, it looks like he waited for you to leave the van in order to take the shot. After he made his shot he dropped the gun and faded into the crowd."

It felt like someone had hit her, it was her, she'd dropped the ball, and as a result her husband and her best friend might lose their lives because of it.

"Captain Searlington?"

Heart turned to the door to find a tall man with a lean build judging by the way his green surgical scrubs hung loosely off of his frame. She stepped away from her officers and walked over to the stranger at the front of the room.

"I'm Captain Searlington," Heart answered.

The man offered her a hand to shake. She hesitated for the briefest of seconds, nothing that was noticeable to anyone but her.

"I'm Dr, Cooper. I'm the head of the team that worked on both your husband and Lieutenant Smyth. Has the lieutenant's family arrived yet?"

"His spouse is in transit as we speak. It may be another couple of hours before Jussy arrives.

As his Captain I'm responsible for him until his family arrives, you can ask me anything. Is he all right?"

"Let's talk about your husband first. Mr. Searlington suffered very little damage as a result of the bullet wound. Mostly, that's because Lieutenant Smyth acted as a shield for your husband. There was only one bullet, it entered through Lieutenant Smyth posterior shoulder and existed through his pectoral muscle then entering your husband's lateral abdomen. Abdominal gunshot wounds can be very tricky, but because your lieutenant stepped in front of your husband he slowed the bullet down, minimizing the amount of damage it was able to do once it entered your husband. He's being moved to recovery now; you should be able to see him in a few moments, as soon as he wakes up from the anesthesia."

She didn't know whether to be relieved, or to cry from worry. Bryan may have saved her husband, and Lord knew she was desperately thankful for that, but her best friend, her second could still in trouble.

"And Bryan?" she whispered, almost afraid to hear the rest of the doctor's words.

"The Lieutenant held his own during the surgery. He lost an enormous amount of blood before he arrived and we had to transfuse him. The bullet tore through a major artery and it was messy. Touch and go, but my team was able to stabilize him and repair the damage. Now we just have to wait and see what happens. We're keeping him sedated and he will remain intubated and connected to a ventilator until we're certain he can breathe on his own."

She walked back inside the room to the team and relayed most of the doctor's message. They were both alive; Kenneth had suffered minimal damage because Smyth had jumped in front of the bullet.

They were all relieved, cautiously anyway, turning their focus on the investigation rather than their colleague.

"Grazzo," the newly appointed sergeant locked eyes with her at the sound of his name,

"...you're in charge of my house while I deal with shit at the hospital."

She watched the young man blanch a little as he looked around at his fellow detectives on the team.

"Me, Cap?" he asked, still looking around the room at his colleagues. "I'm the newbie on the team. I've only been here a few years. Wouldn't you feel more comfortable with someone else on the team?"

"Grazzo, I don't really care how long you've been on the job. I care how you do your job, and as your ranking officer, I say you do it damn well. And don't think you're getting a cushy assignment by doing this. This is going to be the hardest thing you've ever done. And don't worry about the other members of your team giving you hell, 'cause trust me, none of them wants the headache you're about to walk into."

She glanced around the room and watched as the remaining four detectives nodded and laughed.

"See Grazzo, they know what you don't, that I'm going to be all over you like a second skin.

There aren't many things or people I love above my house, so if you fuck it up, I fuck you up."

She allowed her message to penetrate the air and when she was certain it was received, she smiled and asked, "We clear?"

Grazzo nodded, and she returned her gaze to the other detectives.

"And if he destroys my house and the rest of you don't help him save it, I'm fucking all of you up too."

Her message received, she thought about events that led up to the shooting. She'd seen the laser sight on her husband's lapel and leapt into action. It had been the wrong thing to do, and hindsight made that abundantly clear now that she was standing in a surgical waiting area praying her friend and husband made it through this terrible ordeal. Not only had she fucked up, but her subordinates knew it, and that was something she wasn't sure she really knew how to handle. She was Mac, the famed supercop that solved the hard cases, and she'd been duped into leaving her post by a simple trick of flashing lights. How was she supposed to look them in the eye again?

"You suck that shit up, admit your mistake, and move the fuck on," she heard Big Willie say when she'd voiced her concerns about taking on the top cop position and being under such oppressing scrutiny. "You're going to fuck up, MacKenzie. We all do. But the mark of a good leader is not always doing shit right, it's being able to admit when you've fucked up and when you're out of your depth. Own that shit and show them you're human, and then you move the fuck on."

"I fucked up, I did exactly what that bastard wanted me to do and I followed the dancing light. But he fucked up too, because now we know something we didn't know before. Smyth was wearing his vest. A regular bullet wouldn't have gotten through that. He was shot with a high powered rifle with armor-piercing ammo. We won't know the specifics until the doc hands the bullet over to forensics, but just the fact alone gives us a way to eliminate people from our pool of suspects. It gives us a place to start. That's not shit that you're regular Brooklyn thug carries around. That shit is professional and expensive. Apparently someone wants my husband dead and you're going to find out who it is and why."

CHAPTER 3

*T*he first thing Kenneth noticed was sound. There was an annoying repetitive beep that seemed to be somewhere in the distance, pulling him from the comfort of his sleep.

What the hell is that sound?

He moved his eyes from side to side and saw nothing but darkness. He tried to open his eyes to find light, but nothing worked. His head was filled with dense black fog and he couldn't seem to find a way out of it.

Where am I? What's going on? Where's Heart?

His heart rate inched up a little, the pulsing of blood getting louder by the minute inside his head.

He heard a closer beep and then a muddled, "I think he's waking up." *Waking up?* Waking up had never felt this difficult.

"Hey Baby?"

Or at least he thought that's what he'd heard. The sound of the voice was still muffled, like it was traveling through water.

Was that Heart?

He wasn't sure until he felt the familiar warmth of her touch. A touch he knew almost better than his own after four and a half years of marriage.

"Baby, come on. Open your eyes for me. Let me get a look at those crystal blue eyes I fell in love with."

"Was…" he tried to speak, but his throat felt burning hot, clamping off his attempt to move air past his vocal cords.

"Ssh, take a sip of this before you try to speak."

He felt the press of soft plastic against his lips and opened slowly for the straw his wife was guiding between his lips. He gave a slight pull and cool water flooded his mouth and eased down his throat.

"Wasn't my eyes you fell in love with," he growled, the remaining gravel in his throat making his voice almost unrecognizable to his ear. He took a breath and tried to open his eyes again. This time he saw a sharp blade of light cut through the dark haze, making him wince in pain.

"Damn, how long was I out? Why do I feel like a truck ran over me?" He tried to pull himself up and immediately regretted it when a searing slice of pain radiated through his midsection.

"Shit!"

He felt Heart's hand on his shoulder, pushing him back down into the mattress.

"Baby, you need to relax. Don't try anything stupid like that again."

He settled back into the cushion behind his head and breathed carefully until the pain receded to a more tolerable level. He tried to open his eyes again, this time forcing them to adjust to the blinding light in the room.

He waited for his eyes to focus and took a careful look around the room. This wasn't their bedroom. He was in a single bed; Heart was leaning over him sitting on the side of it. There was a small TV positioned on the wall in front of him, and a small window with ugly bars secured around it. He looked to his periphery and saw machines with different color digital displays that flashed strange squiggly lines and bold numbers.

"Kenneth, do you know where you are?" Heart asked softly.

"It's either the worst looking hotel room ever, prison, or a hospital," he groaned.

"You're in the hospital, do you remember what happened?" He shook his head.

"You were giving a speech. You announced the treatment facility opening today. During that speech, someone took a shot at you."

Kenneth fastened his eyes onto her face.

"Someone shot me?"

"Actually, someone was aiming to shoot you, but Bryan got between you and the bullet. The bullet went in through his vest, the back of his shoulder, his chest, then his vest again, and finally passed through to your abdomen. The bullet didn't really do much damage to you, just pierced you really. The docs removed it and cleaned you up inside before closing you up. You were so fortunate. The doctor said there's all sorts of stuff that could have been hit inside your gut that could have taken you out permanently."

He watched each muscle in her face, something wasn't right. She was working hard to put her work face on, the one that gave away nothing, that kept all the important details of things behind her professional mask. It was one of the things that made her such a good cop; people could never really tell what she was thinking unless she wanted them to. But him, he was always able to see through her layers, and right now, he didn't like what he was seeing.

"Please tell me he didn't...he is..."

"He's alive, thank God for that, but...it isn't very good," she breathed.

"What happened?"

"He's fighting hard for his life right now and the doctors don't know if he's going to make it. I've been running back and forth between the two of you. Now that you're awake I need to go and check on him. The Amares and I are the only family he has, so I gotta make sure he's all right."

He wanted to go with her. Bryan wasn't just her friend and colleague, over the years they'd become close, trusted friends. The man had literally taken a bullet that was meant for him and Kenneth needed to thank him for that. But the minute he thought about sitting up again his abs protested with a throbbing ache.

"Tell him thank you," he whispered. "Tell him as soon as I can move without popping a stitch I'm going to be right by his side."

She nodded and leaned in to press her full lips against his. She rested her forehead on his and he felt a warm drop of wetness on his face. When she pulled back he saw the fresh tracks of tears spilling from her tired red eyes.

"I love you. I was so scared we'd lost you. Don't ever scare me like that again. I don't know what I'd do if…"

He wiped her cheek with his thumb and wrapped the rest of his fingers into her brown tresses of hair.

"You don't have to worry about if. I'm not going anywhere anytime soon." He kissed her again, and then gave her a lazy smile. "Go check on B."

She nodded and smiled, then lifted off of the bed and walked to the door. He settled back into his pillows and let the details of the day wash over him. He'd always known that in her line of work there was a possibility that his wife could be fatally injured on the job. Hell, he'd seen it happen before his eyes when she was shot in the shoulder during his niece's kidnapping. But this, him being the target of someone's plot to kill him had never crossed his mind.

Kenneth was a lot of things, arrogant, mildly annoying—if his wife were to be believed— but none of those attributes should have been enough for someone to try to kill him over.

"Fuck, what the hell did I do to make someone want to kill me?"

CHAPTER 4

*H*eart walked into the dimly lit room and stood at the foot of the bed, just looking at the still man positioned so perfectly in the center of it.

God this isn't Bryan, she thought as her eyes traversed the full length of his tall and muscular frame. Bryan Smyth was lively, always moving, always doing, always loud. This figure, still, silent, unmoving, looked like a poor, broken imitation that she could barely recognize.

She inched closer to the side of the bed and slowly slipped her fingers under the motionless meaty hand lying flat against the sheet. It was so cold, so eerily devoid of life. How could this be the man she'd spent the last fifteen years of her life partnered with. He'd held her down for so long, had always gone out on a limb to protect her, and today, today he'd protected what was most important in her life, with no thought to the sacrifice he would be making.

She looked at him and was overcome with such love, such gratitude, and such guilt. How could she be grateful for her husband's survival when her partner was the only reason Kenneth was barely harmed?

She squeezed the cold hand in her palm as she sat in the stiff plastic chair at the bedside. She brought warm lips to his knuckles and kissed them lightly.

"Thank you," she murmured. "Thank you for saving him." She pulled the cold hand up and placed her cheek against it. "I will never be able to thank you enough for what you did, Bryan.

Never. But even though you've already given more than anyone should ever be asked to, I'm going to be greedy and ask you to do one more thing. I need you to wake up. I need you to fight."

She wiped away her falling tears and tried to control the shakiness in her voice. "You have so much to live for and there are so many of us who are out here fighting for you. But it doesn't mean anything, none of it, none of the prayers, none of the hope, none of it means a thing if you aren't fighting as hard as we are."

She looked around at the machines that were attached to him, hoping for some indication that he could hear her, that he was still in there somewhere, still within her reach. But there was nothing but the same monotone beeping she'd encountered since they'd attached the machines upon his arrival in the surgical I.C.U.

"When a real leader speaks, his followers listen," Porter had told her when he was grooming her to take over his command. "Doesn't matter how you speak or what you say, if you're really their leader, they'll answer your call."

She sat straighter and braced her hands flat against the bed next to his unmoving body. "So get the hell up off your lazy ass, Smyth," she ordered, her voice firm, filled with authority and confidence. "...and do what the hell you need to do to get up, and get back to work. I'll be damned if you're going to leave me now to deal with that fucking house and brass all by myself.

Porter had Big Willie, and when Willie couldn't deal with his crazy ass, he had me," she barked.

Porter was probably the only person she knew of that was just as crazy and weird as she was if not more. Everyone knew it was his two lieutenants who'd kept him grounded as a captain all those years. The same was true now. "There's no one out there that can deal with my crazy the way you can, so whatever ideas you have about taking a permanent vacation…that shit is nixed.

I'm not approving any leave."

She looked up at the monitors again and noticed no new movement. The stubborn bastard was ignoring her and that shit she just wasn't going to have.

"You wanna play hardball, Smyth, act like you can't hear me? Well I got a trick for that ass. You lay there all you want but know this. I. Called. Jussy." Laughter filled her as she looked down at her wristwatch. "And since we both know Jussy drives like a bat out of hell, I'd say we'll be joined by the second youngest Amare sibling very soon. So lay there and rest up, 'cause we both know if you're not up when that force of nature blows through here, Jussy is just going to kick your ass until you stand at attention and fall in line."

She heard an errant beep push through the monotone rhythm that Bryan's vitals had been playing and a drop of happiness splashed in the pool of her soul and rippled until a small cautious smile crawled on her lips.

There's nothing like threatening a man with his significant other to make him do what you want him to do, especially when that significant other is an Amare child.

~

Colonel Justice Amare rushed from the elevator as soon as the door gave way to a wide enough opening that exiting was possible. Spotting the nurse's station in the middle of the round, open floor plan, Justice was about to ask where Bryan's room was when the sight of two rooms flanked with armed officers in front of them came into view.

Justice stepped in front of the first set of officers. "Colonel Justice Amare here for Lieutenant Bryan Smyth." One officer looked down at a clipboard and then back to the military ID. It was still dangling from the pocket of the Marine Corps utility uniform Justice hadn't bothered to change out of before jumping in the car and driving from D.C. to New York in a short two and three-quarter hours.

"Go right in, Marine," the officer nodded and stepped aside giving Justice access to the door. A quick slide of the glass door and Justice was standing inside of the room watching some freakishly still version of Bryan displayed center stage in a hospital bed.

"Cousin?"

Justice heard the familiar sound of Heart's voice calling, but couldn't find the will to turn from the garish vision of Bryan lying in that bed.

Justice felt the comfort of Heart's familial touch break through the ice of the shock that seemed to be sucking all of the air from the room. As soon as Jussy turned around the cousinsiblings fell into each other's arms in a violent embrace, each holding onto the other seeking strength that they couldn't muster alone.

"I'm so sorry, Cousin. I'm so sorry."

Justice pulled away from Heart, staring into brown pools filled with worry, fear, and...guilt.

"What happened, Cousin? What happened to my husband?"

CHAPTER 5

" *He* protected my husband when I couldn't."

Justice watched Heart so carefully, not wanting to miss even one detail that led to Bryan being shot and fighting for his life.

"Start from the beginning, Cousin," Justice said calmly, giving Heart the opportunity to gather her thoughts and calm her nerves enough to relay the events.

"Kenneth was dedicating a new treatment facility as an annex to Mac's Place. It's something he's decided to do in honor of his late sister, Karolyn. From the moment he told me he not only wanted to do this, but he wanted to be the public face pushing this, I've just had a bad feeling. I didn't like the idea of everyone seeing his face and knowing who he was. But I couldn't change his mind. So this morning the press and the community came out to witness the official opening and dedication. I had no official leads, but something just felt off. In addition to the normal unis I'd have out for crowd control for an event like this, I also added Bryan's D.T.'s as a protective/surveillance detail. Bryan and I were sitting in a dummy news van and the rest of the team was placed strategically throughout the crowd. Bryan hopped out of the van to do some recon when I saw a sight laser on Kenneth..."

"A sight laser? In East New York?" Justice asked. For all the rise in criminal activity in that part of Brooklyn, guns with sight lasers were expensive and not the usual choice of weapon for the residents that operated on the other side of the law in that part of town.

"I know, that was my reaction too," Heart answered. "But I saw it, and Bryan saw it too. It was coming from the rooftop of the building across the street. The team went active and Bryan got to Kenneth first. He speared Kenneth in his abdomen to take him out of the shooter's sights, but it didn't work."

"Your guys couldn't get to him before he got off a shot?" Justice queried.

"No, we later found out there was no shooter on the roof. All we found was some sort of remote laser device that was intended to draw us away from the real shooter who was positioned on the corner behind our surveillance van. The fucker set it up so we'd all go running to the roof and toward Kenneth. The shot came from the side and tapped Bryan in the back of his shoulder.

He was using some serious ammo; it pierced his vest and still managed to end up in Kenneth's abdomen."

"Shit," Justice uttered, turning back toward Bryan's immobile form. "You think this was a hit, don't you?"

"Yes, my people are looking into it now, but it seems that way. I don't know why someone is out to get Kenneth, but we're searching for the bastard now."

"Find them, Cousin," Justice stated. "Find them before I do. Because if I ever come across the man who did this, there won't be enough of him left for you to prosecute. Now if you'll excuse me, I want to spend a few minutes alone with my husband before I go talk to his doctors."

Justice watched as Heart turned to leave the room. Just as she reached for the sliding door, Justice called her name again.

"Heart, I can see the guilt you're wearing like a fucking coat. This isn't your fault. Bryan did what any Marine would do; he sacrificed himself to save his brother. The only person responsible is the person who pulled that fucking trigger. Shake that shit off, and go find that motherfucker now."

Heart straightened her shoulders, pulling herself up and out of the emotional mire she'd been covered in when she came into the room. She looked more like the cousin Justice knew, strong, confident, and most of all, determined. Now this cousin, this cousin was the one that Justice needed, this cousin would get shit done.

Heart left the room and Justice retrieved the cell phone hiding in one of the many pockets of the utility uniform. Tapping the small thumbnail on the screen, Justice waited as one ring passed before the other party answered.

"Didn't I just talk to you this morning?"

"True," was all Justice needed to say before she recognized something was wrong.

"What happened?"

"Bryan's been shot, and he's not looking good. Heart called me as soon as it happened and I tore ass out of D.C. to get back to New York."

"Why didn't she call the rest of us?"

"Because Kenneth's been shot too."

"Fuck is going on over there? Is he all right?"

"Yeah, he's recovering from surgery, but he's all right."

"What are the details on Bryan's condition?"

"I don't know, I'm about to find the doctors now and get some answers. I just need..."

"We got what you need," she said. "We'll always have what you need, Jussy. I'm on my way and I'll touch base with the rest of the sibs and Pops. When you talk to the doctor, get me on the line so I can hear what's being said. Jussy, just tell that sorry ass brother-in-law of mine that if he's still lying around when I get there, we're gonna have us a problem."

The line went dead and Jussy laughed a little. If there was one person that could get you to laugh in the middle of your heartache it was True Amare, sister, friend, protector, and warrior.

And that's who Justice needed right now, a warrior, or four.

CHAPTER 6

*H*eart sat close to the hospital bed, as close as the side rails and I.V. poles would allow. She ran gentle fingers through the messy array of soft ink black locks. If her prissy-ass husband could actually see what the disorganized chaos looked like, he'd be asking her for his conditioner, wide-toothed comb, and paddle brush to detangle it and restore it to its normal state of sleek and perfect.

As sexy and manly as her husband was, when it came to his hair and manscaping, he was worse than most women, including her. Truth was as much as she loved the result of his grooming routine, because Lord knew that the man's hair did strange things to her, she could care less about the tangled mop it resembled now.

Kenneth was still here. He was injured, he was healing, he was currently sleeping, but he was still here with her and for that she was grateful.

She stood up from her chair and leaned down, allowing her cheek to rest against his. The warmth radiating from his face a celebrated reminder that life still resided beneath the smooth porcelain cloak of his skin.

"Hmmm," he moaned a bit and she tried to pull back to inspect him for pain. He placed a tender hand on her cheek to keep her from pulling away. "I never want to wake up without the feel of some part of you touching me."

She smiled down into his cobalt gaze and her heart squeezed a little tighter than normal. She took several short breaths and then let her lips meet his, needing more of the physical connection that bound them to each other, reminding her battered nerves that he was still with her.

He's still here with us...with me.

"How long have I been in here?"

"It's only been about seven hours since the shooting. I'm sure with all you've been through it probably seems like days."

"Have you checked on...?"

She raised a hand to halt his sentence. "Yes I did, and everything is fine. I spoke with Elvia this morning and she said she could stay as late as I needed. Everything is fine at the house. Elvia told me to tell Mr. Kenneth she was going to pray to all the saints for him and Lieutenant

Bryan."

She watched as the mention of her second's name pulled the smile from her husband's face. His easy smile replaced with sharp worry lines. She was sure if she bothered to look in a mirror there would be a similar mix of concern and fear painted across her features as well.

"How is he? I want to see him," Kenneth stated in as firm a tone as he could muster in his currently weakened state.

Heart shook her head and placed both hands at the top of Kenneth's shoulders as he attempted to sit up.

"Kenneth, stop before you hurt something. You can't see Bryan right now. He's a police officer that was injured in the line of duty. The only people allowed to see him are medical personnel, law enforcement, and immediate family. If it wasn't for the fact that I'm his captain, I wouldn't be able to get in either."

"But we're his family; he doesn't have any family other than us."

Heart watched the light pink flush blanch across Kenneth's face and a little part of her loved him just a little bit more. Her husband knew the importance of a family of one's own making, especially when your own blood wanted nothing to do with you. He loved her partner, and when Kenneth loved you, he protected you, no matter the sacrifice to himself.

"Searlington, calm down," she asserted. "I know most of the time he acts like he was hatched, but Bryan actually has family members. The most important one arrived a little while ago. You need to relax, and get yourself together. I need you out of this place and home as soon as I can get you there. Don't fuck that up by popping a stitch and setting your recovery back."

"For once, your wife and I actually agree on something."

Heart didn't need to turn around to see who the voice belonged to. The very precise pattern of enunciating every syllable in a sentence only belonged to one person.

"How'd you manage to get past security, A.J.? I could have sworn I told them to keep trouble away from my husband."

The petite woman with the Café au lait complexion and the brown/blond curls that were bound in a tight bun leaned casually against the doorway to Kenneth's room. She shrugged a shoulder as she walked in and offered an easy smile to Heart and Kenneth.

"I flashed my old D.A.'s badge and they let me right up," A. J. offered.

"Weren't they supposed to confiscate that from you when you left the district attorney's office?"

A.J. waved an unconcerned hand through the air. "Details, details, Captain."

"You do know impersonating a law enforcement agent is a crime in New York, punishable with prison time?"

A.J. smiled and pointed a manicured finger at herself. "Best lawyer in the country," she beamed. "...arguably the world," she quipped. "Not really concerned about being brought up on criminal charges." A.J. teetered in on her precariously skinny, pink floral, open-toed stilettos that perfectly complemented the white fitted linen dress with a ruched penciled skirt and pale pink blazer.

Fuck, I've been with Kenneth's rich ass too long if I know what the fuck the designer shit this bitch is wearing is called.

Heart watched A.J. carefully as she sat down on the opposite side of the bed and carefully crossed her short toned leg over her knee.

God this bitch just loves to be seen.

Heart heard the growl slipping from her clenched jaw and damn near squeezed the bed rail hard enough to have it break off in her hand. *God why couldn't this bed rail be her skinny ass neck?*

She felt Kenneth's calming hand on her arm and she swallowed the insult that was waiting on the tip of her tongue. This was her husband's friend, someone he deemed family, and like it or not, she was always going to have a presence in Kenneth's life. Unwilling to upset her injured husband, Heart decided to opt out of the verbal sparring match she knew A.J. would try to goad her into during this visit.

"Come stai mio fratello?" A.J. spoke in her preferred Italian.

Heart was fluent in Spanish. The two languages shared Latin building blocks and so she could often piece together what that uppity bitch was saying when A.J. was in Kenneth's presence. But today Heart just wasn't up for the bullshit and so before Kenneth could respond to what Heart figured was a friendly greeting she pointed a finger at A.J. and in no uncertain terms let the lady litigator know that, "The only language that all three people in this room speak fluently is English," she bellowed. "That's all I want to hear coming out of those botoxed lips of yours."

A.J. rolled her eyes and Kenneth just laughed his usual reaction when the two women went at it.

"How are you feeling, Kenneth?" A.J. asked.

"Like I was tackled by a two hundred pound weight and then cut open so people could poke around my insides with sharp metal sticks," he said with a raised brow. "How about you?"

A.J.'s usual expression was a mixture of haughty annoyance due to superior intellect. She always looked like she was just this side of being bored to death by the inferior specimens of the average person's cerebral abilities.

Heart watched her drop her eyes and fiddle with the expensive jeweled bauble wrapped around the woman's wrist as if the answer to

Kenneth's question was somehow woven into the jeweler's intricate patterns of entwining precious metals and stones.

"Right now, I'm relieved," she answered quietly. "But earlier today, I watched one of the people I love get shot right in front of me. It was one of the scariest moments of my life and I'd thank you to never make me have to experience it again."

"A.J., I'm fine," Kenneth offered.

The woman lifted her eyes and locked gazes with Heart. There was a question behind those sad hazel eyes that were framed with long, dark lashes. "Is that true, is he going to be all right?"

"If he follows doctor's orders and takes it easy for the next few weeks, he should be fine. The surgery was mostly exploratory to retrieve the bullet and make certain it hadn't caused any damage. He was very fortunate."

"And your lieutenant?"

Heart ran a firm hand over the knots beginning to form in the back of her neck. Just the thought of Bryan and his situation right now made her tense.

"You were a D.A. once, you know I can't discuss Bryan's situation with you. All I can say is if you believe in a god or higher power, my brothers and I would appreciate you putting in a good word for Bryan."

A.J. nodded her head. "I do and I will."

"Speaking of protocol, did you give your statement to any of my detectives yet?"

A.J. nodded again. "Yes, that's part of the reason I headed over here. I figured they would be coming to interview Kenneth soon, as his attorney I wanted to be here."

Heart shook her head. "He's the victim counselor; I don't think he really needs a legal mouthpiece present to tell the investigators why someone would want to shoot him. It's usually only the suspects who require that."

A.J. leaned forward and pulled her glasses and her leather-bound tablet from her purse. Once the glasses were secured on the very tip of her nose she pulled a stylus from some hidden compartment in the tablet case and began scribbling across the illuminated screen. She looked up briefly to acknowledge Heart and then quickly returned her gaze to the screen.

"It's been my experience that the NYPD sometimes confuses the roles of victim and suspect, so I'm here to make certain that clarity prevails."

Heart was about to speak when she heard a strong tap on the door behind her. When she looked, Detectives Grazzo and Ramirez were standing in the doorway each with a notepad and a pen in their hands.

"Mr. Searlington," Grazzo stated. "Detective Ramirez and I are here to take your statement regarding the shooting on Autumn Avenue this morning."

Heart rose up out of her seat, leaned down and placed a gentle kiss on Kenneth's lips. "I'll see you later."

"You're not going to stay?"

"Kenneth, I'm the captain of the investigating precinct in your attempted murder. I can't touch this case. You'll be safe here now that your pit bull is here to protect you." She looked directly at A.J. as she uttered the last part of her sentence. "Besides, we both know I have to check on things at home if either of us is to have any peace today. "If everything is okay, I'll slip back in tonight after hours. Want me to bring you anything back?"

She watched him run a tentative hand through his hair before he said, "Yeah, my conditioner, wide-toothed comb, and paddle brush. My hair is a wreck."

CHAPTER 7

By the time Heart actually walked through her front door it was hours later, and darkness had settled in the evening sky. She'd decided to stop at the precinct just to check on a few things and of course between conversations with brass and providing her officers with updates on Smyth and scheduling a department vigil with their house chaplain, shit just got out of control and here she was, creeping into her own home at nearly minutes to eleven in the night.

The house was still and dark on the first floor. She removed her shoes and walked softly up the stairs to her bedroom. She secured her weapon, stripped out of her clothes on the way to the bathroom and ran the shower as hot as her tired skin could bear it.

If this were any other day, with any other victims, she would have lingered in the soothing spray for as long as her weary bones would have held her up, but tonight, she couldn't dally. She had to get back to Kenneth and Bryan as quickly as she could.

She gave her wet skin a quick lotion job, threw on a comfortable pair of sweats and packed two more spare sweat suits just in case she had to stay the next couple of days in the hospital.

She grabbed Kenneth's grooming kit, and packed his beloved hair products and tools in a second grooming kit for him.

Worse than a fucking woman.

Satisfied that she'd grabbed most of what they needed. She walked outside the master bedroom and stopped in front of the first bedroom down the hall. She placed the duffle gently on the floor and slowly twisted the knob to open the door.

She met the soft glow of the nightlight as she inched into the room one quiet step at a time.

Not wanting to disturb the room's inhabitant, she just needed a peek to reassure herself that everything was all right.

She softly touched the top of the smooth frame of the honeyed wood, peaked through the slits between the bars and saw tiny feet kicking. The smile already curving her lips in anticipation, she looked over the railing and met the most perfect set of blue eyes looking back up to her. The small cerulean gaze grew wide with excitement and a round cherub's face beamed a bright smile in her direction.

"Da-da," the small voice called and punched out uncoordinated arms through the air.

Heart leaned further over the cribs railing and placed a flat palm on the rounded belly of the little imp lying face up in the crib.

"I am Ma-ma," she said the word slowly, broken in to two separate and long syllables.

"Say it with me now little man, Ma-ma."

The baby must have found her performance entertaining because his limbs went into a quick frenzy of movements as he kicked and giggled and then said with a devilish little grin, "Da-da."

Too amused at the infant's antics, Heart leaned down and picked him up out of the crib and held him tightly to her chest.

"That's all right; Mama still loves you even though you're a traitor."

She secured the four-month-old on her hip and ambled across the room to the rocking chair. She sat down with him and held him around his waist as he practiced standing on his chubby bowed legs.

"What are you doing up this time of night?" she asked the infant who was currently bouncing up and down while trying to shove his entire fist into his mouth. "If Elvia catches you up, she's going to skin both of us alive." "Da-da," the baby answered.

"Is that the only word you know, kid?" At four months, she knew it was, but it didn't stop her from having these kind of conversations with the little boy every night. "You miss Daddy too, right?"

The baby answered with an indecipherable coo that she took to mean yes.

"Well, Daddy is going to be spending the next few nights out. He's got a little boo-boo on his tummy. But I promise you he misses you so much, and he can't wait to come home and play with you."

She marveled at the small being in her hands. Amare Kenneth Searlington had been an absolute surprise to his parents. After suffering an ectopic pregnancy prior to his conception, Heart didn't believe she'd be able to ever conceive again, let alone carry a child to term. But here in her arms was a perfect blending of her and the man she loved, with his father's face, eyes the color of blue fire, and a head full of inky black hair. The only reminder that she had anything to do with his creation was the smooth mocha skin that covered his perfectly round little body.

Looking at him, there was no denying the boy was all Kenneth. It was so evident at his birth that Heart had suggested they name the boy Kenneth Junior. Kenneth had declined her proposal, and told her he wanted to name the child after the thing he admired most about the child's mother, her strength. Heart, still a little lightheaded from the anesthesia, was a little confused and asked, "You wanna name him Strength Searlington?"

Kenneth laughed and gave her a light kiss on her forehead. "Didn't you tell me that your family's name Amare meant strength?"

She thought about it for a long while before nodding her head and smiled. She almost sang the name, "Amare Searlington," to test out the sound and found it lacking something vital. "Amare Kenneth Searlington." She smiled brightly. "Now that's a powerful name if I ever heard one." Then she'd dropped off into a morphine-induced sleep leaving their new son and her exuberant husband to become acquainted.

Her mind drifted away to nearly three years ago when her life took a very dark turn. Their road to parenthood had been paved with so much secrecy, uncertainty, and pain the first time around. It had nearly destroyed their marriage. Leaving their bond broken and in tatters.

Fortune had smiled on them the second go 'round. By the time they'd discovered she was pregnant again, the two were intensely involved in couples therapy, shoring up the weaknesses that had nearly torn them apart.

The chill that always washed over her when she thought about that very painful page in their history started to crest over her, then she felt tiny fingers grip her bottom lip and dig themselves inside her mouth and pull.

"Ow," she hollered, sending the little boy into a fit of giggles. That smile, it healed all that was wrong with her. Whenever she saw it, thought about it, all the bad in her world just drifted away.

"Hey, let's see if we can get Daddy on video chat. I bet he'd love to see you."

Heart removed her phone from her pocket and tapped on the app to open a video call to her husband. She waited for a few beats and then she saw Kenneth's tired face fill the screen from his hospital bed.

"Babe, I'm sorry to bother you so late, but I have a little man here who says he wants to see his daddy."

Kenneth's eyes turned to the same electric shade of blue that filled their son's excited gaze.

"Is that true, Amare?" Kenneth asked the baby, his voice taking on that unnaturally high pitch that all parents spoke in when addressing their happy little hobbits.

The baby rewarded Kenneth with a jubilant, "Da-da," followed by flapping arms and a long string of drool sliding from his chin.

Pink lips pulled into a wide grin as Kenneth watched their son dance around in her lap. Only a few minutes into a video call with their son and Heart could already notice the sickly pallor she'd left her husband with being slowly replaced by the warmth of his love for their son.

"Ah, Daddy misses you so much, Amare," Kenneth uttered happily to the little cherub before lifting his eyes to Heart. "Is he all right? Was Elvia able to stay?"

Heart nodded her head. It always amazed her how involved Kenneth was in the day-to-day care of their son. He didn't just come in to play with him and dump all of the work on Heart, no, he was always right there with her in the trenches of dirty diapers and sleepless nights.

"You tell her she's got a special bonus coming for being so understanding."

"Thank you, Mr. Kenneth."

Heart turned around in the chair as their nanny walked into the nursery. Elvia was a recently retired Latina woman who after nearly thirty-five years as a Nassau County police officer, decided she wanted to change direction in her professional life and take care of children. She was everything Kenneth had wanted in their nanny; kind, patient, nurturing, plus she could carry a firearm and was trained in close-quarter combat. That certainly sealed the deal for Heart and after an extensive police background check, Heart had happily signed off on hiring her. What cop wouldn't want to know that their kid was in the hands of someone who was trained in the business of protecting and serving?

"Hey Ms. Elvia, did we wake you?"

"No, I was checking the perimeter and locking up the house when I saw you come in on the security camera. I finished up while you were in with the little one; I figured you needed some time alone with him after today." Elvia moved closer and looked down at the phone in Heart's hand. "Praying to the saints for your speedy recovery, Mr. Kenneth."

"Thanks, Elvia," Kenneth answered.

The middle-aged woman with kind brown eyes and a little sprinkling of grey mixing in the jet black waves that she kept tightly confined by an immovable bun stuck her hands out and the excited baby sitting in Heart's lap lifted his arms for his beloved companion.

Heart took a moment to lean over and kiss the top of Amare's dark curls and pulled her phone back in front of her face.

"Babe, see you in a few. Everything's good here."

~

*K*enneth let the phone drop to the bed. His eyes closed and his smile broadened, he let the vision of his wife and his son pour over him and fill him. He was stuck in a hospital bed, with a hole inside of his gut, but all of that seemed secondary to the image floating around his head. His family...his family.

After all these years of feeling like he was on the outside, no real anchor to the family he was born to, he'd finally found purchase with Heart and their son. His godparents, David and Pam Porter and his friends, the Tenettis had been the only real semblance of family Kenneth had experienced growing up.

When he'd married Heart, the Amares had been added to the family of his own making, and in his late-thirties, Kenneth found himself surrounded by more family than he'd ever imagined he would have. But even though he loved every single member of his personal band of misfits, there was always that little link missing, that blood of my blood connection that he couldn't claim to anyone except his niece who lived a continent away in France, and his mother who was currently serving a life sentence for crimes connected to his niece's kidnapping and his wife's shooting.

Blood had only ever seemed to bring him pain. Whether it was from loss as in the cases of his father and sister, or from betrayal as evidenced by his mother holding him, his niece, and Heart at gunpoint, blood always made Kenneth hurt.

But with Amare...with Amare, there was only love...so much more than love. That small boy with Kenneth's mirror image stamped across his face, just the thought of him made Kenneth's heart hurt with an ache to be near him.

"You look like you're about ready to float off that bed," the familiar voice filled his ears and pulled him from the happy vision dancing behind his closed lids.

"I just got to see my boy," Kenneth answered as he turned his still-smiling gaze at his friend and attorney, A.J.

"That boy has really been good for you, hasn't he?" A.J. asked.

"Best medicine for anything that ever ailed you, even a bullet wound."

"So has your wife considered my request yet?"

Kenneth turned his eyes away from A.J. and pinched the bridge of his nose. "No," he answered. "But that's because I haven't mentioned it to her yet."

"Kenneth, how long are you going to wait. The kid is going to be in college before you guys make a decision. This would be so good for him," she pleaded.

"And good for you too," he countered. "Don't think I don't know what you're trying to do." "What, throw wealth, love, and attention at your son?" she offered.

"Yes, but also throwing Jeovonni and Gracelyn a bone, and getting them off your scent at the same time."

She rolled her eyes, a standard for A.J. "I don't have to throw them anything, that's what the girls are for."

"Yes, the girls have bought you some time, but a brand new baby boy that you know your parents already love, now that would buy you at least two to five more years."

She squinted her eyes and poked out her bottom lip. It was what Kenneth and her brother John coined her disappointed princess look.

"A.J., this isn't a casual decision, Heart and I feel very strongly about this. We have to really weigh the candidates before we just name someone guardian and godparents to our child. I'll tell her you want a shot at the godmother position, but considering everything that's happened today, I think I should probably bring it up at a later time."

A.J. rolled her eyes again. "With the way your wife hates me, now is probably the best time. You laying up looking all pitiful in a hospital bed might be the only way I get that stubborn woman to agree to let me be godmother to your son." "She doesn't hate you," Kenneth murmured.

A.J. face twisted into a surly pout that said, "Yeah, sure you're right." "Really, she doesn't," he continued.

"I think the jury is still out on that one," she answered.

Kenneth laughed, "You may be right."

"You agreeing that someone else is right. We need a vat of whatever they've got pumping in that I.V. at the office."

Kenneth raised a lone middle finger to greet his friend and work partner. "A.J., you remember my vice president and soon-to-be former friend, Alan Quillen?"

She briefly nodded her head. Kenneth noticed a minor flush under her cheeks. Maybe she's hot? He was sure the room temp was fine, but being shot was probably messing with his internal thermometer so he shrugged his shoulder and turned his gaze back to the tall blond man now standing at the foot of his bed.

"Alan, you remember my attorney, A.J. Tenetti."

Alan nodded. "We've met a couple of times in passing over Searlington Realty contracts."

He thought he saw a strange and silent look pass between his two friends. He closed his eyes and attempted to refocus. When he looked again, it was gone. Kenneth gave himself an internal shake.

Gotta be the morphine.

"I let you out of the office for one damn day and you end up shot. How're you doing man?" Alan asked.

"I've been better," Kenneth laughed. "Thank God for Bryan. He's the only reason I'm still here," Kenneth answered. The thought of his friend lying in the room next to him hurt almost beyond repair and began chopping at the light mood from a few moments before. All the warm and happy that had been infusing his body and circulating through his system with the surprise video call from his wife and son started leveling off, replaced by a slow, cold sorrow. "I'm just praying Bryan will be able to say the same when all of this is said and done."

~

*J*ustice sat in the darkened room looking at the beeping monitors placed strategically around the head of Bryan's bed. They played the same display and sounds repetitively, the waves on the heart monitor going up and down and back up again over and over until the little blip disappeared off the end of the screen and magically reappeared at the beginning again, starting the process all over.

Next was the digital display on the infusion pump of the I.V. Justice watched as the bars ran from full to almost empty, soon the machine would be screaming for attention, beckoning someone to come change its bag of whatever solution was dripping into Bryan's veins.

Then there was the ventilator. The screen was covered with somewhat of a lopsided loop that appeared and disappeared every time the machine pushed a breath into Bryan's chest. It was the loudest sound in the room, its motor a reminder that even though he was broken, Bryan still lived.

Justice looked at everything in that room, over and over again, everything except Bryan. It hurt. There was no other way to describe the searing pain that stabbed Jussy over and over in the same spot. The husband Justice had loved so dearly, even throughout their problems and separations.

Their problems, Justice couldn't even remember what those were right now. They had never been about loving each other enough; they were covered in that department. But somehow, they'd managed to let the outside world seep in through the cracks, and what had started as a tiny fissure had widened over time into this massive canyon that neither of them had been able to cross.

He's here now; you can reach him now, just try.

Justice stood up and placed a tender hand on Bryan's thigh. "I'm here, baby, I've been here. I'm never leaving again. This should prove to you that there's nothing you can do to push me away. You're never going to be rid of me."

"Or us for that matter."

Justice heard the strong voice coming from behind and sank into the relief that came only when you were at the end of your own power and in desperate need of someone else's.

"Six hours since I last spoke to you little sister and you made it across the country already?"

"You know I move through heaven and hell when my family is on the line. And this time I brought reinforcements too."

Justice turned around to find True standing next to their two older brothers, their cousin

Heart, and their father, Hunter. With the exception of Heart's son and husband, the entire Amare clan was present and accounted for.

Justice felt the first tear spill. So small, the tiny pebble of fluid being the last bit of pressure needed to crack through the emotional dam that had been in place for so long.

Hunter was the first to step forward, wrapping familiar arms around Jussy, providing the blanket of security that felt like life at this moment.

"Daddy," was all Justice could mutter before the torrent came and washed the last little bit of resolve away. Justice and the rest of the Amare kids had always referred to their father as Pops, but tonight, the scared child living inside the adult just wanted to be protected from all the bad stuff by the hero-father who always made everything better.

"He's tough, Jussy, he's always been tough. He'd have to be to love one of my children so perfectly. He will get through this, but he's going to need you. He's going to need all of us."

The rest of the family all gathered around Justice and Hunter and closed ranks around them in a protective wall. Just a few moments in the presence of the Amare clan and Justice felt the internal battery that seemed to be flashing empty a few moments ago quickly refuel, its stores rising through the fear and worry and breaking through to the hope the dreary image of pain had begun to smother.

"Has there been any change since I last spoke with the surgeon?" True asked.

"No," Justice answered. "His vitals have been pretty much borderline and he still hasn't regained consciousness."

"Have you talked to him?" True queried.

"Who?"

"To Bryan," she answered. "We don't know why, but sometimes, when people are

unconscious, they respond to the voices of the people they love."

Justice took in what True was saying and thought back over the hours spent perched at

Bryan's bedside. They'd been filled with quiet. Justice pulled out of the family embrace and turned to Bryan, still quiet, still motionless, still teetering between life and death.

"Marine," Justice began with their pet name for one another. They'd met just after basic training on Paris Island booked on the same flight to their initial duty assignment. The connection had been instant, and after only a few hours on a plane together, the bond they'd created was unimaginable.

They'd been busy in their respective details, no real time for dating. But that thing that had their souls locked together forced them to carve out time whenever they could to allow their link to flourish. Deciding to keep the world out of their business, they'd only referred to one another as Marine to keep anyone off their romantic trail. It was something that had stuck even though Bryan had opted out of the Corps after four years, while Jussy remained on a twenty-year career track.

"This is Colonel Justice Amare of the United States Marine Corps," Justice bellowed in that proud Marine voice that basic training had beaten into a newly indoctrinated private seventeen years ago. "I've been told you did a brave thing today by saving Kenneth's life," Justice continued. "My response, you're a Marine, my Marine, and that's what we do. We get shit done, and lay down our lives for our country and the ones we love. But here's the thing, Marine, your mission isn't over.

"I know you're tired," Justice said as the struggle to keep a quivering voice as steady as possible was almost lost. "I can see how tired you are. But Marine, we don't do shit halfway. We finish the job. Always. So you finish this job, you come back to me. I need my husband back and I want him back now. Do you hear me, Marine? That is a direct order from your C.O. You get your shit together, you get up off your ass, and you bring me my husband back. Once you've done that, you'll have completed your mission. Finish the mission, baby, come back to me."

Justice looked for any change and saw none. Bryan still lay in the same eerie, frozen position since Justice's arrival so many hours ago.

Defeat, that's what this perpetual torture of watching Bryan wobbling on the brink of death felt like. As an officer in the military, Justice knew tone of voice was enough to make the troops fall in line. *Why doesn't that shit work in the civilian world? Why can't it work now, when I need it, when Bryan needs it?*

Justice placed a hand inside Bryan's digits and turned slightly away from him, hoping to tap into a little of the Amare strength, when the feel of cold meaty fingers tightened once and then twice in quick succession around shaking fingers.

"Bryan?" Justice cried.

"What happened, Jussy?" True asked.

"I think he just squeezed my hand."

CHAPTER 8

"Sir, you really can't do that," Heart heard a female voice that she didn't recognize speaking in a frantic tone.

"Watch me," answered Kenneth in that, "I'm beyond playing with you," voice he used when he was about to skate past mad to ignorant. "You either get me a wheelchair and roll me the few feet next door or I'll walk there under my own power, but I'm going to see Lieutenant Smyth today."

"What the hell are you doing?" Heart asked as she stepped into Kenneth's room.

"Captain Searlington, I'm trying to keep your husband from hurting himself—"

Heart waved a hand stopping the nurse from continuing. "I was talking to him, sweetie," Heart pointed an accusatory finger at Kenneth. "It's very obvious you're trying to keep him from doing something incredibly stupid, like setting his recovery back."

"They didn't care about setting my recovery back when they woke me up at the ass crack of dawn and told me I needed to walk around. Now I want to walk and all of a sudden I'm too fragile?"

She watched as her husband sat on the edge of the bed holding his injured side. His broad chest covered in a white tee, long legs dangling over the edge of the bed, covered in loose sweatpants. Her eyes continued their trek, finding his feet wedged into his favorite pair of thong sandals.

If it wasn't for the fact that he was in a hospital bed, this is exactly what he looked like when he woke up at home.

"Kenneth, you'll have plenty of time to see Bryan."

"Just not right now?" he answered. "What's wrong with him, Heart?" Why won't you let me see him?"

"Kenneth..." she couldn't finish the sentence. Didn't even really know how to. Saying the words out loud just made the situation all the more real. Considering how much of a bitch reality was being right now, Heart didn't feel the need to speak existence to anymore of her bullshit at the moment.

Kenneth stood up, placing a strong hold on the wheeled I.V. pole at his side. He took gentle steps away from his bed, and when he seemed comfortable enough that he wasn't going to fall on his face he walked past his wife and out into the hall. He looked from left to right and then headed to the right where her officers were guarding Bryan's door.

This stubborn man was going to be the death of her. She dragged in a ragged breath and turned to follow him. She stepped inside the room just moments after him, her heart ratcheting up to a panicked irregular beat when Kenneth turned to her, his bright Azure eyes dim and heavy with hurt.

He snatched his eyes away from her and passed them across the other inhabitants in the room.

"Law, Free, True...Justice?" he asked carefully. "What are you all doing here?"

Four pairs of careful brown eyes moved past Kenneth and looked to her, all asking the same question. *Is it all right?*

She gave them the only answer she could, there wasn't really much else she could do in this situation, the truth always did have a way of catching up with her.

"Bryan is our brother-in-law, Kenneth," Law answered. "Of course we would be here in his time of need, that's what family does."

She watched him from the side as he began to calculate the pieces that were being thrown at him.

Heart watched Kenneth turn to her cousin True. His eyes were still questioning even though words had not yet crossed his lips.

"True, you and Bryan are married?"

Heart felt her breath catch in her throat. Why couldn't it be any of the other Amare kids except True? Her reckless mouth was not what was called for in this situation.

"Me and Bryan married, nah. He likes dick just as much as I do, it would never work out."

All eyes in the room fell on True, all with the same expression buried in them. *Really, really, who the fuck says shit like that at someone's deathbed?*

"What, am I lying?" True asked.

Heart watched Kenneth carefully, her cousins did too. He was piecing it together, understanding was just in reach.

"What?" Kenneth whispered. He looked back at Heart for confirmation, but before she could speak she heard Justice's voice fill the quiet of the room.

"He's their brother-in-law Kenneth because he's my husband," Justice uttered. "And I'm his."

~

*J*ustice felt uncomfortable in the silent room. There were too many bodies in the small space for there to be so little noise. He raised himself to his full height of six feet three inches and waited for Kenneth to say something.

Being a black man who'd spent the last seventeen years in the military, Justice was often wary of the first few moments after someone discovered he was gay. In those few minutes you learned who you were really dealing with in that time.

Kenneth had always been good people. He had always been supportive of Heart and the people she served. He never seemed to be defined by his wealth or breeding, always open and welcoming to all people. But for some people, their tolerance had limits. Although he was married to Justice's cousin, and trust, looking at Heart you could never mistake her for anything other than a sista, but that didn't mean he could accept his wife's gay cousin and his husband. *Come on Searlington, show me who you are?*

Justice watched Kenneth lift a shaky hand placing it around Bryan's. "He saved my life," Kenneth murmured.

"That's all you have to say?" Justice replied.

Kenneth held Justice's gaze, a beat, then two passed before he spoke again. "That's all that matters."

"So you don't have anything at all to say about finding out that Bryan and I are gay?"

"Oh trust me, there's an entire conversation that you, me, and Bryan are going to have. And the topic of you being gay might come up, among other things," Kenneth answered. "But right now, the only thing I care about is finding out what's going on with my friend, the man that saved my life. If that's not what you want to talk about then I'm afraid I've got nothing else for you right now."

Justice took in Kenneth's words and nodded his head. It wasn't a glowing endorsement of tolerance, but it was better than some of the hateful things he'd heard come out of people's mouths when he came out to them.

He looked down at Bryan and smiled at him. *We might have to kick his ass later, Bryan. But for now, at least Kenneth's head is screwed on straight. At least I don't have to kill him today.*

Justice let his muscles relax and he could see the poised readiness of his siblings slowly dissipating. They'd been ready to go on attack for him and his, just one more reason he loved his family. You fucked with one Amare, you got them all.

God save the poor fool, who got them all, because that was a man whose end was near. Too many had found that out the hard way in the past, and the next person to learn that very painful lesson would be the man who put Justice's husband in this bed.

∾

*K*enneth hurt. Yeah, his body wasn't feeling its best right now, but if it were just the physical pain twisting him in knots he'd be able to deal with this situation that left him feeling like he couldn't carry his own weight.

He turned gingerly looking for the nearest chair and was immediately flanked by Law and Free helping him fall carefully into it.

His eyes collected the pieces that made up this awful image. Machines and tubes tangled all around Bryan.

Bryan...

A large man, similar to Kenneth in height with the added bulk of thick muscle that Kenneth would never possess no matter how much weight he lifted, Bryan filled up the much too small hospital bed. Kenneth sat there for the longest time attempting to figure out how someone so strong could manage to look so broken and fragile.

"I always thought that if we ever ended up here it would be because you were protecting my wife. I never thought...I never thought it would be to save me. I never would have asked you to do this for me. She's everything; the world needs her, but me..."

Kenneth took in a slow breath trying to quiet the pain that was threatening to overwhelm him. "I'm so grateful for what you did, but if you think you're getting a thank you right now, you're wrong. Get up, talk the usual shit you would to me when we share the same space, and then and only then will I thank you. Just in case you didn't know it, you're more than just my wife's partner, you're my friend..." Kenneth turned his head and affixed eyes on the Amares and his wife. "...my family."

~

*J*ustice stepped into the hall watching his cousin as she spoke to the officers on duty in the ICU. With a quick slant of his head he caught her attention, and when he stepped out of the unit and into the family waiting area she was only a few steps behind him.

"You worried about Kenneth?" he asked.

She shrugged her shoulders. "Not really, not the way you're thinking anyway. Kenneth's not homophobic, Jussy. It's just, this is big, and he's my husband, and I never mentioned it."

She moved further inside of the room and slumped down into one of the hard plastic chairs that lined the walls. "If he didn't know Bryan, it probably wouldn't be an issue, but he and Bryan are boys, and you know he loves you too. He just doesn't do well with the people he loves keeping secrets from him."

"You sound like you have experience in that. Everything all right between you two?"

His cousin was never one to provide an overabundance of details about her life. Coming from a military and law enforcement family, it was a fatal flaw that all of them seemed to possess. But standing here watching his cousin, he could see concern all over her. He knew that they'd had a rough patch after losing their first baby to an ectopic pregnancy. A pain like that, something so deep it embedded itself into every molecule of your being, it could definitely change you, change the dynamics of a relationship.

But they seemed happy despite their loss, and little Amare was the single most adored baby on the planet. Until this moment, Justice would never have questioned the bond his cousin and her husband shared. But the subtle creases in her brow and the sad lines making her mouth hang just this side of worried made his protective instincts crawl beneath the surface of his skin.

"You want me to talk to him, Heart?"

She looked up at him with weary eyes. She'd been through hell with him these last few days. Heart worried right along with him about her husband and his with the added pressure of trying to spearhead a massive manhunt and protection detail. Now that her husband was out of the woods she should be relaxing in blessed relief, not borrowing trouble that hadn't quite found her yet.

"Nah, it'll be fine," she whispered. "Kenneth and I will be fine. He's going to be pissed at me for keeping this secret, but we'll be fine."

"Why did you?" he asked. "I've never asked you to keep my sexuality a secret. Outside of my work I've never been in the closet. The few times it's come up on the job I've never hidden who I was, what I am. And the truth is, since 'don't ask, don't tell' took effect, there's no need for me to hide anymore. Trust, it ain't easy being a gay Marine. For all the new equality laws passed, the military is still homophobic and racist as hell, but I don't have to hide. But you know all this cousin, so I'm sitting here wondering, why would you keep this from your husband? I know you're not ashamed of me, I know I've always had your love and support, and I think the only person happier than Bryan and me when we took our vows was you. So why hide us from your husband?"

"Because Bryan..."

Her answer settled in his gut like a hard brick splashing down so heavy, the bile in his stomach rose up in a powerful wave. He put a closed fist to his mouth and tried to stifle the wretch that was working so hard against his gag reflex.

Because Bryan is still in hiding, it wasn't a question; he knew the answer was yes. Of the two of them, Bryan had always had the harder time embracing his sexuality publicly. When they were with Jussy's family, Bryan was able to relax, let down that carefully placed façade that he always wore. But elsewhere, in front of other people, he just never managed to just be who he really was.

"Jussy, you of all people know it isn't that simple. You know what he's been through; you know what he's lost. His experience with being a gay black man was totally different from yours."

Justice nodded, his cousin was speaking truth. Bryan had gone through hell and back because of who he was, and it was so difficult not to bear soul-deep scars when you battled the devil and won. But that still didn't make the knowledge that his husband had never forgiven himself for winning that battle, had never been truly able to live a free life since he'd escaped from the battleground any easier to swallow.

"I know, cousin, I know." He reached over and gave Heart's hand a light squeeze. "But we're not talking about me and mine. We're talking about you and yours. Are the two of you going to be all right? Is protecting my husband's secret going to damage your home?"

"Kenneth and I will be fine," she laughed. "He'll be pissed, there's no doubt about that. He already is. But I ain't the only one that's going to suffer the rich boy's wrath. He's gonna be gunning for you too. And let me tell you, he may be pretty and all, but that man is no joke, having him mad at you is not going to be fun. So, get ready."

"I'm a Colonel in the United States Marine Corps. I think I can handle a rich boy with a ponytail that sits behind a desk for a living."

"Yeah okay," his cousin answered. She gave a hearty laugh as she raised up and headed for the door. She took one final glance at him, and began laughing again as she walked through the door.

It can't really be that bad, can it?

CHAPTER 9

*H*eart parked her cruiser on the sidewalk in front of the station house. No time to be bothered with driving around to the parking lot, she wanted inside her precinct fast. She shoved the door open and headed through the squad room without stopping.

"Grazzo," she bellowed not breaking her stride until she was inside her office, preparing to sit behind her desk. She didn't need to look for her third, as his commanding officer she knew that when she spoke, he did. It was as simple as that. She looked up just as the backs of her thighs met her high-backed chair to see Grazzo closing her door behind him.

"What'cha got for me, Grazzo?"

"Cap, what're you doing back here? Shouldn't you be at the hospital with Mr. Searlington?"

With a cocked brow she focused on her sergeant. A small smile pulled at the corner of her mouth as she motioned for him to take a seat in front of her desk. "Your concern about my whereabouts notwithstanding, I asked you a question and I'm expecting an answer, Grazzo."

She watched the sergeant fidget a little in his seat. Grazzo was a great investigator, way better than she and Bryan were at his age, but he still had a few things to learn, like knowing how to get down to business when his commanding officer asked for a situational update.

Grazzo pulled his notebook from his pocket and began flipping pages. The image taking her back into her past when she was the sergeant and it was her duty to report to Big Willie or Porter. It was almost comical how things had changed in a handful of years. Now it was her job to lead, a job she wasn't always certain she was succeeding at.

Her Captaincy had not been easy, she'd worked hard for it, but it had been a ridiculous struggle to balance life with work, especially on cases like this when the two intersected in a loud cataclysmic crash.

Her best friend, her partner had been shot as he protected her husband. Still unconscious, still hanging on to the tiniest sliver of life by his fingertips, Bryan's case was paramount. The attempted murder of an officer was what needed to come first, but everything in her told her that following the why, following the initial target, her husband, would bring Bryan's attempted killers to justice.

"We've been scouring through the surveillance, and street cameras as well as security camera footage from any of the local businesses in the area. We got an image of someone setting up the laser on the rooftop after our people cleared it during the pre-press conference sweep you ordered."

Grazzo opened a folder and placed a clear color picture of a darkly dressed figure with a skull cap, hood, and bandana covering his or her face from the nose down in front of her. The only distinctive feature she could make out was a pair of slate gray eyes.

"Well this is useless," she countered. "This could be anyone."

"I know," he answered, raising a hopeful finger as he pointed to the next photo he'd placed on her desk. "But from the surveillance shots we picked up something that piqued our interest.

Take a look at this."

She looked down at the photo and followed his finger to a man who appeared Latino or Caucasian with a black baseball cap on, jeans, a plaid button down, and construction work boots. His face was covered in a full dark beard and she could see short, dark locks licking out from under the cap. She looked at the picture again to see what she was missing, then smoke-tinted irises called to her from the image.

She said nothing, just raised knowing eyes to Grazzo and waited for him to continue. Heart took another glance at the green eyes looking back at her from the original photo. "Please tell me we have something else?"

"We do. The man with the baseball cap goes inside the deli on the corner, five minutes later, this woman walks onto the scene."

Another darkly dressed figured, it appeared to be an Islamic woman dressed in a hijab that covered her head, chest, and face entirely with the exception of her eyes.

"There's nothing overwhelmingly alarming about an Islamic woman being on scene. In that area of East New York there is a huge population of Islamic residents. Just look up and down

Pitkin and Ave. What's so..."

A quick glance down again and she had the answer to her question.

Her eyes...she has the same eyes.

"Give me more," she uttered quickly making a 'gimmie that' motion with her hand. It wasn't a question; the tiny glint of light that danced around his coal eyes told her he had more information for her.

He opened the folder again and gave her a still shot of the apparent 'woman' pull a rifle from beneath her robes, take aim, and fire.

When she looked up from the picture again, Grazzo eyes were reflecting her very own thoughts.

Got him.

"Any idea who he is?"

"No, I don't," he answered carefully, then moved out of his seat and headed toward the door. "But I contacted someone with bigger resources than ours that seemed really eager to help us find this bastard."

Heart sat back as the tall figure sauntered into her office with a heady mix of confidence and arrogance that seemed to be par for the course in his particular line of work.

"Captain Searlington," he asked with a sly smile. "How can I be of service?"

Heart laughed, walking around her desk to offer the man her hand in greeting. A wary smile graced her lips. "Supervisory Special Agent, Caleb Weaver. How the hell are you?"

Caleb Weaver had been slightly problematic the last time they'd worked together a few years ago. He'd been assigned to her precinct by the governor to assist in finding a serial killer that was terrorizing Brooklyn. His work was exemplary, he'd hit the streets with her detectives, never once putting on airs about the importance of his lofty FBI badge. But he and Kenneth didn't always see eye to eye after he'd unknowingly let some inappropriate remarks slip in front of her husband.

Be that as it may, Kenneth was going to have to suck that shit up because the only thing

Heart cared about was finding out who'd put a bullet in both Bryan and Kenneth, and making them pay for it. Everything else was secondary.

"I'm eager to get to work and figure out who was stupid enough to cross you. You got a spare space you can lend me so I can get to work?"

She nodded. "For now you can take Grazzo's desk, he's going to be working from Smyth's while he's out."

Weaver nodded his head and made his way back to the door where Grazzo was standing. He was almost halfway out the door before he turned around to face her again. "Captain, this has to be the biggest fool in the world. He hit two of your people on the same day," Weaver let out a slow whistle. "He must have a death wish."

"He certainly must," she answered. "And I'm about to grant him his wish, just as soon as you tell me who the hell I'm dealing with."

❧

*I*t had only been a few days since Kenneth had last stepped on the winding staircase that led to his front door, but it felt like months. The landscape was all familiar, the almost sweet smell of the grass on their front lawn, the large white stairs that wound a path to the front porch, all things he recognized as part of his home. But as he took his first step toward the house, strangeness permeated his chest making him halt his accent to the house.

"You all right?" his wife asked.

The truth was, he didn't really know. Standing here on the steps of their home had always been the cue for the calm and relaxation of refuge to push away the day's anxieties and worries.

But now, where was that feeling? After everything he'd experienced in this short span of time nothing should have been more welcoming than the sight of the place where his family lived.

He looked down at his wife briefly as his thoughts traveled to the dark place his heart had been visiting over and over since the family dropped their bombshell in Bryan's hospital room.

Maybe that's because it doesn't really feel all that much like family right now. Family doesn't lie to you. Or at least they shouldn't.

Why this news that Bryan and Jussy were married came as such a shock to him, he didn't know. He also knew it wasn't really about them being married that bothered him; it was the collaborative effort of the entire Amare clan, his wife included in that number, to keep him out of the loop. Because obviously the only people that needed to know were family members. And apparently, he wasn't family.

"I'm fine," he uttered and continued his hike up the stairs. Placing his foot on the last step, he leaned against the wall to catch his breath.

Damn. He'd never quite noticed how many steps or how deep of an incline there was from the street to his front porch.

The opening of the front door pulled his attention away from his current state of exertion. His father-in-law, Marcus MacKenzie stood in the doorway ushering Kenneth into his own living room.

"How are you feeling, son?"

He'd heard Marcus call him that for years. It was probably pretty typical of all fathers-in-law to address their sons-in-law in such a familial fashion. But today all Kenneth could wonder was if Marcus was in on the conspiracy too to keep him out of the loop.

"Marcus, what are you doing here?"

"I've been bouncing in since you went into the hospital to check on things for you and Heart and help Elvia with my grandson."

Kenneth looked back over his shoulder to watch his wife closing the door behind herself as she entered the house.

"Heart must have forgotten to mention it. Seems she's been forgetting to tell me a lot of things recently," he replied. "Where's Amare?"

Marcus pointed up the staircase. "He went down for his morning nap about ten minutes ago."

Disappointment settled inside of Kenneth's stomach. If his son wasn't awake, he didn't see much cause in him staying up either.

"I'm going to head to the guestroom and take a nap. Those stairs look a bit daunting right now."

Heart took a step in his direction, but Kenneth held up his hand to stop her.

"I'm fine," Kenneth snapped. His face burning with what he knew was a pale rose hue, "I'm not a child, and I can decide what I need for myself. Right now I just need some rest."

He turned around without speaking and ambled slowly into the guestroom and closed the door. When the soft click of the lock filled the room, he sighed a relieved breath and climbed into the bed, toeing off his shoes. His mind tried to stir, attempting to find some meaning in his actions, but Kenneth refused to allow his thoughts to take form. Instead he rolled over onto his back and kept a pillow at his side to give his healing abdomen a little cushioned comfort. Soon, sleep called him and he answered its summons without hesitation. At least in sleep he didn't have to worry about pesky secrets rocking his ability to trust.

~

*H*eart could feel her father's eyes on her, the questions he had loudly knocking around the silent room.

Kenneth was pissed, there wasn't much getting around that, but this silent thing he was doing was disturbing. Running and throwing up passive-aggressive behaviors was her bag, how she dealt, or in most cases didn't deal with the shit life dumped in her plate. Kenneth usually wanted to talk shit out, hammer at it until it was laid bare before them.

She hated that shit most of the time. Especially when they had to do it in front of that miserable therapist they saw intensively for the first few months after their marriage nearly exploded into a very ugly scene. Hell, the word ugly was a kind way to describe what actually happened. The truth was things could have very easily tipped over into physical violence if her husband hadn't had as much control over himself as he did.

"He all right?" Marcus asked.

She put on her cop face, the one that hid all of her secrets behind a cool and calm mask. "He's fine, just tired and worried about Bryan. Once he wakes up from his nap and has a chance to play with Amare I'm sure he will be fine."

Heart felt that very familiar darkness trying to enter her soul again and she refused to allow it entry.

I'll give you the day to get your shit together, Searlington, but after that. We hash this shit out.

"You home for the day?"

Marcus' voice pulled her out of her thoughts and forced her to focus on the moment at hand.

"Yeah, if you need to bounce you can."

He shook his head. "Nah, I cleared my schedule. Unless you want to me to leave, I'd never pass up an opportunity to spend some time with my family."

Family, there was that fucking word again. It kept coming back like a bad fucking burrito. Her devotion to her family was unwavering, always had been. There was never a question of her protecting those whom she loved, including their secrets. After all, they did the same for her, buried her secrets in the bottom of their souls and never brought them to daylight again. Her family kept her secrets safe from those that would seek to destroy her, doing the same for them was something that came as naturally to her as her gun on her hip. But now there was a slight fissure in her situation, she was forced to protect family from family and either way she turned, she risked hurting someone she loved.

"Hey," she heard Marcus say, concern coloring his usual tenor with a little more depth and fullness. "He's fine, he's home."

"I know it's just..." she shook her head and turned around to face her father. "Marcus, I

don't understand how you don't hate me."

"What? Where the hell did that come from?" he asked cautiously.

She and her father hadn't experienced the traditional father-daughter connection. Her mother dying at birth, leaving him to care for her hadn't worked out so well for either of them. She'd spent fourteen years thinking her father had made an attempt on her life that left her emotionally broken and unable to bear the touch of another person. Fourteen years' worth of hell all due to a secret her father and her family had kept from her. A secret that had festered until it nearly destroyed her and the people she loved.

It had taken years for Heart and Marcus to rebuild. Brick by brick they had built something comfortable. She couldn't say they were as close as Marcus wanted them to be, but they were close enough that having him in her life, in her family was a gift she cherished.

"I took the woman you loved from you. My life meant her death. I don't think I really recognized what a huge loss that was until I was waiting in that family room filled with cops, wondering if I'd ever see my husband alive again. The thought of losing him…"

Marcus walked closer to her, extending his arms open, hands palm up and exposed. She watched them with care, eyes dancing back from his hands to his face. Soft brown eyes called to the child that had spent so many years aching for the father she'd thought she'd lost.

She moved cautiously into the embrace and let relief seep through her when those protective arms lightly hugged her. It had taken nearly twenty years, but the touch of the man holding her didn't make her want to run. Instead she tucked into the warmth of his chest and arms and nearly purred as his slow hand gave a tender pet to her head.

"Baby, there has never been a day that I hated you. I might not have known the best way to express it, but you were always the child of my heart. Why do you think I named you that?"

She was too raw to speak, if she did the wall of tears she was stemming by sheer will would tumble down. Instead she shrugged her shoulders quickly and settled back into the touch her father was supplying.

It was amazing; she'd spent so many years without any touch, unable to bear it even in its briefest forms from anyone except the kids she worked with at Mac's Place. But Kenneth's touch broke the spell, and since he'd shown her the necessity of touch all those years ago, it was like her body and mind constantly craved safe ways to fulfill that need.

Marcus continued to stroke her hair, seeming to be in no rush to evict her from her space between his arms. It felt good to be there, her soul unwinding the tight knots that it had bound itself in throughout this horrible ordeal.

"I gave you the name Heart. Your mother wanted to name you Constance. She said there were too many odd names in your family and she wanted a normal name. I'd fought her tooth and nail, but your mama was an Amare child, and being stubborn is a birthright for you people."

She couldn't have argued with him if she'd tried. It was second nature for the Amare clan to dig their heels in and demand their way. Although she'd never met her mother, she could definitely believe she shared their famous stubborn streak.

"She walked around all nine months of her pregnancy calling you Constance. Finally one day, just before she went into labor with you I told her I hated that blasted name and that I wanted to keep up the Amare tradition of choosing a special word that we hoped you'd live up to as you grew. I told her I wanted to name you Heart, because two hearts had made one, and because you were the center of both our hearts.

"Your mother rolled her eyes and laughed at me. She said she'd never heard anything so silly and corny all her life. But when you were born, and for the few minutes that she got to hold you and love you, she finally agreed with me, that you were much more Heart than Constance.

Her last words were, 'You are my Heart, and I'll always love you'

"I gave you that name because even before I knew you, I loved you. I have always loved you. And even though it broke me to lose your mother like that, I never once regretted having you in my life. You were my heart then, and you still are now. Never doubt that, little one."

She pulled out of his embrace and looked up at him. She hadn't heard those words cross his lips since she was a very small child. It was always how he soothed her when she was upset as a kid.

"I don't know if I could have been as strong as you. I don't know if I could have survived losing him like that."

"And fortunately you don't have to find that out. The only thing you need to focus on is the fact that he is here. Whatever it is that has you so worried, as long as you're both here. There's always a chance to get it right."

"How can you be so certain of that?"

He stepped forward and put a light peck of a kiss on top of her head. "Because I'm standing here holding my daughter that I feared would never find her way back to me."

They heard the stirrings of her son through a nearby baby monitor and smiled at one another.

Whether he knew it or not, that little boy's timing was just the ray of sunshine she needed in her spirit. He was living proof that love could barrel through even the most solid strongholds.

"Can you check on him for me?"

Marcus' smile widened showing a full set of white teeth. His usual disposition when he was around his grandson.

"You don't even have to ask," he beamed as he made his way up the steps.

Heart took the short few steps to the guestroom and opened the door slowly. Kenneth was laying across the bed in a diagonal fashion hugging a king-sized pillow to his side. She stepped into the room and sat near his head. Her fingers found the dark strands of their own accord. Whenever she was near him, they ached, almost itched to touch his hair. She stroked and stroked until the uneasiness she'd been carrying since Kenneth found out the truth left her. She looked down at him, noticing the flutter of his eyelids as he worked his way through sleep and back to wakefulness.

"You keep doing that and I'll never get up," he muttered.

She stopped the motion of her hand. "Well we can't have that," she answered. "I need you awake in order to have a conversation."

"I'm sure my doctor forbade me to engage in any deep conversations for at least another week. In fact, I think it's expressly written in my discharge instructions." "Kenneth," she chided.

"Heart," he replied.

What were they doing? They were always able to talk to one another, even through the worst of times. When it had been her who had fallen victim to a crazy person's bullet, he'd used his words to soothe her, keep her sane, and to work her body back into fighting shape. When she'd fought against the love and attraction that blossomed between them, he'd talked her through that too, eased her fears with the calm timber of his voice. When they'd lost their first child he talked and talked, even though she'd fought him every step of them way, even when she'd lashed out at him in an unthinkable way. He'd talked and eventually, with the help of their therapist, she learned to listen, and then talk for herself as well.

"Heart, if you're gearing up to talk to me about Bryan and Justice, then don't. I don't want to talk about it. You've spent the last four and half years of our marriage lying to me, and I'm not really ready to address that yet."

"Kenneth, all you need—"

"Stop fucking telling me what I need," he bellowed. "I'm a grown man; I know what the hell I need. What I need is for my wife to be straight with me, for her not to keep secrets from me. You've had more than four years to figure out how to explain your choices and actions to me; I think you can wait a little longer until I'm actually ready to hear that explanation."

She wanted to defend herself, to explain that she hadn't lied to him at all. But then that quiet little voice inside her head chastised her with a firm, *he's right, you did lie. A lie of omission is still a lie.*

She looked down into clear blue eyes and opened her mouth to speak. She was moderately intelligent, she should be able to come up with something to make Kenneth understand. She worked in law enforcement for goodness sake; she of all people should be able to come up with a sound enough argument to get her out of this emotional predicament with the man she loved.

But when she looked down into those hypnotic eyes…those disappointed eyes… She couldn't stand it. They were so filled with sadness and disappointment. Reading his disillusionment, coupled with the knowledge that she'd placed those murky clouds there, all thoughts to save herself ceased and she could only think about saving her husband.

"You're right, I did lie to you and we do need to talk about that. But if you're not up for it now, we can do it another time."

The relief that eased through him at her declaration was almost palpable. The previous tightness he carried in his body seeming to bleed away with each passing cleansing breath.

"So if you don't want to talk about my fuckup, then what do you want to talk about. 'Cause just because I'm letting you off the hook with that conversation doesn't mean you get to not talk to me at all."

A sharp glint of light flickered in his eyes and he carefully maneuvered himself into a sitting position then he said, "I want to talk about making Alexis-Jeovonni Amare's godmother."

CHAPTER 10

*E*motional blackmail, that's what this was. There may have been some fancy name for it that a shrink would use, but in its simplest terms, that's the only reason she was sitting at the food court at the Valley Stream Mall on Sunrise waiting on this fancy ass bitch, A.J. Tenetti, to show up.

She'd fucked up, both Heart and Kenneth knew that, and he knew she would do just about anything to stay in his good graces right now. He'd thrown this fucking wildcard at her and it had stuck, because above all else, she loved her husband, and she wanted his happiness. But this shit was cruel and unusual punishment as far as Heart was concerned.

She peeked into the transforming monstrosity that closely resembled an armored truck rather than the infant's stroller it was supposed to be, checking on their sleeping son. Fucking True, she'd rolled that big ass thing into their baby shower and declared that her nephew-cousin— because only True could come up with some silly ass name for what was technically termed her first cousin once removed, should ride in luxury, but be protected like he was in a tank.

Her eyes scanned the crowd again looking for the designer clothing whore, but still, she saw nothing.

"She'll be here," her husband offered.

"It would suit me fine if she didn't show."

"Heart, you know what this means to me. I don't understand why you just can't be nice to A.J."

"You don't understand?" Heart questioned. "Is this not the same chick that tried to get me to sign some shady pre-nuptial agreement without you even asking her to draw one up in the first place?"

Kenneth shrugged his shoulders. "Heart, she is my attorney, and I am ridiculously wealthy.

We'd only known each other six months when we got married. A two-week engagement didn't lend a great deal of confidence to our being together out of love. She was just doing her job."

"Kenneth, you believe that bullshit if you want to. Doing her job would have been sending a messenger to deliver the papers, or making an appointment with me and encouraging me to bring my own attorney with me. That bitch showed up at my precinct unannounced and used her past connections with the district attorney's office to push past my desk sergeant and ambush me in my office. She slapped papers on my desk and tried to get me to sign them without reading them.

That shit was sneaky, and it was personal.

"I haven't figured what her angle is yet, maybe it's 'cause she always wanted her big brother's best friend, or maybe it's because she really looks at you like a brother she needs to protect, that bitch is too personally involved where you're concerned. Not to mention, I don't trust her sneaky ass. Something ain't right with them Tenettis and I don't want you and Amare around them."

"Aww, Captain. You wound me, really you do."

Heart rolled her eyes; she couldn't even find it in herself to be ashamed the subject of her conversation had heard her rant. She'd meant every bit of what she'd said, and if A.J. needed a recap from the beginning, Heart would be more than happy to start from the top.

"You really don't like me, huh?" A.J. asked with a playful smile.

"I don't trust you," Heart responded.

"You don't know me. Whenever I come around, you all of a sudden become scarce."

"That's because I'm trying to keep from ringing your neck. What I do know of you rubs me the wrong way, why would I invest more time in you?" "What do you know about me?" A.J. asked.

Heart let her eyes take the short walk down the petite woman's body. Standing at just over five feet, Heart was sure she could use A.J.'s head as some sort of coffee stand if her busy ass would stop flicking her long perfectly coiled curls enough to keep her damn head still.

She wore a sleeveless cloud gray wrap dress that was belted at her tiny waist with a pewter belt to match the expensive handbag and six inch stilettos of the same color. When A.J. sat down directly across from Heart, dangling one dainty leg over the other, she could see those classic red-bottomed shoes that screamed to anyone who knew what they were that the owner of those shoes was paid.

"A.J. we're at a mall, everyone else in this mug is dressed in jeans, t-shirts, sweats, what us commoners call casual wear. It's comfortable, it's utilitarian, and it allows us to run in to all of the stores in the mall with speed and ease. You just stepped in this piece wearing a designer dress, and shoes that cost more than the living expenses of most of the shoppers here.

"Every time I see you you're either talking about the latest and greatest, or modeling it for our pleasure. Doesn't matter whether is cars, clothes, or housing, you always have to show folks that money is your god. I don't really want to be around someone like you, because if money is the only thing you respect, you'll sell anyone out just to get more of it."

The quiet at the table seemed to drown out the surrounding mall sounds. She could see the muscle in her husband's jaw ticking his displeasure. A.J. on the other hand looked smooth and unfazed. Her reddish-brown skin was glowing makeup flawless, honey-blond and brown curls hanging perfectly over her shoulders. Not a thing out of place, always so cool, calm, and unaffected.

"Assume much?" A.J. asked. A tiny quirk of the corner of her mouth let that, "smart as sin and sly as the devil" expression she wore in the courtroom flourish. "Yes, I like very nice things, mostly because I can afford them. I can afford them, because I work eighty or more hours a week getting shit done for my clients that no other attorney can do. I'm a fixer, when shit explodes,

I'm the one that not only calls the cleanup crew, I manage those motherfuckers so that the mess is discarded in such a way that you'd never have known how fucked up things were before I stepped my pretty ass shoes on the scene. People like your husband pay me unimaginable amounts of money because I do the unimaginable. Money is not the god in this situation,

Captain. *I* am."

Heart bit the inside of her lip. The bitch was arrogant, there was no denying that, but Heart certainly couldn't argue about her tactics. Heart had seen the woman in the courtroom as both a prosecutor and a defense attorney. It didn't matter which side or position, the woman was a beast. She knew it, her competitors knew it, and somewhere deep down, Heart knew it too.

"Now, quit stalling and tell me why you really don't like me."

"My reasons are the same as I stated. You're just superficial and I can't entrust my kid to someone like that. I want my child to know that money is cool, but that it doesn't define who he is or make him better than the next human being. I want him to embrace qualities that can't be bought, like integrity and compassion."

"There you go assuming again," A.J. answered. "I don't know why you think I'm some cold hearted princess who doesn't care for anything other than the amount of zeros in her bank account."

Heart watched A.J., she was still the perfect rendering of what money could buy. But somewhere behind the mound of flawless makeup a flash of fire sparked in her hazel eyes.

"You really do want to do this?" Heart asked. "Don't you?" Heart crossed her arms over her chest and leaned her head to one side as she watched the young woman sitting opposite her. Beneath that perfect image Heart saw a little bit of need. It licked out and disappeared just as quickly as it had come, but Heart had definitely seen it.

Why does a woman like this want my son so bad? Why does she want to be a godparent so much?

A.J. remained silent, probably afraid that whatever bullshit she laid out Heart would see through. She wouldn't be the first lawyer to trip up in her own words.

Maybe it's time to get a little closer to the counselor? Maybe it's time I found out exactly what she's up to.

"All right counselor, you want the chance to stand up for our son, here's how you earn it. Kenneth and I are going to wait three months to Christen Amare; it's the only time I can get all of my family in the same place at the same time. So you've got until then to prove me wrong about you."

"And just how am I supposed to do that?" A.J. replied.

"By volunteering at Mac's Place."

"What?" the word was dipped in heavy sarcasm. "You want me to provide free legal service for the little criminal-children you babysit?"

"Remarks like that aren't going to win you any points with me. Kenneth tells me you spent many years studying classical forms of dance. I want you to pick two Saturdays a month for the next three months and create dance workshops for my kids. Show them how to do something other than make it clap on the dance floor."

A.J. appeared to be rolling the proposition over in her mind. She smiled and her eyes lit up brightly before she spoke. Heart's stomach stirred just a little. Anything that made that bitch smile like that was sure to give Heart an ulcer, so she prepped herself for whatever conniving scheme the woman was thinking up.

"I'll volunteer my dance services, but only under one condition, you take my class too. And if I were you, I'd hit the gym and work off the rest of that baby weight because Mistress Tenetti does not allow jiggling body parts on her dance floor."

*K*enneth must have seen the signs that Heart was about to jump over the table and choke the shit out of that designer label princess, because just as Heart was about to open her mouth he stood up and began pushing the baby's stroller out of the food court and toward the stores.

"I think I saw some shops up ahead that I want to look into."
Fucking liar.

Kenneth was as much a label whore as that barracuda in heels was. He didn't shop in malls, he had people shop for him and the findings sent either to the house or the office. She tuned out the yapping sound of the woman beside her and allowed her eyes to pass through the crowd and people watch.

Mentally processing a scene was always second nature to her. After spending so many years as a police officer, she always paid attention to detail. Didn't matter where she was, or who she was with, or how much of her attention seemed to be on whatever or whomever she was engaging, she always paid attention to her surroundings.

For instance, she could see the teenage couple by the ice cream stand arguing. By the look of the phone the young girl was waving back and forth in front of the boy's face, he was probably receiving some texts from someone he wasn't supposed to be.

Then there was the woman walking out of the nails salon inspecting her new manicure for any imperfections as she attempted to navigate through the empty mall traffic.

A few hundred feet in front of them she could see the kids playing on the stationary car rides and the moms sitting on the bench watching them like a hawk.

And behind them, she could see two men that seemed to be walking in the same direction as them.

The exact same direction.

The threesome walked in and out of ten different stores since meeting in the food court. Even though her prissy ass was too good to shop in a place like a local Long Island mall, that fact didn't stop her from needing to walk in and out of every store in the facility. Every time Heart looked up, those two were close. Not close enough that the average person would be worried, but close enough that her cop sense tingled and put her on alert.

She decided to test her theory. She pointed to the large department store at the end of the path. The place had several exits that opened to different sections of the huge parking lot. It would be easy to get Kenneth, the baby, and A.J. to safety from one of the ground floor exits.

They were in a mall, and these men could be innocently shopping right along with the rest of the consumers, but an attempt had already been made on her husband's life and she wasn't about to take his or their child's safety for granted.

Being safe means you're never sorry.

"Hey guys, let's head in here for a minute." The two followed Heart and she stopped near the makeup counter and turned to her companions. "When I say what I'm about to say I don't want you to react. No matter what I say to you you're going to stand here and smile and you're not going to look around. Got me?"

They both looked at one another then turned concerned eyes toward Heart. She greeted them with a toothy grin and soon Kenneth and A. J. followed with their own wide smiles plastered on their faces and nodded. Heart let her eyes pass quickly over the two large men that were currently in the hosiery aisle attempting to blend in with the sheer and opaque stockings. She could easily make out the distinct outline of a handgun through each of their blazers.

Heart pulled out her phone for both utility and appearance. "Kenneth," she whispered while still looking down at her phone as if she were just checking her notifications. "There are two armed men that have been following us all through the mall. I need you to unstrap Amare and pick him up in your arms. Do it slowly, no sudden moves. When I tell you, you're both going to head out the door and get into the car."

"And what are you going to do?" Kenneth asked her.

"I'm gonna do what I do."

"Heart, I'm not going to just leave you here. I'm not some weak—"

"It's not about that, Kenneth," she pled. "Please…let me do what I'm trained to do."

She picked up her phone, tapped a few numbers and placed the phone next to her ear. "This is Captain Heart Searlington of the seven-four precinct in the NYPD. I'm in Matties Department store in the Valley Stream Mall. I've got two unknown white males approximately six feet in height. One dark haired, one blond. They've been following me and my family inside of the last few stores we've entered and exited. They're each armed with at least one holstered handgun. We are currently at the C.A.M. makeup counter. I'm attempting to exit to the east parking lot through the side entrance. I'd be real grateful if some of my Nassau County brethren could give a

Brooklyn girl a little assist."

Getting the confirmation she'd hoped for she held her phone up and pretended to take pictures of A.J., Kenneth, and the baby. She made certain the field of the camera was wide enough that every shot she snapped included the two strangers that thought they were undetected.

Gotcha.

She glanced down at the phone as if she were admiring photos she'd taken and whispered,

"Get out now."

The two of them left on her word quickly walking toward the exit. They'd just pushed through the door when Amare let out a sharp wail and drew all eyes to their port of egress.

One of the men pointed to the other and they each headed for the door after Kenneth and A.J.

She saw one of them reach under his jacket and her fingers instantly wrapped around her gun. As she withdrew it from the holster hanging on her hip she identified herself as a police officer and demanded they stop moving.

"Don't do it," she shouted. Both men, standing still, one with his hands in the air, the other with his hand still concealed inside his jacket. "Don't be stupid, I will put you down. Put the guns on the floor and kick them over to me."

Hands locked around her weapon, she watched the two men, trying to think up a scenario where she didn't actually have to lick off a shot inside of this department store. There were too many civilians around, too many people that could end up as collateral damage.

The skinny guy was ready to surrender, but the one that look liked he was suffering from 'roid-rage was a potential problem. She could see him attempting to size up the scenario for his benefit too. He was planning something, and in a situation like this, the last thing she needed was some fool thinking he could outthink and outrun the police.

She recognized the moment that fool made his final decision; she saw it all happen in slow motion. He reached further into his jacket to grip his gun and before he could pick it up to aim it at her she'd tapped him twice in his chest.

Before the thugs body could fall to the floor she heard sirens closing in and voices yelling for her to put down her weapon and get on the floor.

A little more than pissed that this day wasn't really going the way she'd planned she put her weapon on the floor kneeled down and placed her hands on top of her head. "I'm Captain Heart Searlington of the seventy-fourth precinct in the NYPD. My badge is on my hip next to my holster.

While an unknown officer patted her down she kept eyes on the remaining suspect being cuffed and led out of the opposite doors. She watched him walk-stumble out of the doors surrounded by several officers as she felt the clink of metal bracelets around one, then both of her wrists.

She bit her lip at the cinch of the metal around her skin and wondered just how she'd ended up in this particular situation. Shortly after that thought crept across her mind the answer followed. Her husband had insisted she meet with A.J. Tenetti. It seemed like every fucked up day she'd had as of late had started that very same way.

As she was pulled to her feet and led through the doors, a hand on her head pushing her down into the backseat of the patrol car only one thought repeated on a loop in her head. "This day just keeps getting fucking better and better."

CHAPTER 11

Bryan Smith hurt, there was no mistaking or deny the fiery burn in his back and his chest.

*W*hat the hell that pain was from he didn't really understand, but it was there loud and throbbing and making him want to run back into the fog that kept trying to drown him.

The fog was everywhere, dark, rolling billows of cold hazy nothingness that permeated every inch of wherever the hell he was at right now. Was he dead; was this hell, had he really ended up in this place after all?

Bryan felt his muscles tighten into a shiver from the cold. He folded his arms around himself and tried to unsuccessfully block the feel of the chill surrounding him.

"I never thought hell would be this cold. Where's all the fire and brimstone I was promised."

His mother and father had assured him he would burn in a fiery pit for all eternity unless he repented from his evil ways.

An amused humph jumped from his throat. Every time his family had told him that, he'd think back to all of the crooked shit he'd witnessed his family perpetuate. Like the time his dad figured out how to fiddle with the dials on the gas pumps at his station so that customers never really got as much gas as they were paying for. Yeah, the government had officials that were supposed to regulate that kind of shit, but when they were getting a cut of the pie, who was going to tell?

Or what about his uncle Ray, the jack legged preacher in the family that was using the church's building fund to finance his luxury vehicles, summer homes, mistresses, and extramarital children? Those were two fine, God-fearing upstanding men as far as his family was concerned, despite their ongoing hypocritical behavior they were still the right kind of men. Straight men. Something that Bryan could never be.

It always seemed so ridiculous to him. That out of all the things in the universe that God had to worry about, that Bryan's sexuality would be the most important problem on that list.

Well according to his family and their twisted interpretation of the Bible, that was the situation. Everything else was forgivable, redeemable, interpretable, but being gay was a one way ride to hell.

"Well if this is hell, I guess I'd better get used to it. As long as it's got a bathroom, Wi-Fi, and a flat screen, I think I could spend eternity here."

Could you really? Bryan heard a voice surrounding him. *Could you really stay away forever knowing you'd never see him again, hear his voice, touch him?*

Bryan felt the shudders racking his body again. He couldn't tell if it was the cold, or the spooky ass voice talking to and around him at the same time.

You haven't answered me, could you really leave him...for good?

Bryan didn't need to ask who the 'him' the disembodied voice was referring to. There was only one him that ever mattered in his life. Justice Amare, his husband, the man he loved.

Just the thought of Justice chased the chill filling him away. Bryan thought about that happy smile Justice always wore. Justice could be in the middle of a military briefing planning the details of a determined target's demise when he'd notice something—didn't have to be anything big, could have been something funny someone said in passing a few days prior—but he'd stop whatever he was doing and just smile.

That was his Marine, capable, determined, and skilled. But his most beautiful quality was his smile. It was wide and bright, lifting his full cheeks, warming the smooth brown skin that Bryan loved to touch and taste.

Bryan had teased Jussy mercilessly about his smile. The truth was he couldn't smile small. No matter how hard he tried; there was always a full set of teeth on display when Jussy smiled at you. He'd smile and no matter how sour a mood you were in, you'd join in because really when that man smiled at you, happiness blossomed on the innermost parts of you and just fought its way on through to the outside. That smile was just so perfect and full of warmth that you never wanted to leave its presence.

Yet you did...voluntarily so.

Who the fuck was this in his head? The voice spoke truth; there was no doubt about it. But

Bryan didn't need to be reminded of his past fuck ups. He'd lived them...way too many of them as far as he was concerned.

The age of seventeen is rather innocuous for most teenage boys. You go to school; maybe you play sports, or possibly hold down an afterschool job. That's really all there was to do for a boy that age growing up in a small backwater town in the Southeastern states.

Until that age, Bryan had lived a rather uneventful life. He went to church, he went to school, and he went to work. Day in, day out, that was his life. It was simple, clear-cut without much fuss or drama.

He worked hard, not leaving much room for anything else because he had one goal in mind, go to college the following year and get the hell out of dodge. He had to leave; the only other alternative was dying.

Since the age of thirteen when Bryan noticed his interest in the local varsity football quarterback went way beyond the hero worship and adoration a little kid held for the hometown sports god, he knew that he would have to leave his home.

There was just no room in his world for the kind of person Bryan was.

For four long years Bryan hid behind an iron wall of his own creation. He didn't allow himself to indulge in any single thing that could make someone question his sexuality. No gay porn, no going out on night trips to the hidden places in the city that catered to his kind of interests. Nothing.

Living in a severely religious household it was actually kind of easy to remove himself from all the social situations that required one to express or experiment publicly with sexuality. There were no school dances because his parents didn't believe in him attending any secular social gatherings. If it wasn't church related, he couldn't go. Their church-Nazi mentality provided an instant excuse for him not asking any of the girls in his school to go out, or make out. He was a church boy; everyone knew it and expected him to walk the straight and narrow. And so he did, with a precise and finely-tuned ability to avoid anything that could result in his family knowing who he truly was.

Then he'd made the first big mistake of his life. Uzziah Conway was the local judge's son. He was known for being a trouble maker, but he had two things that made him acceptable in a way that Bryan never could be. The first, his father was the town Judge. He pretty much made the law in their patch of dirt. Second, he was white. Having a complexion and the family breeding that protects you from persecution and prosecution meant Uzziah could pretty much do and be what he wanted, and no one would say a thing.

Bryan ran in to Uzziah one day while running some errands for his father. From the moment those steely gray eyes winked at him through a fan of low-hanging black bangs, Bryan was lost to his spell.

Uzziah pursued Bryan relentlessly. He showed up at Bryan's school which was on the opposite side of where Uzziah lived. He'd pop up at the local fast food places; he'd even show up at Bryan's part time job at the hardware store pretending to be a customer.

Bryan fought so hard to stay away from the man. But in the end, Uzziah proved to be a formidable opponent. He showed up at Bryan's house one night while his parents were at their weekly couples' Bible study meeting.

To this day Bryan couldn't explain why he'd let Uzziah into the house. He'd known he'd pay for it the moment he stepped back from the door and let the man enter his life. His seventeen year-old mind couldn't really explain it at the time, but maybe it was the ache to step outside of the lonely world he'd created for himself that made him relinquish control to Uzziah that night. Or maybe it was the fact that he was a sexually repressed teenager whose hormones had riddled his brain addle. Whatever it was, he'd quietly stepped aside and let the wolf into the henhouse.

Uzziah had crossed the threshold of Bryan's family home and had attacked him with his whole body. Lips, hands, hips, tongue, legs, he'd pretty much mastered Bryan before he'd stripped one article of clothing from either of their bodies. Once those full pink lips had surrounded Bryan's cock, Bryan lost all control to think, the haze of arousal so thick he thought he would just about choke on it. Before long, Bryan was surrendering to the fast glide of that perfect mouth on his dick and his balls exploded into the first release he'd ever had that didn't include his own hand.

Just as his brain was waking up from the sex-induced coma Uzziah had forced on him, Bryan opened his eyes to find his parents standing in the living room with their mouths hanging open in shock and disbelief.

As soon as Uzziah realized they were no longer alone, he ran from the house and left Bryan alone to deal with the aftermath.

Standing there alone with his dick out and his head still a little fuzzy from his first and only sexual encounter with another human being, Bryan was at a loss.

He still couldn't remember what happened exactly after that moment. He knew his father attacked him; remembered some of the blows that rained over his body. He recalled covering his head with his hands and curling into the fetal position, folding into himself to protect his major organs. Then there was darkness and silence.

When Bryan awoke in the same spot his father had discovered and beat him in, the old man was sitting across from him with a pistol sitting on his knee.

"No way in hell I'm having a fag for a son. You will end this sick shit, or I will end you."

The older man motioned for Bryan to stand up. "Go upstairs and get yourself cleaned up, then we're going down to that Marine recruitment office and you're going to sign up and they're going to make a man out of you. Because trust me when I tell you, you are going to be a real man."

There had been no further discussion, they'd headed to the recruitment office and Bryan's father had signed on the dotted line for the underage boy to enlist in the Corps.

His father had meant it for punishment, and every second of basic training felt like it, but then something wonderful came from all of it. When he'd finished his basic training, he'd met the love of his life.

His father had thought the Marine Corps was a way to scare him straight. What it had actually done was lead him right into the arms of the man that would be his soul mate. Funny how life worked out some times.

Justice Amare was worth every blow he'd taken that night; he was worth every miserable moment of basic training in the Corps. Simply put, Justice was worth everything.

Well if that's true, why did you leave him; why are you leaving him again?

≈

*K*enneth paced back and forth in an empty interrogation room of the Nassau County Police station. He gave a passing look at the one-way mirror imagining the detectives who'd spent the last two hours questioning him watching him like some sort of sideshow

Scheduling this meeting between his wife and his friend had taken a herculean effort on Kenneth's part. Knowing how much these two women rubbed each other the wrong way, Kenneth certainly understood fireworks should probably be expected—gunfire was something totally different.

How had an easy day at the mall turned into a shootout between his wife and two armed henchmen?

Why the fuck were those two men following them or him in the first place?

Kenneth's head ached. Everything in him wanted to scream and rage at that fucking mirror that separated him from the rest of the buzzing precinct. But then the sleeping bundle of fourmonth-old baby that rested so contently in his arms kept his temper intact and his anger reasonably restrained.

"Excuse me," Kenneth murmured to whoever might be sitting on the other side of that mirror—if anyone at all—fighting to make his voice sound as calm and neutral as he could. "Can you give me any news about my wife? It's been hours since we arrived here."

Silence, it should have been familiar by now after sitting in this concrete-gray room all day.

He'd have to ask Heart later if this was part of standard police procedure—make people wait all damn day long just for amusement.

Kenneth's position as the head of a business empire meant waiting for anything wasn't something he experienced on a regular basis. What he wouldn't give to have this dreary room morph into one of his offices so he could push a button, speak a couple of words, and have his staff magically produce whatever he required instantly.

Amare stirred within his arms forcing Kenneth to attempt to control the worry and frustration racing through him at the moment. He took a deep breath and repositioned the sleeping baby in his arms until the tiny cherub snuggled into a sweet spot and dropped back into unconcerned sleep.

Kenneth heard the creak of a door and his eyes followed the sound until he saw A.J. and Heart stepping into the interrogation room heading in his direction.

A.J. fell behind Heart and allowed her to step through the door first. Moving their son to one arm, he pulled his wife into the other and held her until the press of her body against his was almost painful.

"What the hell happened in there?"

Heart waved a carefree hand. "Nothing, just standard S.O.P. My story adds up to the witnesses' accounts and it was a clean shoot. The video tapes corroborate my story as well."

He let her step out of his embrace and let his eyes pass down the length of her body. He was sure she was fine, but the last time he'd seen her she'd been handcuffed, being placed in the back of squad car by an officer.

God his blood boiled at the thought of what she'd had to endure, or some other man putting his hands on her and feeling the flesh that belonged to him and him alone.

"Did they—"

She held up a hand halting him. "I'm fine, Kenneth. The officers were professional, they treated me with respect. The handcuffs were standard protocol. They came on to a scene finding me and two others armed. They needed to secure the scene and sort it out later."

She held her arms out to her sides and took a simple spin around. "See, I'm leaving just the way I came in."

He watched as she completed her revolution. Make certain to catalogue as much of her as possible when his eyes stumbled over the sight of her empty holster on her hip.

"Where's your gun?"

Heart looked down and ran long fingers over the empty sheath and looked back at him.

"They confiscated it."

"But I thought you said they're ruling it a clean shooting? Why would they take your weapon?"

She must have read the fear in the trembling of his voice, in the sharp lines of his face. She stepped closer and ran a gentling finger along his cheek.

"Baby," she answered. "It's all protocol. They have to test my weapon for ballistics. Once they're done, they'll give it back. I'll pick up a loaner in the meantime when I go back to work."

He nodded, accepting her response. He laced his fingers into her dark mane and pulled her to him, placing a relieved kiss to her forehead. Holding her there, treasuring the feel of her against him. This was the only place she was safe, with him, in his arms.

Heart pulled back out of his embrace just enough to lean down and press a soft kiss to their son's dark curls.

"As long as you two are fine, I'm all right," she whispered. Then she raised her brown eyes to him and squared her shoulders. "And to make certain you stay that way, NYPD, and the FBI are going to join forces to figure out who the hell is after you, Kenneth and why."

She stepped to the side and movement from the door pulled his attention to the new occupant in the room.

"Kenneth, I believe you know…"

"Agent Weaver," Kenneth answered, his jaw automatically locking. He drew in a steadying breath through his nose trying to waylay the memory of the man standing in front of him trying to go after what was his. It didn't matter to Kenneth that the man had never actually had the opportunity to pursue any of the illicit thoughts he was having about Heart. It only mattered that Kenneth knew first hand that Weaver in fact had them at all.

Heart took their son from his arms and walked across the room and placed him in A.J.'s arms. It was a sight he'd never thought he would live to see, but she did. She whispered something in his friend's ear and soon the young woman was gone with their child.

Kenneth pointed a finger in question, but Heart pointed toward the chairs surrounding the lone table in the room.

"An officer is going to escort her to our house where Elvia is waiting."

Kenneth nodded his head and sat down next to his wife and watched as Weaver sat down opposite them.

"All right, Mr. Searlington," Weaver began. "Why would someone want you dead?"

CHAPTER 12

enneth walked into their home two steps behind his wife. This day could go straight to hell right along with the day he'd been shot. He walked past his wife in the hall and headed directly up the stairs to their son.

When he cracked the door he found Elvia sitting next to the crib with her long legs stretched out and blanket resting over her lap. The epitome of the unassuming nanny, he'd bet money there was a weapon or two hidden under that blanket.

He'd battled with Heart about hiring this woman. He'd not really seen the need to have someone who carried a firearm near their child, but Heart wouldn't be swayed. And now, standing next to his sleeping son's crib, after a day like today, he was grateful for the nanny that packed more than sweets and goodies.

He leaned down into the crib and settled his fingers lightly on the child's chest. He felt the tension bleed out of him at the gentle up and down movement of the baby's small torso.

"Is everything all right, Mr. Searlington?" Elvia asked.

He looked up from his sleeping son and gave her a weary nod. Every time something like this happened, the opportunity to spend moments like this with his child, with his wife, they could have been snatched from him.

He let his finger stroke his boy's round cheek and then he smiled at Elvia.

"Everything is fine, Elvia. Looking at him just reminded me that I needed to do something before it's too late."

The tie around his neck was gone before he closed the door to the nursery behind him. He stepped the few feet down the hall and sprinted into the master bedroom with renewed strength.

"Heart?" He waited for an answer, looking around the room for his wife.

He'd been home a few days, but not all of him, not the important part that made their family complete. He stripped the clothes from his body and made a direct line for the shower.

From the moment the shower heads opened above and around him, he felt the sodden layers of this godforsaken day slide down his skin and hopefully into the pit of hell via Nassau County's sewer system.

There were so many unanswered questions in his head. The biggest and loudest one to date was who was after him. Kenneth didn't delude himself. He didn't count himself as a saint. He knew there were people in this world he'd pissed off just by breathing.

His competitors definitely wouldn't shed tears at his demise. They'd dance their happy dances and try to steal whatever business they could manage to before his body was cold. Yeah, they'd benefit from his death, and they'd be happy as hell about that benefit, but they weren't going to borrow the trouble necessary to actually off Kenneth.

There was only one person Kenneth could actually think of that would have the motive and means to make something like this happen. Jacqueline Searlington, his mother.

Agent Weaver had called her name first on the list of possible suspects. The mention of Kenneth's mother's name across that man's lips made the muscles of his jaw grind together. Was the man wrong to bring Jacqueline's name up? Probably not.

After all, she was currently serving a prison sentence for crimes she'd committed against him, his niece, his sister, and Heart. There couldn't have been a more perfect suspect in fact.

Jacqueline's greed and hatred for Kenneth as the sole heir of his father's fortune drove her to abduct Kenneth's niece.

The fact that her antics had led to the death of his twin sister disabused him of any fantasy that his mother cared too much about him to make an attempt on his life. Jacqueline was a viper; she'd eat her young sooner than nurture them. This was true, but he wasn't sure he could really blame this on her either.

It had been years since she'd been convicted of her accused crimes. He'd heard nothing from her in all this time. She'd never asked for anything, never asked for him to visit, nothing.

Up until now, he'd been grateful for that fact, grateful that he no longer had to deal with his mother's messy and criminal behavior. He just hoped his readiness to wash his hands from her madness didn't get him, or the people he loved hurt.

The subtle touch of fingers so familiar to his skin he could confuse it for his own grazed the slick skin of his shoulder until it slid down his back as smoothly as the droplets of water raining down on him.

"You okay?" she asked softly into his ear. "I was afraid today was too much for you. You've only been back home a handful of days."

He nodded his head, eyes still closed to the streaming water saturating the thick strands of his hair.

He felt her hand crawl back up the length of his back, the movement making the muscles that rested just beneath her digits twitch in anticipation. Heart was right, he had returned from the hospital several days before, but in that time the two of them had barely spent any alone time together.

They'd both been physically present, and usually that was all it took to stoke the embers that always seemed to be on a low simmer just waiting for an excuse to fan the flames to full blaze. But since his release there had been something there, something that was keeping them from being them.

Kenneth turned his head slightly toward the sound of her voice. He opened his eyes just enough to see the water-sprinkled vision of her standing to the side of him. He pulled her into his embrace and pinned her back against the wall between his outstretched arms.

There was nothing like the sight of his wife naked and waiting for him. No matter how difficult things were between them they'd always had this. It baffled him that he'd allowed whatever this was between them to fester to the point where he hadn't touched his wife in days.

The knowledge that she'd kept something so important from him fucked with his head in a way he hadn't anticipated. Truth was he really hadn't even given serious thought as to why her omission of the facts about Bryan and Justice impacted him so much.

But to deny himself this, this connection, this reassurance that his world was grounded, that they were whole, what the fuck was he thinking?

He positioned her directly under the spray of water and watched the fullness of her hair flatten against her scalp and back. She would bitch at him later about having to go to the hairdresser, but the thought of that conversation alone was pulling up the corners of his mouth into a wicked smile.

He allowed his fingers to rest at the base of her head, fingers caressing her nape in just the right way to make her fall into his touch. His heart tightened slightly. They'd been stressed and their connection strained, but underneath all the bullshit, it was still there and he was grateful for it.

Their connection is what kept his soul intact, what kept him sane enough to deal with the rest of his life when dealing with the craziness that wealth brought.

"We have a lot to discuss, Heart."

"Kenneth I—"

He leaned down and pressed a hard kiss to stop whatever it was she was about to say. Words weren't what they needed now. He giggled to himself. If their shrink could hear his thoughts she'd be jumping up and down screaming her opposition to his line of thinking.

Kenneth wasn't against therapy. It had definitely worked to get the two of them back on track, and he definitely wanted them to sign up for a session or two after this latest fiasco, but this wasn't something that needed fixing. This was the one way that their communication was perfect and they were absolutely in sync.

He plunged his tongue inside the warmth of her mouth and savored the sweet hint of apple juice that danced on his taste buds.

He pulled back just a moment to give them each a chance to breathe.

"I'm not avoiding the conversation we need to have, and as soon as we're finished in here we're going to throw on some clothes and go downstairs in the kitchen and hash this shit out over a cup of coffee. But right now, I just need to feel my wife."

She nodded her head in agreement, and followed him to the bench in the shower. He sat down and pulled her into a straddling position over his lap tightening his grip around her waist when the blessed heat of her wet sex slid down over the rigid underside of his dick.

He pulled her into his tender kiss. He tasted from her, slowly drinking in the soft moan she gave in response. He let his tongue slide down her chin to her neck until it found the throbbing pulse point nestled there. He lapped at it, bathing it until she pressed closer to him, begging for more. He allowed his teeth to lightly graze it as he ground his hips up against her slippery folds that were slicking him up flawlessly for the smooth ride he intended them to share.

He pulled her up just a little taking an eager mouthful of one of her breasts. He'd always loved them, loved touching them, tasting them, pressing his face in between them. They'd always been perfect to him. When her body began to change as their son grew within her womb they had grown perfectly plump and just the sight of them gave him pause to stop whatever the fuck he was doing and worship them.

And after the baby had been born, while she nursed him for the first three months of his life, Kenneth had gloried in the fullness they'd possessed.

He moved searching fingers over to its lonely companion and tended to it while he continued to pay homage to its counterpart. Damn, she may have stopped breastfeeding a month ago, but damn if her tits weren't still that perfectly round weight in his mouth and hands.

Note to self, inform that personal trainer she plans on hiring that if she loses an ounce of these, I'm coming for his fucking certification.

He moved his hand down between her legs and let his fingers circle her clit. Her hips instantly bucked in answer begging him to speed up the pace. He refused, tonight wasn't about speed, wasn't about them thrashing about in this shower. This was about connection, securing the link that kept them bound to each other, that kept their family bound.

He grabbed a handful of her ass and stilled her as he slowly popped the head of his cock inside her. When she attempted to drop down on him, he squeezed the mound of her ass harder and made her drop her focus to him.

"I would love to fuck you up against the wall at a break-neck pace, but I've got two problems with that tonight. The first, I want to savor the taste of you, the feeling of us. And second...well, let's just say I'm afraid that if I fuck you the way I usually do I'll permanently damage something."

A wide grin spread across her lips and she sucked her bottom lip in between her teeth to try to hold her laugh in.

"You're such a big baby," she answered. "A little scratch and you're acting as if you should be on the disabled list."

"A scratch? Were you not there when they sliced into my stomach to take a bullet out?"

"Kenneth, the doctor told me he used a set of tongs to pull the bullet out. The only reason they actually cut into you was to make certain the bullet hadn't damaged anything in your gut. They spent more time exploring than anything else. Stop bitchin', Bruh."

He looked up into laughing brown eyes lit with amusement and desire and said a quick thank you to whichever deity responsible for dropping this woman into his life.

"I don't know who 'Bruh' is, but keep that motherfucker's name out of your mouth tonight." He pushed into her slowly and watched the smile drip gradually from her face and her lips form a *perfect* circle as each inch of his dick slid deeper inside of her. "The only name I want to hear crossing those sexy lips of your right now is mine."

He forced her hips down the rest of the way and braced himself for the taut fist-like grip she was about to have on his shit.

"Say it with me now, Kenneth," he uttered.

He ground his hips up into her at the perfect angle and she spasmed around him, her breath breaking his name into individual syllables.

He lulled his head back and languished in the silky sound of his name on her lips. It sounded like pure sin and he was an eager convert just waiting to fall into temptation. She begged him for more and he willingly gave in to her hungry demands. Shit if she called his name like that again, he'd give in to just about anything she could ask.

Kenneth had never been pussy-whipped. He'd never met a piece of ass he couldn't enjoy one second and forget the next. But Heart, you'd think her shit was laced with some sort of opiate the way the smooth drag and pull of her walls always made his cock sing. But the most addicting part of the dance they did was knowing she was just as strung out over his dick too.

Fuck what the experts say, codependency is a wonderful thing.

If this were their usual, this would be the perfect moment for him to pick her up fuck her against the wall, or turn her over flat on her back and pound into her over and over until she broke apart.

But this wasn't their usual and despite his wife's earlier bullshit, his fucking abdomen was killing him and wasn't about to cooperate with any lifting beyond the ten-pound little cherub that was asleep down the hall.

He slapped a flat palm against her ass and motioned for her to lift up. He turned slightly to his side and in one smooth motion he was lying flat on his back on the bench. One look at the hunger in her eyes and his fingers itched to touch flesh, his...hers, really didn't matter, he just needed to touch. He wrapped careful fingers around his sensitive cap and he hissed when his nails made contact with the responsive flesh.

He motioned for her to climb back on and she did with vigor and heat and so much need he could smell it billowing off of her in thick waves. He wrapped strong fingers around her neck and pulled her down to him, drinking from her mouth, savoring the taste that was unique to her.

He planted his foot at the base of the bench when her pussy lips kissed the base of his cock to give himself purchase. He might not be able to do this like they normally did, but fuck if he wasn't going to make sure this was just as satisfying as it always was.

His hips set an unhurried but tantalizing rhythm that she followed with practiced ease. When his muscles tightened, hers released producing the most delicious glide. There was something to be said for slow, his hands were usually all over her when they made love, but the touching was always frenzied, rough, and desperate. Tonight, tonight there was no rush, so his hands took the time to rediscover his wife, much like that very first time he'd shared this with her.

Hips still dancing to their unique rhythm, his fingers slid down from her neck over her collar bone. He continued his tactile journey, over her shoulders, down her arms, the silky softness of her skin tickling his fingertips. He joined his fingers with hers and brought them to his lips and kissed them.

Heart twirled her hips and somehow the simmering fire that kept his passion at a slow but steady boil increased the flames tenfold.

He felt the tightness of her heat increasing around him, she was so close, each contraction of her sex drawing him closer to his edge.

The soft mewling sound spilling from her lips signaled her need. She was close, but just out of reach of what she needed.

He pulled her down to him again, captured her lips in his and then moved his mouth to her ear.

"Sssh, baby, it's all right."

He held her tightly to him and ground his hips into her over and over until she finally broke apart in his arms and he followed her within seconds. Each spurt drawn from him by the glorious pressure her locked muscles held him with drained his balls empty and left him limp against the cool tile of the shower bench.

He was sated, and the inviting weight of his wife pressed against him made him feel like he could conquer anything, like he'd finally regained his superpowers. Hopefully those rediscovered powers could help him deal with the shit that had been brewing for way too long between them. Because if they couldn't...well, the alternative just wasn't something he was willing to entertain, not when there was so much at risk.

All right Mr. Superhero, time to battle the evil villain and save and get the girl in the end.

~

*K*enneth brought two cups of coffee and sat down next to his wife. He allowed her to take a few sips of the smooth brew before he twisted in his seat spread his legs, and pulled her chair toward him until they were sitting in each other's personal space.

This was their ring. This small space between them was where they worked out their issues.

They'd learned the hard way that space just created more opportunities for shit to go wrong. Close together, leaning on only each other, this was how they worked out their demons and made things work.

"Shit hasn't really been right between us since I came home from the hospital." It was a statement, sugarcoating the situation wasn't going to fix this problem that was festering beneath the surface of their relationship.

She shook her head, admitting what they both already knew, they needed work.

"Trusting someone after all the secrets and lies I was buried under by my own family, I never wanted to live like that, Heart."

"I know that," she countered. "I know that and I never wanted to willingly keep secrets from you, Kenneth."

"Then why did you? I love Jussy and Bryan just like you do, why wouldn't you tell me they were married? Why did the entire damn family keep that a secret?"

She looked at him with regret and contrition in her eyes. "It wasn't about you, Kenneth, not for any of us. It wasn't about hiding their relationship, not like you're thinking anyway."

"Did you think I would have a problem with it? Did you think I'd turn the two of them away after everything they've meant to me?"

She shook her head again; this time with quick sharp movements that helped quashed some of the doubt sitting in the bottom of his stomach.

"Kenneth, if I thought you were homophobic, I never would have married you. I love my cousin and I have no issue with who and what he is, none of us do."

"Then why?"

She pinched the bridge of her nose and went to stand up. When she attempted to break their contact by standing he stopped her, causing her to sit back down in front of him.

"If you want to know the answer to your question, we have to go downstairs in the basement."

He might have thought she was joking if he hadn't seen the hard etched lines of concern color the previously relaxed muscles of her face.

He released her and followed behind her as she led him down the stairs to their basement. She stopped in the linen closet at the bottom of the stairs and removed what looked like a small black electronic device.

She walked into their gym and motioned for him to mimic her moves and straddle the workbench she was sitting on. Once seated, she placed the device between them and pressed a button. The device silently came to life flashing an electric blue wave from one side of the rectangular shaped box to the other.

"What's that?" he asked pointing to it.

"It cancels out listening devices. I brought us down here so that our voices aren't carried beyond the soundproof barrier of this room," she declared.

"Is this something to do with police work?"

"Sort of, but not really."

He watched her look around the room before she raised her eyes to him. There were few times in their marriage where he could literally see the walls his wife erected around herself crumble. When they'd first met it was learning about her traumatic past and the dysfunctional relationship she shared with her father. Then it was the pain and insecurity that surrounded the conception and loss of their first child.

All of those things were so intense and personal, and so difficult for her to acknowledge and verbalize. When those issues came to head he could always see her need to share staked against her ability to keep herself safe. But now, this was different. There was no fear, just…reservation.

The warmth that filled him after their lovemaking slowly dissipated into a chill that seemed to permeate from the inside out.

What the hell is going on?

"Jussy and Bryan met in boot camp in the Marine Corps. They literally fell in love from those first few moments on a plane together. Being in the military and being gay wasn't cool. And no matter how much of this PC bullshit you see in the media, it is a scary place to be a gay man, let alone a black gay man in that motherfucker. At first it was a matter of their jobs and not getting kicked out. Justice always knew he was a career man; Bryan went in because his homophobic asshole of a father forced him to go in at seventeen. Bryan lasted about four years in before leaving the Corps and entering the police academy.

"They were together for years, over a decade when the marriage equality law was passed in New York. They had a small ceremony in Ida Mae's backyard and the family was thrilled to share in their happiness."

She pulled out her cell phone and tapped the screen a few times before she turned the screen to him. There was a picture filled with all of the Amares, Ida Mae included, all surrounding a smiling Justice and Bryan, both dressed in identical gray suits smiling at each other as if no one else existed in the world.

Looking at this photo it was so obvious now. He spread two fingers across the screen widening the picture until only the smooth brown faces of both men remained. How hadn't he seen this before? How hadn't he recognized this truth with his own eyes? This look of love and happiness beyond belief was the same look he wore every single time he laid eyes on his wife, but yet he was so blind to it in the faces of these two men.

Every time the family was in town, Bryan dropped by. He'd always thought it was because

Bryan was "like" family, never really knowing that he truly was. He was family, just like Kenneth was family.

"That kind of love, happiness, it changes you. Sometimes blinds you to the ugliness of the rest of the world. After they were married Bryan called his mother. He hadn't spoken to her in over a decade, but he wanted her to know how happy he was. He told her they'd married and that they were having a baby via surrogate, that he was the bio-dad. She said some very evil and hateful things and hid behind her Bible while she criticized, humiliated, and decimated her son. And then just for shits and giggles she told him that God was going to strike him down for his sin and he was going to smite that abomination that was growing inside some heathen's womb."

Kenneth closed his eyes. Not wanting to imagine the rest of this story. He knew the pain of losing a child that still rested in the womb. He wouldn't have wished that kind of pain on his greatest enemy.

"What happened to the child?" he asked quietly, already knowing the answer. Bryan was dedicated to his job and his friends. There's no way he would have hidden his own child. "Seven months into the pregnancy, the surrogate stopped feeling the baby move. When they rushed her to the hospital there was nothing that could be done. The little girl was stillborn and

Justice and Bryan were devastated."

"And Bryan blamed himself for his daughter's death because of what his mother said."

"Yeah," she answered. "It wrecked him, ate at that secret place inside of himself that had been poisoned since his father threw him out of the family for being gay. Every nasty thing his family had ever told him about himself and his kind was validated. I think somehow he twisted that into believing God hated him and never wanted him to be happy, that God was punishing him for being gay. So when you're afraid that someone is going to snatch the things and the people you love, you start pushing them away yourself."

Understanding dawned on Kenneth. "Is that what happened between Justice and Bryan?"

"Yeah, Bryan pushed him away, tried to deal with his grief and pain on his own. Jussy was pissed, but he loved Bryan...loves Bryan. He tried to give him the space he needed, the nature of his job keeps him gone from New York for months at a time. But Bryan still hasn't agreed to let
Justice come back home."

Kenneth rubbed the back of his neck. It all made sense now, the way Bryan tried his best to talk to both Heart and Kenneth when they were battling through their grief. The way he always encouraged them to hold on to their love and protect it at all costs. He was speaking from experience, speaking from a place of understanding. He knew what it felt like to lose what you loved the most and he didn't want Heart and Kenneth to experience it themselves.

"I can't believe Bryan has been holding all this pain and history inside all these years. I would never have thought he knew this kind of pain," Kenneth murmured.

"There's something you have to understand about Bryan, Kenneth. He's always happy, even when he's not. He often uses humor as a way of dealing with the pain in his life."

So many of the puzzle pieces were clicking into place, shining much needed light onto a dark spot that he hadn't even known was there for most of his interaction with these two men. But even though she was providing enlightenment, it didn't really make the reason for this conversation make sense; there were still things that didn't add up for Kenneth.

"What does this have to do with why everyone in the family knows Jussy and Bryan are married except me?"

"Once he decided to put their past behind him, once he walked away, he didn't want anyone to know he was gay. He'd never been out at work and he'd always kept to himself. Most people just assumed that he and I were secretly a thing. We let them think that to keep folks off his back."

"When did all this take place?" he asked.

"Shortly before I met you."

"And you never once thought this is something you should share with your husband?"

"Kenneth, it wasn't my story to share. I wanted to tell you, but Bryan asked me not to tell you he was gay. I couldn't reveal one thing without disclosing the other. I was trying to protect him. Yes, under normal circumstances I would have told you everything. But Bryan has the right to deal with his sexuality as he sees fit. He didn't have the opportunity to come out to his family on his terms. His parents caught him in the middle of his first sexual experience at seventeen.

That's how they found out he was gay, and less than twelve hours later, after nearly beating him senseless, his father shipped him off to the Marine Corps. That power was stolen from him once before, I wasn't about to do that to him all over again."

He watched his wife. There was remorse in her eyes. She was sorry, for keeping this from him, yes, but not for honoring her friend. And no matter how much it pissed him off that she'd kept her friend's secret, he couldn't really find the anger that had been bottled up inside of him since he'd discovered Bryan and Jussy's secret.

"I don't like it, Heart, I don't like it when we keep secrets. But I get it, I do, and I don't hold it against you."

She smiled and lifted her shoulders. "Well, let's hope you continue to feel that way when you hear the rest of what I've got to say."

He scrutinized her; they'd never had this type of conversation, not even when she was investigating his niece's abduction. This was beyond Captain Searlington the police officer, this was something... someone he hadn't ever seen before.

"Kenneth, what I'm about to tell you has to stay between us. You can never talk about this to anyone outside my uncle and cousins, and Bryan. No one else can know this." He nodded his head in silent agreement.

"I never anticipated having to explain certain things about my family because I never expected this life that you've given me. I never thought I would have a husband and a child to share my life with, people that I would be held accountable to. So I'm going to tell you about Jussy and Bryan, then I'm going to tell you about everything that you should have known a long time ago about my family."

CHAPTER 13

"You know my family is in the military, right?" she asked.

"Everyone except True, yeah," he answered.

She shook her head slowly. "Everyone...including True," she responded. "My aunt and uncle met in the military, and when they had kids, she became a civilian, and my uncle Hunter continued on his career in the Army. When Hunter began to climb the ranks he was assigned to this post where it was his job to create, train, and dispatch these special ops teams.

"Legend has it he became exceptionally good at it, better than anyone else across the different branches of the military. So he was charged with creating this inner-branch training program. They wanted him to teach all the military instructors how to train their respective special ops teams how to use my uncle's playbook. Well whatever it was that he taught them, supposedly it revolutionized things in their community and Hunter became a shining star in the military and the Army.

"Upon his promotion to General, he was tasked by the joint chiefs to create five teams that would go in for dark missions that none of the other special ops teams could or would tackle.

"These were the types of ugly secret ops that couldn't be publicized in the media, the type of ops that the American public could never know about."

"So what happened, did he do what he was asked?"

She nodded. "Yeah, he did. He put out the call throughout the Army, Navy, Marines, and Air force for the best people they had that worked special ops. Each branch was to send four people that were to be vetted through some form of competition. The other branches sent their people and when Hunter walked into the training facility where these sixteen service members were sent, four of them were his children."

Kenneth wiped his face with his hand and tried to calculate the unlikely odds against something like this happening. A million to one probably didn't cover it.

"Hunter tried to have them excluded, but the chiefs said this wasn't a usual command, and so some of the usual rules, like family not serving together, didn't count. Well, you know my cousins, they were training for the military since they were in diapers, so each one of them killed the competition, and in the end, they were the four left standing. They were made team leaders and were allowed to put together individual teams from the people they had beaten in the qualifications."

"That only leaves four teams then; you said there was to be a fifth."

"There was a second part to all of this madness. Although these four were created to clean up the nasty jobs of the military, some jobs are nastier than others, and some require closers that can do shit no one else can do. My uncle took the four leaders of the individual teams, and he created sort of an alpha team."

Kenneth processed all that his wife was sharing. He'd always known there was something different about the Amare children, especially True. He'd never actually witnessed her lift a single finger in violence, but it was there, that keen sense of her surroundings that always made him feel she saw and knew shit that the rest of the world just didn't get.

"So what are you telling me," he laughed. "Your family's like SEAL

Team Six, or something?" He continued to laugh until he saw the serious lines pulling at her features.

"No Kenneth, my family isn't like SEAL Team Six," she responded. "My family is who they call when SEAL Team Six can't get the job done."

He watched her for a moment. Looking for any signs of sarcasm, but found none. She'd meant every word that had crossed those luscious lips of her.

"Why are you telling me this?"

"Because I don't want there to be secrets between us," she answered. "I want us to be transparent, and I haven't been. I can't tell you I will always share every thought or piece of knowledge I have. My job at times prevents me from sharing things. But I can promise you that when it comes to family, I will always try to be as open with you as you have been with me."

She leaned across and ran her finger through his hair, nails lightly scraping his head just the way he liked.

"And in the interest of being completely open with you, I have something else I need to tell you."

"What?" his voiced dripped with speculation waiting for her to drop whatever hammer she was about to pummel him with.

"Things have been crazy. Inside of a week one attempt on your life was executed and another was thwarted. We have one suspect dead, and one that refuses to utter anything but name, rank, and serial number. I don't know why this is happening, and frankly I'm scared. I'm afraid I won't be able to protect you. So I need to call in back up."

"What do you mean? Someone else to investigate the case?"

She shook her head. "No," she answered. "Someone else to protect you. I'm adding a full protective detail to you, one outside of my command that not only has experience with these types of circumstances, but will do everything and anything to keep you safe."

Kenneth was about to respond when he heard the doorbell ringing. He looked up at the clock, it was late, and people just didn't drop by their house without the benefit of a call at this hour. Not if they didn't want Heart handing them their tails on a platter.

He stood up and walked to the door, hearing his wife follow behind him. He moved the curtain slightly to look out on the porch and then turned back to his wife.

"Really?" he asked, while she shrugged her shoulders.

Kenneth opened the door to the four well-known faces standing on his porch and stood aside as Hunter, Law, Free, and True Amare all piled into his living room.

He closed the door and turned just as they were sitting and making themselves comfortable in their seats. He looked at his wife once again for an explanation when he heard True's voice crack the air.

"So, white boy, my cousin tells me you've got yourself a situation and are in need of a little muscle."

~

Kenneth stood at the door watching his wife's family trickle in one by one. He slammed the door, crossed his arms and faced his wife.

"What the hell is this about, Heart?"

He ignored the other people in the room. This was his damn house and if one of them thought he wasn't going to speak his damn mind then pity for them.

"Kenneth, I need someone watching you, protecting you."

"Heart, I'm a grown man, not some child. I'm not going to be followed like I'm some airheaded princess who can't figure out how to protect himself," he spat the words out with force, his displeasure more than evident.

"Kenneth…"

"No, Heart, I'm not agreeing to this," he answered. "I'm sorry you all wasted your time coming here tonight," he spoke in a controlled tone, too afraid that his anger might get the better of him. "But my wife should have discussed this with me before she called you over here."

He said nothing more, just kept walking through the house until he found himself walking through the back door. He stood there in his yard, his anger brewing when his mind started twisting, wondering exactly when his wife had begun to think of him as helpless.

Kenneth wasn't a violent man, not usually anyway. He was skilled in martial arts, but in all the years of his training he'd never found a reason to have to use those skills outside of a dojo or competition. He could usually diffuse most situations with a level head and smooth tongue. But had his choice of weapon, his tongue versus his fists led his wife to believe he needed to be saved?

He'd never bought into the Neanderthal belief that women were the weaker sex. He'd never treated Heart as if she were weak. He'd offered his assistance in any way that would help her, but he'd never treated her as if she were unable to think for herself.

Did a non-life threatening bullet wound to the gut render him helpless, balless to his wife?

When did he become the bitch in this relationship?

≈

*H*eart stood at the kitchen counter tapping some unknown rhythm on its smooth surface. Her husband was outside blowing off some steam and she was in here…hiding. She was hiding from him, hiding from her family, feeling weaker and less in control than ever.

Giving control of her husband's protection to someone other than herself was killing her. The moment she'd realized she needed to make this call had cut her in half. No cop wanted to believe they couldn't protect their own. She was a decorated officer, top cop in her house, and yet she couldn't protect the man she loved.

Every natural instinct she had screamed for her to stand in between Kenneth and whatever trouble came for him. Even if he couldn't see the trouble, she could, and as furious as he might be right now, she had to make certain he was protected.

No, it didn't feel right letting someone else take over his protection detail, even if it was her cousins. But she couldn't split herself in two any longer. She needed to focus on finding whoever was responsible for the shooting. She needed to know what the hell they wanted with Kenneth and how to stop them. Because one thing was for damn sure, she was going to find these bastards and end them. There was no other way she was willing to let this shit end.

She took a sip of her coffee and thought back over the conversation she'd had with Kenneth about Bryan and Justice. He was hurt, like he wasn't a member of the family he loved.

Heart had known this day was coming, had known it since the day they'd married. She'd always known she was going to have to either break the confidence of her closest friend, or lie to her husband.

She'd also known that Kenneth could end up resenting her for keeping Bryan's secret as well. Fucking Jacqueline Searlington and her crazy plans for world domination had fucked with

Kenneth's head. He didn't trust everything he saw now, and if he did trust you and you lied to him, it was really difficult for him to get beyond that.

She'd explained herself, and he seemed to accept her explanation, but there was no telling if he would get beyond this.

She shrugged her shoulder. She couldn't really spend more time worrying about this. Not when there was someone after her husband. She lifted the cup to her lips for a sip when she heard footsteps. They were quiet, barely noticeable in fact, but her ear picked up the displacement of weight against the floor tiles.

She caught hold of a wrist before it could rest itself on her shoulder. Turning quickly, and twisting the wrist so that soon the individual's arm was wrung behind the back and they were on their knees in front of her.

"Good job, soldier; now let an old man up."

She smiled at her uncle. "I'm not one of your soldiers, Uncle Hunter."

The older man stood up with the speed and agility of someone half his age. Shining bald head, deep brown skin, his form was a mix of hard lines and carved muscles. Her uncle may have been aging, but he was still the strongest man she knew, and by his appearance, it didn't really appear that age had changed that at all.

"Who says?" he asked as he pulled himself up from his kneeling position. "I trained you, doesn't matter to me if you choose to use that on the police force instead of in the service, you will always be one of my soldiers, niece."

There was comfort in his words. She wasn't always confident she had what it took to get the job done, but hearing her uncle's words reminded her she was capable. She'd been taught by the best, forged to perfection in Hunter's fire. So during those moments of doubt that crept up from the ground like a weed seeking to choke the life out of her confidence, she would turn to her best asset, the strength of her family.

"How's Kenneth doing out there?" he asked.

"I don't really know, he hasn't come in yet and I don't think he's all that thrilled with me at the moment. I'm trying to give him some time to cool off before I try to talk to him again," she answered.

Hunter's clear brown eyes sparkled with understanding. Maybe it was because he was a man and understood Kenneth's perspective a great deal better than she did. Or perhaps it was because he'd spent a hell of a lot of years married that he understood how things like this worked between couples. Either way he gave her a supportive nod and smiled at her.

"You guys figure out a plan yet for Kenneth's detail?"

"You sure you really want to implement this, Heart?" Hunter asked. "It's a dangerous thing to mess with a man's pride."

Pride. That's what all of this bullshit came down to. She was trying to save Kenneth's life and he was worried about looking like less than a man. Was she sorry that Kenneth was upset, yes, but she couldn't give a fuck about the fact that his pride was hurt. This was about his life, preserving it. Beyond that, nothing else mattered.

Why was Hunter even questioning this? He was a general in the

Army, if anyone should understand the type of danger Kenneth was in, or the lengths she was willing to go to in order to keep him safe it should be him above all others.

"Heart, you could always just bring him to me. Maybe it's time he learned to take matters into his own hands. Maybe that would help get rid of some of the tension between the two of you? He could win back some of his independence, you would feel better about him being out there on his own."

The muscles of her face locking into a hard-set jaw and sharp lines must have been enough to convey her thoughts. Hunter held up his hands in an I-surrender motion and nodded. He pointed toward the warming coffee carafe on the coffeemaker instead, silently asking for a peace offering. She collected herself and pulled a mug from the cabinet and poured her uncle a steaming cup of the brew motioning him to the island in the middle of the open kitchen.

"For right now, Law and Free are going to tag along with Kenneth everywhere. Considering what's going on with Bryan, I think True's time is best served at the hospital with Justice."

"How's Jussy doing?"

"He has a lot of regret. He blames himself for not being more aggressive with Bryan and forcing this issue of reconciliation. Did you know that Bryan sent him divorce papers?"

Her eyes rose from the coffee cup in her hand to the concerned father sitting across from her. Hunter was always strong, stoic, a pillar they all looked to for guidance and direction. But sitting here with him, watching the slump in his shoulders and the resignation in his eyes, it was a clear indication that he was worried for his son's marriage.

"When did this happen? Neither of them told me."

"Maybe six months ago," Hunter answered. "He sent them with no warning; Jussy rushed back here on a weekend pass and told Bryan in no uncertain terms there would be no divorce."

"Does Justice know why after nearly five years of separation Bryan decided to officially end things?"

"Probably has something to do with Jussy's reenlistment. Jussy's got one more mandatory tour to reach his twenty-year mark. Twenty years in and he leaves with a full pension. With that reenlistment will more than likely come promotion, which will lead to a new command. Last I spoke to Jussy, he was having reservations about being shipped off somewhere. At least being stationed on this task force with me in D.C. he can be back up to New York in a moment's notice. Anywhere else and he might not be afforded that opportunity. I think Bryan was trying to make it easier for Jussy to go if he needed to."

Heart could definitely see her second making that kind of sacrifice to help his husband reach his full potential, to set him free. She just wished Bryan would understand that Justice didn't want freedom.

Damn, Bryan, stop wallowing in your martyrdom. Grab some happiness for once in your life.

She shook her head; she'd never thought she'd be having those kinds of thoughts regarding anyone's love life. She certainly hadn't worried about grabbing her own bit of happiness before Kenneth walked into her life. But now, she'd sell her soul to the highest bidder if it meant Kenneth remained by her side. Without him, nothing else mattered.

"Bryan really needs to wake up so I can slap the piss out of him. How could he throw away his happiness like this?"

"He's a man, Heart. I don't know if you've noticed, but sometimes we don't always make the best decisions under the best of circumstances. After dealing with the death of a child, not to mention coming from that fucked up family of his, it's a wonder the man can think straight enough to tie his own shoes."

She could certainly agree with that. That family of Bryan's...no, she could never think of them as his family. She was Bryan's family, the Amares were his family, the precinct was his family, never those people. Those miserable, hateful assholes that had attempted to destroy him would never be family to Bryan as far as she was concerned. But somehow, even though he hated them, they'd still tarnished the shiniest part of his soul and convinced him to let go of the one thing that would make him the happiest. She just wished he would open his eyes again, wake up and rebuild his life...with Jussy.

The snick of the doorknob twisting pulled her focus to the back-door. Kenneth walked in and snatched the keys to his SUV from the hook on the wall.

"Where are you going?" she queried.

He didn't spare her a look. "Out."

"Kenneth," she replied slowly. "Now's not the time for this, you should—"

"Stop trying to manage me," he responded. "I'm not one of your cops. I'm going out and if I see one of your so-called ninja cousins anywhere near me I'll call it in to nine-one-one."

The door slammed and he was gone. She reached for the cup of coffee sitting on the counter. Hunter anticipating her next move snatched it up just before he fingers could lock around it.

"Not gonna let you do it. You'll be pissed when you can't find a replacement to match the

set."

She slapped her hand against the hard granite countertop instead. "Dammit, Hunter, I know what you're trying to do. Why can't that fucking man just listen? I'm trying to save his ass." "Trying to save him, or tell him what to do?" Hunter asked.

For some reason she couldn't fathom, thinking about the answer to that question pissed her off more.

CHAPTER 14

*J*ustice stood at the window looking down into the busy Brooklyn Street. He could see the B12 bus running up and down the block and the small moving people scurrying across the street, dodging oncoming vehicles.

He'd been all over the world during his service as a Marine, but nothing ever felt as comfortable as being home in Brooklyn.

He remembered the first time he'd brought Bryan home on furlough to meet his father and grandmother. He'd known that no matter how much he loved Bryan, if he couldn't make it beyond the elders in his clan, then their love was a nonstarter.

Bryan was a country boy, hadn't stepped out of Small-town, Nowhere before his father signed him up for the Corps. Stepping out of a cab and onto the eclectic streets of Brooklyn had been culture shock to him. The girls jumping double-dutch in the streets, the boys kneeling down on the chalk-outlined sidewalk with their wax-filled milk bottle caps playing skelly, the fellas on the corner kicking it to loud hip-hop music, and the neighborhood hens sitting on the stoops watching everything on the block go down kept Bryan's eyes wide with wonder as they climbed the steps to his family's house.

It had all been like something out of a blaxploitation movie and

Bryan had taken it all in one image at a time. From that moment on, he'd fallen in love with Brooklyn, promising that they would settle down here when they'd both retired from the service.

That memory seemed like it happened only seconds ago, not nearly the two decades that had passed. Justice stood there doing the math in his head, seventeen years in love with the same man, his one and only. Justice had known from that first glance that he would ride to the grave loving Bryan, he just hadn't figured that the journey could come so soon.

It was odd, especially considering how they'd met and their career choices. Even though both of them faced real dangers performing their professional duties, Justice had never once thought they wouldn't make it home to each other. He'd somehow known that they would grow old together. That was probably why he just couldn't wrap his head around the fact that Bryan might not make it out of his hospital bed.

The doctors had told him there was no change. Bryan was breathing on his own now, the ugly ventilator a happily discarded memory, but he still wasn't awake yet. He still wasn't responding. They were hinting to Justice about making decisions regarding Bryan's care and rehabilitation. They'd given up and wanted to put Bryan out to pasture in a long-term rehab center. He'd told them the only decision he would make is the one where Bryan lived and walked again on his own power and since then they'd left him alone.

Justice felt the shift in the air. "There's been no change, Pops, you didn't have to come all the way down here."

"My sons are here, one of whom is fighting for his life, the other his heart. Where else would I be?"

Justice felt a quick ripple in his soul. His father's support never ceased to surprise him.

There wasn't even a time Justice could remember his father giving him anything but his genuine support.

As a young teenager, Justice was so afraid of his father discovering the truth about his sexuality. Hunter Amare was a decorated soldier climbing unbelievable heights in the Army. He was strong, he was bold, and he was built like a Brahma bull. He was also a religious black man who had grown up in the Baptist church. Justice's little mind just couldn't grasp how Hunter would accept having a son like him.

He'd decided that hiding was the best way to deal with the situation until a better idea came to him. The only thing that had tripped him up was that damn junior high school dance. Hunter had taken him out to the backyard to shoot some hoops and questioned Jussy's decision to not attend.

When Justice had shrugged his shoulders in true pre-teen fashion and answered with a halfassed, "'Cause," Hunter had sat him down on the steps and made him have a conversation he'd never wanted to have.

"Is it because you just don't want to go, or is because you're afraid of what people wills say if you go with the person you really want to go with?" When Justice didn't answer him, Hunter continued. "With Michael?"

Eyes wide with fear, Justice sat rigid and afraid of the blow he assumed would follow his father's revelation. Instead he felt a soft but strong hand on his shoulder comforting him rather than bringing harm.

"I know, son, I've known for a good while now. I just didn't want to say anything until you came to me."

Tears sprang up in Justice's eyes. He shut them tight fighting the visible signs of his weakness.

"I'm so sorry, Pops. I've tried...I don't want to be like this...I..."

Justice felt himself being pulled until his cheek met the hard wall of his father's chest and he was being imprisoned by his father's muscular arms.

"Baby boy, there is nothing wrong with you. You are who you were always meant to be. And if anyone else in the world ever gives you a problem about that, you tell them to come see your daddy. Is that clear?"

Justice couldn't remember if he'd actually answered his father, just that he couldn't seem to stop clinging to him, so overwhelmed by the paternal love he was being showered with, so relieved that his father hadn't turned away from him.

From that moment on, Justice had never been ashamed of his homosexuality, and if his father hadn't already been the young boy's hero, he'd certainly become so then.

"Come here, boy." Hunter's deep baritone carried the command on silent wings that wrapped around Justice and brought him back into the present. The Marine in him trained to yield to command; he turned around and walked to his father. Stoic and proud, he stood with his shoulders back, and chest out until his father opened his arms, then just like that young boy all those years ago, his resolve crumbled and he fell into his daddy's strong arms.

"As long as I have breath, Justice, you will never have to face hardship alone."

Justice shook in his father's arms, the cry silent at first, but the tremors were vicious. His entire being just shook in silence as hurt and fear stole his breath from him. The more he shook the tighter Hunter held him, securing him from the rest of the world while it collapsed.

"I just want to tell him I love him, Pops. I was so angry the last time I saw him, so pissed about those damn divorce papers. I just want the chance to say it again and to have him hear it, and to hear him say it back to me. I just don't want that to be the last time we had together. I just need him to know I love him and that he loves me."

In nearly seventeen years in the service Justice had known injury. Every time he'd come home on leave, Bryan had taken to cataloguing any new scars Justice acquired. He would wait for Jussy to come out of the shower, rub him down with whatever lotion or oil was closest as he looked for new battle wounds.

It had become their customary interlude to welcome home sex, every time without fail. But that last time had been so different. Bryan was different, cold, and distant he wouldn't even look Justice in the eye.

Profane language wasn't something Justice shied away from, he was a Marine, and sometimes profanity was the only thing that could accurately depict the emotions he was attempting to convey. But Lord help him the words that came out his mouth when Bryan wouldn't even acknowledge them trying again. The things he'd said...he just couldn't let that be the last words Bryan heard from him.

He stepped out of his father's embrace and pointed toward the door. He needed a few minutes to try to compose himself. He made it as far as the doorway when he heard a ragged breath being drawn. The sound was small, almost imperceptible, but when you've been aching for something for so long that you were beginning to doubt you would ever get it, the slightest sign that it had arrived filled you with unimaginable joy.

"I heard...I...I know," the scratchy voice was quiet, but managed to fill the room like a loud boom.

Justice turned around looking toward the bed for confirmation.

Is this my imagination? Did Pops hear it too?

When Hunter's careful smile widened into a relieved grin he said the words Justice hungered to hear.

"Yes, I heard it too."

The two men turned to the bed and watched as Bryan slowly blinked the fog of unconsciousness from his brown eyes. He turned his head just enough to lock eyes with Justice and beckon him to his bedside.

"Bryan?" he whispered.

"I'd better be," he forced out. "Or as soon as I get my legs under me there's going to be some furniture moving."

Justice leaned down and placed a gentle kiss on his husband's lips. He'd done that several times over the weeks Bryan had been trapped in his hospital bed. But today, he pressed back, and lifted a hand to the back of Justice's head, pulling him in deeper, closer, letting Justice know he was alive, and awake, and most importantly, still in love with him.

"Pops," Justice uttered without taking his eyes off his husband, "... go get the doctor."

~

*H*eart stood in the back of the auditorium and watched the focused movement on the stage. Several of her girls, including LaQuisha were in full ballet garb, with their varying hairstyles all twisted into a tight bun at the back of the head. Even 'Quisha's with her jumbo electric blue and black box braids was pulled into the severe style that seemed almost mandatory for the ballerina. They all twirled and pointed their toes in a practiced synchronization that all seemed to flow from the poised instructor dancing on stage with them.

This far from the stage Heart couldn't make out the prima ballerina's features, but her skill, her focus, that was very apparent. The control she had over the dancers was also evident by the adept way they followed her lead step for step, movement for movement. She had them all in line resembling Debbie Allen during her *Fame* years.

God she's beautiful up there with my girls.

She almost let a smile creep onto her face until she remembered it was Alexis-Jeovonni and

Heart couldn't stand her.

"Go on and smile, you know you want to." The surly old man standing next to her nudged her arm breaking her train of thought.

"Willie, I don't know shit except that woman is a potential problem for me," she answered.

"What could that little woman up there do to give you a problem, MacKenzie?"

Heart wasn't ready to answer Big Willie's question, partly because she didn't have an answer, and secondly because she didn't believe in sharing her inner thoughts on someone she was watching carefully.

"How's she doing with the girls?"

Willie blew out a low whistle followed by a quiet chuckle.

"She got them gals in check. The first day she showed up 'Quisha called herself checking A.J. Well, not only did A.J. read little missy, but then she floored her with her ballet skills. Them girls couldn't do nothing but stand with their mouths open while she pranced around on her toes all over that stage."

Heart was secretly impressed. 'Quisha could be a handful when she wanted to be. She was also the ringleader of the group. If you couldn't win her over, there was no way the other kids were going to follow your lead.

"How does she interact with them? You catch her belittling them, looking her snobby little nose down at them?"

Big Willie looked at her with squinted eyes trying to read her. She kept her face blank, not willing to give his cop's mind fodder for looking beyond the picture of calm she was presenting.

"A.J.? Nah," he answered. "She's real good with the kids, Mac. She honestly seems to love the time she spends with them as much as they enjoy her. I don't know what your deal is with her, MacKenzie, but whatever it is it's not about her bringing harm to none of our kids."

Willie gave her a final nod and turned to leave the auditorium before he stopped and looked at Heart again. "I know you've been busy trying to take care of this shit with your husband and Smyth, but the kids were asking if you're going to be able to make it to their spring concert."

Heart pulled out her phone and looked down at the calendar. How the fuck had she managed to lose track of that much time that she hadn't realized how close to the concert they were.

This concert happened twice a year. A spring concert at the end of May and a holiday concert at the end of December where the kids showed off their abilities. They sang, they danced, the performed martial arts, and created visual art for the audience. It was an opportunity for the community to see that the kids that frequented Mac's Place were doing something positive with their lives. It was also an opportunity to get guilty rich people seeking an outlet for their self-reproach over the accident of their births to spend some of their stacks on her center and her kids.

"Willie, shit. I've been so out of it I didn't even realize how close this was. I need to get started with making calls for donations."

Willie shook his head. "No you don't. When that young lady

discovered what was going on, she got to work on it. Apparently she knows some folks with some deep pockets, 'cause we've got donations coming in that we've never had before. That little woman is connected."

Heart turned back to the stage. The music ended and A.J. was talking to the girls. She looked over her shoulder once catching a glimpse of Heart at the back and waved her to the stage.

Before Heart could push off the doorframe Willie's voice stopped her.

"You know, Mac, when Porter and I first met, I couldn't stand his ass. Hell, most of the time I still can't stand his fucking ass. But when we first met, I'd sooner had put a bullet in him than admit he actually knew what the fuck he was doing."

She laughed; it took most people a while to warm up to Porter. It didn't surprise her that her two mentors hadn't been the best of friends in the beginning.

"What changed things?" she asked. "'Cause y'all mofos are bosom buddies now."

Big Willie nodded his head and joined in her laughter. "It's true, that man is my brother. The only person closer to me than him is my wife, and even then...sometimes I wonder. But what I realized was that although he was an arrogant son of a bitch, so was I. His police work was just as solid as mine. After looking at things for a while I realized that the reason I couldn't stand him, is because he was too much like me. Sometimes MacKenzie, when like recognizes like, it's not always a good time. Maybe you don't like that young lady because she's too much like you?"

Heart rolled her eyes and waved a dismissing hand at her former lieutenant. "You don't know what you're talking about, old man. That chick is nothing like me."

"Really?" he asked. "'Cause I see one major personality trait that you both share in spades."

"Yeah, like what?" she answered.

He turned to face her, granting her the full measure of his cocky grin. "You're a boss,

MacKenzie," he declared. "But that young woman up there on that stage...she's a boss too."

Heart let Willie's words settle into her gut. She couldn't argue about A.J.'s boss qualities. On the surface, the woman had her shit together; there was no doubt about that. But as Heart walked down the angled floor to the foot of the stage, she couldn't shake the fact that it was just a case of two alpha females clawing for the top spot in Kenneth's life.

As far as Heart was concerned, there was no competition is that regard, no doubt in her mind that she ruled her husband's heart. But there was something, something she still hadn't figured out yet, something she honestly hadn't given much thought to once all hell broke loose and some maniac set his murderous sights on her husband. But standing here watching this woman with her girls, watching the delight on their faces as she gave them praise for their performance, she thought once again that she might just have to put this woman down if she fucked over the people that she loved. Her kids at Mac's Place, or her husband and son, if A.J. Tenetti fucked with either of them Heart was going to end her.

"Stop shooting daggers at me out of your eyes, Captain," A.J. taunted, a self-satisfying smile plastered across her face. "What did you think of our performance?"

Heart studied her for a moment taking in the confident squaring of her shoulders, the sure placement of her hand on her slim waist. Willie was right, A.J. was definitely a boss.

"I'm impressed. You guys really do look good up there." The girls preened and posed, putting their confidence on display. All Heart could do was stand back and smile with pride.

When LaQuisha and her crew had come to Mac's Place they were skeptical of her intentions. They didn't trust that there were cops in Brooklyn that actually gave a damn about them. They were afraid they'd either die in the streets or succumb to NYPD and the penal system.

It hurt Heart that those assumptions weren't necessarily wrong in their part of the world. Here in East New York, Brooklyn and other places like it all over the world, those were the only options for kids like LaQuisha. But in this place, Mac's Place, the children had been offered another option...hope.

"Cop Lady, you really like it, or you just tryna' be nice?"

Heart laughed, the girl knew damn well she was good, she also knew Heart didn't suffer from the need to appease those around her.

"You know ain't a thing nice about me, 'Quisha, so stop fishing for compliments." The girl gave an easy smile and nodded her head at Heart.

"How's Mr. Money doing? He coming to see us soon?" LaQuisha asked.

I'd have to see him first to ask him.

Heart took a deep breath and pushed a smile onto her face. These kids loved their Mr. Money. If nothing else, that name alone turned her efforts into a real smile. She'd told the kids that she wasn't really comfortable with them calling Kenneth white boy. She knew they meant it as a term of endearment and that was exactly as he'd taken it. But she felt it was disrespectful and told them they'd have to come up with something else.

LaQuisha, DeAndre, and Jaisyn had taken one look at Kenneth and decided Money was Kenneth's new name. Heart simply rolled her eyes and gave up, telling them they better put mister in front of it. She'd learned to pick and choose her battles where these kids were concerned, and apparently coming up with a respectable nickname for her husband wasn't going to happen.

"'Quisha, you know he was hurt, don't you?" Heart asked.

"Yeah, but he's all right, right?"

Worry filled the teenager's body and Heart was once again reminded of how much Kenneth had come to mean to these kids. He was just as vital to them as she and Willie, another person in their small arsenal they knew they could depend upon.

"He's fine, 'Quisha, just recuperating. You know y'all are a rough bunch. He's not up for that right now. As soon as he's all healed up he'll come spend some time with you guys. You know he wouldn't miss hanging out with you guys if it could be helped."

There, that was close enough to the truth without actually lying to the girl. The truth was after last night, Heart didn't really know where Kenneth's head was, especially when it came to her. But these kids were his heart; he wouldn't turn away from them just because he was pissed with her. At least she didn't think he would.

You didn't think he'd storm out last night and not come back home either, but he did.

"Please ask him to come to the concert; Mistress Tenetti is helping us put together a surprise for Mr. Money and we want him to be here to see it."

Heart's smile grew wider as she watched the excitement in the woman-child. Didn't matter if she had to tie him to a chair and drag him in here, Kenneth wasn't going to miss this. She wouldn't let the bullshit they were dealing with affect these kids.

"He'll be here 'Quisha."

The girl placed her feet close together in what Heart guessed was ballerina fashion, and she made a deep bow from her waist down to the floor before she sauntered off the stage with the rest of the dancers.

"They really think highly of you. They were disappointed when you didn't show up to rehearse with them," A.J. disclosed.

"I can imagine. I'm sorry I missed this. It would have been great to dance next to them. This thing with Kenneth has swallowed most of my time."

"Has it?" she inquired. "Or is it that you just don't want to be around me?"

Heart shook her head. "I don't run from shit, and certainly not you. I might not trust you, but

I wouldn't disappoint my kids just to avoid you."

The attorney watched Heart carefully seeming to measure each muscle movement in her face. Heart figured this was how she obliter-

141

ated witnesses on the stand, that cold stare would cut through a lesser woman, for Heart, it was a mild chill.

"So how are things with Kenneth's case?" A.J. asked.

"Not much I can say. We're investigating," Heart replied.

"Would you tell me if you did know anything?" "Probably not," Heart answered with a shrug.

"He's my brother, Captain—"

Heart stepped up to the stage and hauled herself into a sitting position on its edge. She pulled her knee into her chest and looked up at the small woman standing with her hands on her hips, indignation simmering just below the surface of her skin.

"Kenneth is not your brother, A.J., John is. Kenneth isn't anything more to you than an old acquaintance."

"Are we back to this jealousy shit? I don't want your man, MacKenzie."

Heart cocked her head to the side as she carelessly tapped out a rhythmless beat with the heel of her boot.

"You may not want my husband in a romantic sense, but you want something from him. I just haven't figured out what it is yet."

"God woman, get a hobby and give this conspiracy shit a rest already." Heart ignored her and waved the diva down to sit next to her on the stage.

"Look, A.J., I'm no fan of yours, but I do know this, whatever it is I don't like about you, my kids don't share it. You're doing a good thing here, the way the kids act around you is proof of that. Not to mention, Willie tells me you've raised more money this year than we've ever had in the coffers before. Whatever my issues, you're doing good work for my kids. As long as that continues, you and I are good."

"And if I don't?" A.J. inquired.

"Then all bets are off and I'm coming for you," Heart answered. "Just know this counselor, don't ever let me find out you put one of mine in harm's way, because then...well, let's just say it wouldn't be wise."

Heart smiled at A.J., extending a friendly hand to her. "But for now, while things are good, let's forget about the fact that we don't really like each other all that much and let's focus on giving these kids a great show. You think you can do that, counselor?"

Heart left her hand hanging in the air waiting for A.J. to either shake it or slap it away. With a slow, measured pace A.J. finally accepted her hand and gave it a firm shake.

"Truce?" A.J. asked.

Heart nodded. "Truce."

For now, they both thought.

CHAPTER 15

*K*enneth stared out at the dark Manhattan skyline. From this high up, the usual buzzing of the city seemed almost serene, peaceful. Usually it calmed him, helped him refocus, but tonight his blood still bubbled with anger.

After she'd promised to keep him in the loop, Heart had fallen back to her old tricks, attempting to manage him the way she did her officers. She hadn't even thought twice about his reaction to all of this, no, she'd simply barged through as usual and expected him to fall in line.

A quick succession of knocks pulled him from his view of the city. Company really wasn't what he was looking for and if Heart had followed him here, or worse, had him follow here,

Kenneth wasn't sure if he'd be able to reign in the storm that was building inside him.

The door opened and Kenneth's eyes rested on Alan Quillen. Once his vice president stepped into the room Kenneth turned back to the window, pretending the relief that his wife wasn't following him wasn't filling him.

In their time together, even when things were at their worst,

Kenneth had never relished being apart from his wife. But today... well today just wasn't a good day.

"Not really in the mood for company, Quillen. If Heart asked you to check on me..."

"Heart hasn't asked anything of me. I was leaving my office when I saw the light on in yours. I just wanted to check in and see if everything was all right. Seems like it's not," Alan answered.

"Since the shooting, things have been really crazy at my house," Kenneth replied.

"I would assume so. I'm sure Heart is losing her damn mind right about now," Alan quipped.

Kenneth rolled his eyes, hoping to stamp down on some of his rising anger. "You wouldn't be wrong in assuming so."

Kenneth saw Alan's reflection move closer to him through the window. The firm hand on his shoulder wasn't a surprise when it finally landed.

There were very few friends Kenneth trusted throughout his lifetime. Drew, John, Alan, they were the only people in his life that had always been loyal to him. Not once had he ever found any of them lacking. If only he could say the same thing about his wife.

"Hey, Ken man, what's going on?"

"Heart and I have been at odds since the shooting. I found out she's been keeping some things secret from me. Maneuvering and planning behind my back without consulting me, I just can't take it all right now."

Alan directed him from the window and motioned him to couch. When he was seated next to him he handed Kenneth a clear glass that was half filled with amber liquid.

"Sounds like you could use a little of this," Alan quipped while handing Kenneth the glass. "As I said, it sounds like you've got a great deal going on. Let me ask you this, what's the thing that's bothering you most. What made you leave that wonderful woman you're married to and opt for spending your night in the office?"

There it was, that thing between real friends, that thing that helped those that really knew you to pinpoint the real issues in your life.

"As I said, Heart has been keeping secrets lately. I get why she did, she was in a fucked up situation, and keeping those secrets seemed to be the best way to handle the situation at the time. Well, she finally came clean with me, promised she would never do it again, and in the next breath springs this new plan she cooked up without even discussing it with me. Like I didn't matter, as if I were just some chess piece she was moving around in her fucking cops and robbers game."

Just the thought of how she'd made decisions for him without even consulting him, or taking into consideration how he would feel. Yes, he'd done things for Heart in the past, set things up for her, but never had he just managed her fucking life without any input from her.

"She's decided that I need 'round the clock protection from now until she finds out who's after me."

"I don't think that sounds like a bad thing."

"Have you met her cousins, the Amares?"

"She wants her cousins watching your every move?" Alan laughed loudly apparently Kenneth's current situation was amusing to him, no so much for Kenneth.

"Kenneth, I know True and her brothers can be a little crazy, but honestly, your wife is just trying to protect you. Why is this such a problem for you?"

Why indeed? It wasn't as if Heart had never done her cop thing before. Hell, that's how they'd met in the first place, but this, there was something about this that just felt wrong.

"I just don't like having my life decided for me without consultation. She can't just make decisions for me without including me in the process."

"Kenneth, someone shot you and her work partner. From what I understand Bryan's condition is extremely serious. Heart is a woman who sees the ugliness of the world every day.

She knows how dangerous the world is. Why wouldn't she do everything in her power to protect the man that she loved? We both know your woman isn't the average. She's exceptionally talented, she possesses a strength that few people do, and she always has the best interest of others at heart. Why is this so unexpected for you? Why are you so bothered by it?"

Kenneth was quiet as Alan's words rung in his ears. Alan was right, Heart protecting those in danger wasn't anything new to him, but somehow it bothered the hell out of him that she was doing this.

"The only thing I can figure out, Kenneth, is that your pride has taken a hit. Maybe you don't like the idea of being saved by a woman?"

"I know I told you how Heart and I met," Kenneth answered. "You know that can't be the answer."

"She was a stranger to you then, you didn't have any real connection to her. But now she's your wife. Does that up the stakes at all?"

Kenneth didn't answer, just continued drinking until the glass in his hand was empty and his chest was burning from the alcohol.

"Kenneth, don't let your pride cause you to do something stupid like alienating your wife.

Or worse yet, doing something dangerous."

Yeah, 'cause it's not like dangerous hasn't been a frequent visitor in my life recently.

Kenneth twisted the heavy tumbler back and forth between his hands trying to avoid the questions his friend had posed.

God I just need my life to get back to normal.

Normal, he almost laughed. His life from the moment he was born was never normal. He'd been born to a homicidal mother, and a father who figured out too late that he couldn't protect his children from his crazed wife.

Now his life was in the balance again, a place he always seemed to find himself over the course of his lifetime, and the one person who could help him he was pushing away.

Not willing to focus on the why of that, he set about lines of thought. If the police could just figure out who was doing this, maybe he could have his life back; get things settled in his house again between him and his wife. Maybe the police needed a hand in figuring this thing out and if they did, he knew just where he needed to start in order to get to the bottom of things.

~

*K*enneth pulled through the heavy gates of the prison and slowed to a stop at the security checkpoint. Once his car was cleared; he pulled into an empty parking spot and made his way inside.

After various pat downs and security scans, he finally sat in an empty room that looked more like an old-fashioned telephone booth than a visitation room. He sat in the single chair that faced the safety glass divider and waited for the prisoner to be delivered.

The entire drive here he kept asking himself why he was headed into hell to sit with the devil. Who in their right mind would do something like that? Maybe that was the problem.

Maybe he hadn't really thought this through with a clear head.

He'd been behind at least two glasses of whiskey last night when this thought had come to him, that coupled with the anger he was harboring and he'd come up with this brilliant idea to face his tormentor head on.

If he was honest, he couldn't really blame this trip on the booze, he'd stayed in the office and slept off whatever effects alcohol would have had on him before he'd sat behind his wheel and pointed his car north.

He was mad when he'd stormed out of his house. Heart and her need to control everything and everyone just pushed him to a place where he'd been willing to do anything to prove his independence.

Now that morning had dawned, instead of waking up to his wife, he was in the sleeping town of Bedford, Westchester waiting to walk into a federal prison to visit the woman who was convicted of attempting to murder his wife, kidnapping his niece, and attempted extortion.

Smooth Searlington, most dudes would be sucking on a longneck, you go running to your convict mama.

He heard a startling buzz fill the air and then the thick metal door slowly opened and his mother stepped inside the room.

She looked around until her eyes met his and he saw surprise in them.

So she hadn't been expecting me?

He watched Jacqueline Searlington stand in the middle of the room. She was covered in what appeared to be bright orange hospital scrubs. They weren't flattering; their boxy shape gave her sort of a nondescript look like she could easily be lost in a sea of others wearing the same items.

The last time he'd seen her sitting in her hospital bed, her hair was the same noire black his own locks possessed. But now, nearly five years later it was virtually all white with only tiny slivers of its former black streaking through it.

For the slightest moment the son in him ached to go to her, see if she were all right. But then the image of her holding a gun to his niece's head flashed before his eyes and he remembered why he'd driven to this godforsaken place to begin with.

She sat down in front of him behind the safety glass that separated them and picked up the telephone headset on her side. Kenneth reached for the phone on his side and placed it to his ear.

"Hello Kenneth," her voice was familiar, but no longer drenched in that classist superiority that defined her prior to incarceration.

"Hello…" he paused, wondering what he should actually call her. He hadn't actually thought of her as a mother in so long it almost seemed foreign attempting to address her by that title now.

"How have you been?" she asked, moving him beyond his hurdle of what to call her.

"Up until recently, I've been really good. I got married, had a son."

Her eyes glowed. "A son, do you have a picture of him? Can I see him?"

He couldn't exactly explain why her interest in his son felt good, but it did. He and Heart had never discussed whether she would be involved in Amare's life. When you tried to kill the woman who would become the mother of your grandchild it kind of secured the fact that you weren't going to be invited to watch the child in question grow up.

He reached for his wallet and pulled the small photo from the bill-fold and looked down at his son's smiling face. If he consulted his wife about this she'd be ready to put a bullet in him, but at this moment, he didn't really feel all that inclined to consider her thoughts on this matter.

There was a tiny bit of worry that pulled at the base of his neck, reminding him that Heart had a say in this too. As quickly as the thought popped up, he tried to stomp it down. Should he consider his wife's feelings, probably, but for damn sure she hadn't been considering him in all her plans as of late. So he pulled the photo out and turned it around, laying it flat against the window that stood between them and showed her his son.

He saw the accustomed expectancy that people donned when they were looking at a new baby, that moment where they attempted to figure out which body part the child received from which parent. Then her brows formed in to a perfect V and he watched the questions form in her eyes.

"He looks just like us, same blue eyes same prominent slope of our nose. He is a little dark though, sort of exotic. Is his mother Moroccan royalty?"

Shocked quiet by her ignorance, although he wasn't quite sure why, Kenneth just shook his head. "Did you really just ask me that?" he questioned. "If you're asking me if his mother is from Morocco, the answer is no, if you're asking if she's black, then yes, my wife is an African-

American woman."

Not waiting to see the disappointment in her eyes he pulled the picture from the glass and replaced it to the safety of his wallet. When he returned his gaze to hers she dropped her eyes slightly, almost in contrition.

Yeah right, Kenneth. You know damn well Jacqueline Searlington doesn't do sorry.

"He's a lovely boy, Kenneth," she whispered. "You and your wife must be very proud."

"We are," he answered, the succinct nature of his tone making the words sound sharp. "I'm not here to take up much of your time. I just have a few questions I need you to answer for me."

"I've got nothing but time in this place," she answered as she gave a sorrowful glance at the surrounding metal the room seemed to be encapsulated in. "What do you want to know?"

"Someone took a shot at me, would have killed me if a police officer hadn't taken the bullet for me. Then a short time after I went home from the hospital someone came after me again."

He wasn't really certain how to read the expression on Jacqueline's face, shock, possibly. It looked genuine, but it could just as well be practiced and calculated. One just never knew with Jacqueline Searlington.

"Are you all right? Were you hurt?" She pressed her hand to the glass as if she were reaching for him, attempting to inspect his well-being herself. "Is this why the FBI came to visit me recently?" she asked. "An Agent Weaver came to see me, but he kept asking about European royalty, he never mentioned you."

He watched her carefully, waiting for that moment when she'd reveal her truth to him. The truth that he'd always known, money ruled her, and she hated him for taking it away from her.

"Thankfully I'm fine," he answered. "But I need to know something."

"What?" she asked quickly. "Anything, ask me anything."

"Was it you that put a hit out on me? Did you try to have me killed, Mother?" She flinched. Hard. As if he'd struck her.

"Kenneth," her voice echoed quietly, "I know I wasn't the best mother. I know I belong behind these bars for all the crimes I've committed against my children. I know when I say this to you, you won't believe me. But I've changed."

"Is that right?" he replied. "So being trapped behind metal bars for the rest of your life has made you see the light?" he laughed in derision. No way was he buying this, "I've found Jesus in prison," act she was attempting to sell him.

"No, Kenneth, being here didn't miraculously make me mother of the year. But seeing my daughter lying in her casket changed some things for me. I never thought I cared about her, about any of my family until she was cold and dead in front of me. Being locked away everyday with that image does something to you. I may not like the fact that I'm behind bars, but I never want to know what it feels like to lose the last of my children to death. I didn't do this, Kenneth.

Whoever is after you is still out there."

 ❀

*H*eart sat in her office making her way through much of her neglected paperwork at Mac's

Place. Since Amare's birth it seemed like she'd been pulled away from this place and these kids more often than not.

Since Kenneth was still in the wind, she figured today was the perfect day to take out her frustration on some mind-numbing paperwork. It would keep her sane long enough to keep her from murdering the man she loved.

Just the thought of Kenneth made her want to snap something in half. They'd had their battles before, but he'd never just left like that.

Except for when he did...

Her stomach felt sick just thinking about that time in their lives. They'd lost their child, she'd been swirling at the bottom of a deep depression and she'd lashed out on the nearest person to her, Kenneth. He had born the weight of her pain and heartache for four months before he'd reached his limit.

She took a moment to sit back into the chair, needing to find truth in her thoughts. That's what their therapist had told her, think about things the way they really happened, not the way you wished them to be. The truth was Kenneth had reached his limits; the truth was she'd pushed him beyond his limits. The result was her pressed up against a wall with his hand around her throat after she'd accused him of killing their child.

They'd almost trampled into a place where they would never have been able to return to their happiness, save for Kenneth finding the strength to walk away from her and stay away from her. Those four weeks of silence had nearly ended her. Watching him walking out again without knowing if he was coming back scared her more than she wanted to admit.

She'd played with their son until the tiny boy had fallen asleep in her arms. She'd even broken her own rule of no babies in the bed just to keep from pacing the halls all night while she waited for Kenneth's return.

But this morning she'd been pissed as hell and rather than take it out on some poor unsuspecting fool that happened into her path, she decided she would put all her angry energy to good work and attack some of the center's paperwork.

Kenneth had suggested she hire an assistant director a long time ago, someone to help Big Willie carry the load when her NYPD duties interfered with her ability to stay on top of things at

Mac's Place. With all of the craziness she had going on in her personal and professional lives it was getting harder and harder to handle the administrative details needed to keep a place like this running.

She always made time for her kids, but this mountain of paperwork was getting bigger and bigger and soon Willie was either going to send her a hostile fuck you and quit, or they were going to miss something vital that might impact them keeping their doors open.

Either way, it was time for her to ask for help. Something she was learning more and more she needed since becoming a mother. It wasn't an easy fact to swallow, especially when it came to protecting the people and things she loved. Her husband and son, her kids at Mac's Place, her family, her house, she needed help protecting them all. If she were honest, she'd always needed help, just hadn't recognized it. But now, with those that she loved at risk, for the first time in her life, she was willing to ask for it.

She signed off on the last bit of paperwork for the day and walked over to Big Willie's office. He was talking to one of the regular kids and motioned her to come in as she stood in the door. The teen nodded his head and waved at her as he left the two adults alone.

"You outta here for the day, MacKenzie?" Willie asked. "Yeah, finished up that paperwork you've been asking me for."

"Good, maybe now I can get some shit done around here."

"I know I've been useless around here, Willie. I've just got so much going on. I was actually just thinking of hiring an assistant director for you."

He sat back in his chair and looked up at her for the first time since she entered the room.

One eyebrow standing up at attention, suspicion drawn across his caramel face, it was Willie's typical what-kind-of-bullshit-you-about-to-sling-at-me-now face. One she'd grown to both fear and love over the years.

"I ain't gonna lie and say it wouldn't be nice to have an extra set of hands around here. But honestly, who the fuck you planning on bringing up in here? You know Big Willie can't work with just anybody."

She laughed at him; the fact that this cocky old man spoke about himself in third person didn't surprise her, but hearing him do it was just another reason why she loved him. Crazy liked crazy and they didn't come any crazier than the old man giving her fever from behind his desk.

She was about to answer him when her phone vibrated. "Hold that thought, old man, I got a

call."

"Call me old man again and a call ain't all you 'goan get."

She rolled her eyes and looked down at the unknown number. "Searlington," she answered and waited a beat before a barely recognizable rush of words came at her.

"Hold on, hold on. Who is this? I can't understand you."

"It's Hunter, get to the hospital now."

One hand tightened around the phone while the other braced her body weight against the desk.

"Hunter?" She was afraid to ask; once he answered her greatest fear might come true. Willie must have seen something because he came from around the desk and placed a firm hand at her shoulder. It grounded her, told her it was all right to listen, all right to take on the load.

"What happened to Bryan?"

Hunter talked and her eyes burned with tears. She didn't remember if she ended the call, if her uncle had stopped speaking, the phone fell from her hand and she just let her body shake while the worry and tears raked through her soul.

She turned into Willie's arms and let the anguish she'd been holding on to spill out through loud wales.

"MacKenzie?" he whispered into her ear. "Is he...did Bryan..."

"He's awake," was all she was able to push past her lips before the tears took over again.

The big man that was holding her pressed her tighter into his embrace and before long they were both shaking with relief, happiness. Willie was the first to step out of the embrace, using his forearm as a tissue and wiping the tear tracks from his face.

"Let me finish this paperwork up and I'll meet you over there. You tell that boy if he ever does some shit like this again I'm gonna put my foot in his ass."

She couldn't help the smile that spread across her lips. That was probably about as close as Willie would ever get to saying he was happy and overwhelmed with joy.

"Damn that paperwork, old man!" She smiled as she slapped his shoulder. "Our brother is alive, and we're both going to see him right now."

~

*H*eart headed to the parking lot. Willie agreed to forego his paperwork, but the place still needed to be locked up. She had barely cracked the door open when she heard the rumble of quiet but angry voices in the air.

"I don't really care what you want to do; I'm telling you I'm not putting up with your bullshit anymore. You either come clean about all of this shit, or I'm done, A.J."

Heart listened to the voice, it was familiar, she'd heard it before. She ran through her mental rolodex until the right name fell into place.

Alan? He was Kenneth's vice president. Heart had to wonder if this was some business issue these two were arguing about?

"My brother had no right to give you that information, Alan. It was my business, not his, so back the hell off."

"It was something I shouldn't have had to find out from him. I'm not fucking him, A.J., it should have come from you!"

Heart backed up a little. Okay, apparently this isn't about some business deal. She carefully tiptoed back up the stairs and made sure to make a lot of noise when coming back down.

"Big Willie, Bring you ass on if you don't want to get left," she bellowed, hoping the two people on the other side of the door would hear her. She was filled with all kinds of happy after learning Bryan had taken a turn for the better. She wasn't about to let whatever awkward shit these two had going on fuck with her mood.

She bust out of the door and found the two standing far enough apart that anyone looking would have doubted they even knew each other, let alone had any sort of personal dealings.

"Counselor?" Heart addressed A.J. first. "You're still here?"

"Yes, Alan needed to drop off some contracts for me from Searlington Realty."

"So he came all the way over here instead of seeing you at the job tomorrow?"

Alan ran a hand through his blond locks and scratched his scalp. "It couldn't wait until tomorrow. You know we're always about making your man money."

Heart let her eyes pass back and forth between the two of them. She didn't believe shit either of them had to say, even if she hadn't overheard a portion of their conversation. But she'd let that shit slide for now.

Big Willie ambled out into the parking lot and met up with the gathering crowd. He exchanged salutations with A.J. and Alan and motioned for Heart to head to her car.

"Bring ya ass, MacKenzie," the older man grumbled.

Heart took that as her opportunity to get the hell out of dodge. Whatever was going on between these two she wanted no parts of.

~

*A*s soon as she hit the road, she dialed her husband through the car's Bluetooth system. After the first two rings she was prepared for it to switch to voicemail. After dialing it all night she knew almost to the second his recorded greeting would begin.

She went to tap the end call button on her steering wheel when Kenneth picked up.

"Damn woman," he answered. "I'm trying to sleep."

"It's afternoon for the rest of the world."

"True, but I just laid down," he grumbled.

"Perhaps if you slept at night like you were supposed to you could get up in the morning like a normal person."

"Or maybe if my wife went out and handled the errands that her note said she was going to handle and would stop trying to manage me, maybe then I could get some sleep."

She could see Willie's shoulders shaking through her peripheral vision. The shit that came out of her husband's mouth made her wonder how she ever kept the respect of her fellow officers at times.

"Kenneth, I'm in the car with Willie, and I didn't call you to discuss whatever bug has crawled up your ass this afternoon."

"You think I really care about Willie's ass being in the car?"

"Kenneth," she blew out a long breath trying to control her exasperation. "Hunter called me, Bryan is awake."

"When?" he asked, his voice instantly clear of the sleep that was present just moments before.

"A few minutes ago. I'm on my way to the hospital. You can meet us there."

"Let me call your father to see if he can watch Amare for a few. I'll be there as soon as I can."

"Are Law and Free still there?" she asked already knowing the answer.

"Seems like they're always here lately," he responded. "This protective detail just started and it's already getting on my nerves. I'm not agreeing to this, Heart."

"Not up for discussion, Kenneth. Keeping you safe is the prime directive. I know having my cousins underfoot might seem problematic to you, but right now it's the safest option we have."

She heard his frustration in the long breath he released followed by the quick click of the dial tone. If Willie wasn't in the car she would have been cussing left and right. Kenneth knew how much it pissed her off when people hung up on her. Instead, she bit the inside of her lip, nodded her head and hung up on her end. She held up a single finger in the air. "Say one fucking word and I will make you do a tuck and roll out of this damn car, old man."

She didn't hear a sound from the other side of the car, but she could still see the man's shoulders quietly shaking in laughter.

By the time they arrived at the hospital, Willie was finally able to compose himself. They walked side by side heading directly for the hospital police officer guarding the entrance to the elevators. She flashed her badge and he stepped aside allowing them to cross behind his perch.

She was about to step past the visitors lounge when she heard raucous celebrating coming from the room. She looked at Willie wondering if he knew what the hell was going on, but the shrug of his shoulders told her he was just as clueless.

She stepped inside with Willie on her heels and walked into a room filled with her officers hugging, crying, and cheering. They'd heard the news; there was nothing else that would make them celebrate so publicly.

"All right, people. I know you guys are happy, I'm thrilled too. But you know them meanass nurses are going to boot all of us out of here if we don't keep it down."

"Cap, have you seen him yet?"

She looked around until she found the voice she was looking for.

"No, Jacobs, I haven't. I'm on my way now. Got distracted by all this noise coming from in here," she answered.

She turned to walk out the door when Jacobs called out to her. "Cap, aren't you going to take a knee?"

She'd completely forgotten this ritual they had at the seventy-fourth. In the years since she'd become Captain of the house they thankfully hadn't suffered any causalities or serious injuries.

Taking a knee was a euphemism for saying a prayer of thanks for their recovered brother. She stepped further into the room and slowly took to one knee. By the time she was in position, everyone else in the room was kneeling with her, including that old heathen Willie.

"Dear God, this house comes before You in thanksgiving for the life of our brother Bryan Smyth. Thank You for his life, for his health, and for sparing this house the loss of a comrade. Thank You for this most precious gift. We ask that You bring those who sought to end his life to justice and finally we ask this one final thing."

She heard a collective intake of breath as her officers prepared to join the familiar litany.

"Please protect us as we serve. Amen."

When they were done, the hugging and celebrating continued and she dismissed the idea of trying to get them to quiet down. They were happy, and dammit, so was she.

She left Willie with her men and headed to Bryan's room and gave the two officers guarding him strong handshakes. She kept a forward motion until she was inside the room. The picture of Bryan sitting up in his bed, eyes open, and a smile on his face while he was laughing at something her uncle and cousin were saying was one of the most breathtaking images she'd ever seen.

She took a moment to quell the tears that were threatening to escape her eyes and then cleared her throat to make her presence known.

"You know Smyth, if you'd wanted time off all you had to do was say so. This laying in a coma shit for weeks on end was a little bit much. Don't you think?"

He turned toward her slowly and lifted a skeptical eyebrow. "Would you have approved my leave if I had?" he inquired.

She stepped further inside the room until she was standing at his bedside and her fingers were closed around his.

"Not on your life. You are never allowed to leave me," she whispered. "Never again." Those damn tears she'd been fighting slid down her face and she didn't give one damn that there were people around to witness them fall. Her partner was back, he was alive.

"So I hear your husband knows the truth about our little family situation?" She nodded her head.

"Well, this wasn't exactly the way I wanted him to find out," Bryan offered. "But I guess it was bound to happen. My only question is this, how mad is he?"

"Maybe that's something you should ask him yourself?" Kenneth asked from the doorway flanked by her two cousins Law and Free.

Heart gave Bryan's hand a gentle squeeze in show of her support because the look on

Kenneth's face, that stoic, unmoving look that he usually wore in the midst of his business dealings, the one that said, "I'm not pleased, and there'd better be a reasonable explanation coming my way quick, fast, and in a hurry."

"Come on in, Kenneth. There's nothing like waking up from a coma to make you want to get right with the people in your life. Take a seat, and let's have at it."

CHAPTER 16

*K*enneth stepped into the hospital room and greeted his family. He ignored the little niggle in his heart that crept up every time he thought of that word. Yes, the Amares had kept secrets from him, but he knew there hadn't been any malice attached to that fact. At least that's what his head kept telling his heart.

No one wanted to hurt you. The litany kept replaying on a continuous loop in his head. He wanted to believe it, needed to believe it if he was ever going to feel like he had a place amongst these people that he loved.

He watched Justice stand from his seat and fold his arms across his chest. Kenneth recognized that pose; he'd had to implement it a few times over the course of his relationship with Heart. It was the fuck-with-the-person-I-love-and-see-what-happens look. Kenneth smiled and shook his head.

"Jussy, you don't have to go into guard dog duty. I'm not here to attack either of you. I just wanted to see him."

"I'm the one you should have a problem with Kenneth. Not Jussy. If you're ready to bite someone's head off, come for me, not him," Bryan interrupted.

Kenneth moved closer to the bed and sat down on its edge so he was facing Bryan. "Bryan, you're lying in a hospital bed recovering from a coma and a gunshot wound. Whatever I have to say about being kept out of the loop can wait until you're home and healthy and I don't have to feel like a dick for chewing out a sick man."

Kenneth moved closer to Bryan leaning into him, trying not to hold him too tightly. "The only thing I want to say to you today is thank you. You saved my life, gave me another day with my wife and son. There's nothing in this world I can ever do to repay that debt."

Kenneth felt Bryan's hand rest on the back of his head, holding him in place, almost protecting him from the other sets of eyes in the room.

"You're the husband of my sister," Bryan whispered. "That's what family does; we take care of each other."

Kenneth nodded his head and sat up. Bryan was right. Regardless of whatever issues rested between them right now, they were family, and he would remind himself of that no matter how many times doubt crept up into his heart. If he'd learned nothing else from the Amares and his godparents, it was no matter how many times and how badly family could manage to piss you off, no one loved you or protected you like family either. And being protected by this family was like having a mini Fort Knox surrounding you at all times.

~

*K*enneth walked into the house from the garage into the kitchen. He walked to the half bathroom in the hall, freshened up and returned to the kitchen. He'd left the family in Bryan's hospital room needing a little bit of air.

He was thrilled Bryan was awake, thrilled Justice had him back. Now that he knew about the relationship between Bryan and Justice, his mind just kept wandering to a single morbid thought.

What if Jussy had lost Bryan?

He knew that wasn't the real question his subconscious wanted to ask, but even bending his thoughts in that particular direction was enough to make him ache with dread.

What if you ever lost Heart?

His stomach lurched back and forth threatening to bring up whatever it was that rested inside of an empty stomach. He placed flat hands on the countertop and waited for the nausea to pass. His world would be so empty if that woman were to leave it.

The truth was Kenneth hadn't really known love and compassion until she'd come into his life with all of her crazy family members.

Porter and his aunt Pam had done a wonderful job raising Kenneth; his godparents definitely kept him on the straight and narrow. But it was Heart and the Amares that had pierced his heart with their unconditional love and immovable loyalty.

He couldn't lose that. God forbid he did lose it, he wouldn't be able to handle that loss coming from something as petty as getting mad and storming out on an argument.

He grabbed his phone and dialed the fusion restaurant on Peninsula Boulevard. They didn't deliver, but being one of their best customers came with perks. He placed his order with a promise that if they could have his order at his door in less than thirty minutes there would be a hefty tip for the delivery person.

He ran upstairs took a quick shower and pulled on his standard home uniform, an A-line tshirt and pair of lounge pants. It was comfortable for him and it didn't hurt that his wife loved to see him in this attire either. He'd just finished passing a paddle brush through his hair when he heard the doorbell ring.

"Twenty-two minutes," he uttered as he looked over at the large-faced analog clock on the wall. He opened the door to find a smiling young Asian man with dark eyes and hair, and a slim build. He was probably around college age if Kenneth's assessment was correct.

"Hi, Mr. Searlington," the young man greeted him as he handed a large brown shopping bag to Kenneth. "That will be Sixty fifty-eight."

Kenneth pulled two hundred dollar bills from the petty cash drawer in the hall and handed them both to the young man.

"You gave me too much," he said attempting to give Kenneth back one of the bills while he searched for change in his pocket with the other hand.

"Enjoy your night," Kenneth said with a smile and softly closed the door. He cleared the low-sitting coffee table and placed the bag in the center. After a quick trip to the kitchen for plates and utensils, he set up an attractive table for two. He threw the couch cushions on the floor for them to sit on and headed back in the kitchen for a bottle of wine and two glasses.

He was searching for the wine bottle opener when he felt a tingle of electricity travel down his spine and out through his fingertips. She was home. A smile bowed his mouth as he heard her open up the front door.

Don't get too happy, she might not be so thrilled to see you.

The thought only stilted his happiness for a second before he pushed it away. No matter how angry they were with one another, they always came back to one simple fact. Heart plus Kenneth equaled happiness for the two of them. No other equation worked, no other factors could change the outcome of that expression. It just was the way they just were.

She was standing by the foot of the stairs when he returned to the living room. Her expression was guarded, she didn't seem exactly certain of the atmosphere.

"You ordered from the Fusion place?"

"Yeah," he answered. "I know how much you like their spicy crab rolls with strawberry."

She lifted one eyebrow and pointed toward the table behind him. "You got me crab rolls?" He nodded, amused by the look of disbelief on her face. "Then you must be serious about getting out of the doghouse."

"I am. Very serious," he added. He looked around her to see if anyone else would be joining them. "Are Free and Law with you?"

She shook her head. "No, they're with Bryan and Jussy. I told them you and I needed to talk before we went any further with the current plan."

He nodded his head, a little bit of relief unlocking inside him. A little bit of hope that they could actually have a level-headed conversation even when they were on opposite sides of the issue.

"Go upstairs and take a shower. I'll fix you a plate and a glass of wine."

She nodded in acquiescence and placed her foot on the first step of the staircase when he called her name halting her.

He placed the bottle of wine and glasses on a nearby accent table and met her where she stood. He leaned in and placed gentle lips on hers. The kiss was brief, not meant to excite, simply to connect. He pulled her into a one-armed hug and allowed her beautiful heat to warm his skin, fill the cold emptiness he'd been carrying around inside since he marched out of the house overcome by anger, pride, and stupidity.

"I love you," he offered. "No matter how foolish I am, always remember that."

She gave a soft smile in reply and headed up the stairs. He watched her until she disappeared into their room and returned his attention to setting their dinner table. When he was done and was about to sit cross-legged at the table she came bounding down the stairs in one of his A-line t-shirts and a pair of his boxer shorts she'd confiscated from him when they first became romantically involved.

She'd told him one day while doing their laundry that he wasn't allowed to wear anything but boxer-briefs because she liked the way they hugged his ass and package. The memory of that conversation brought a widespread smirk to his lips.

The one thing he loved about his wife was she didn't mince words, so when the discussion of his choice of underwear came up he'd handed them all to her and made certain every time she saw him he had on a fitted pair of those boxer-briefs she loved so much. That little concession had gotten him laid more times than he could count.

If you could give in to that so easily, why are you having such a hard time with this protective detail issue?

Why indeed? It wasn't that he was some misogynistic asshole that couldn't follow a woman's lead. He didn't need to control his wife, or drag her around on a leash like she were a simple-minded pet to be led around. He adored Heart, all of her. One of the sexiest things about her was the fact that she took no shit from anyone, including him. Well there was that and the fact that she carried a gun.

Weapons had never been his kink, but from the first day he'd seen her pull that fucking gun off her hip his dick had been hard. Nearly five years later and his cock still twitched when he watched her getting ready for work and she secured her sidearm on her hip.

Focus Searlington; you're getting off topic.

He watched her as she moved around him. The waistband of the boxers was rolled over several times so that the band rested just below the start of her hips and the legs ended where ass met thigh.

Fuck me.

He poured himself a glass of wine and swallowed it in one gulp hoping it would take the edge off his desire. Yes, he would love nothing more than to step over to the other side of that table, lay her on the floor, and bury himself so deeply between her thighs that he could forget about all of the bullshit they'd been dealing with as of late. No, that would have to wait. Sex was good, but sex after talking and conquering an issue was even better.

"I was wrong," Kenneth said.

"For?"

"For the way I stormed out of here yesterday. I shouldn't have left without giving you some idea of where I was or if I was all right. There's no excuse for my behavior."

"I was worried."

"I know."

"Why'd you leave like that?"

He tried to think up ways to express his feelings in a diplomatic way, but diplomacy didn't feel right. Not at this moment anyway.

"I felt belittled. Like I was some helpless person whose wife thought less of him," he answered.

"Kenneth—"

"Stop, let me finish," he interrupted. "Logically I know you don't think less of me. I honestly do understand that you're trying your best to protect me. It's just...since the beginning of our relationship, no matter what our roles were outside of this house, I've always been the protector and provider in this place. Last night I felt like you'd snatched that away from me without even consulting me. Like you doubted me."

She picked up her fork and began moving the contents of her plate around in preparation for consumption.

"I don't doubt you, Kenneth," she said calmly. "I'm just afraid. This thing has gotten so much bigger than I ever thought it could have been. I wield a great deal of power as a police captain. But this is beyond my reach. I'm afraid, scared out of my mind that I won't be enough to protect you. So if I'm acting like a controlling asshole, and bossing you around please understand it's not because I doubt you, it's because I doubt me."

He took one look at her and something inside his soul broke apart. He'd never considered that. It had never crossed his mind that she was afraid she wasn't enough to protect him. He didn't like the idea of having people follow him around. He didn't like the idea of someone else he loved being injured or worse yet, killed because they were protecting him. But the weight of this burden she'd been carrying now rested squarely at his feet and he had to make a decision. Continue to let her bear it alone, or be the husband he had always been to her and fortify the visible fissures in her weary soul.

"I can't lie and say I'm all right with this plan, Heart, but if it will make you feel better, I'll do it. I just can't promise I won't snap and kill one of your cousins. On a good day they're barely tolerable."

"True 'dat," she answered. Her eyes filled with mirth and she drew him in for a quick kiss.

"Thank you, my cousins aren't the easiest people to be around, but I know they will protect you in ways that the law doesn't necessarily allow for me to do. I've been without you, Kenneth. Granted, it was only for a month, but it felt like an eternity. I thought I'd lost you, and I was slowly dying inside because of it. I don't know what I would do if..."

She didn't need to finish. He felt the same way. The thought of losing her to the dangers she regularly faced as a police officer caused him actual pain. That kind of fear was tangible, you could touch it. Feel it weighing down on you like a granite boulder. He didn't want that for his wife.

Being a husband meant you did what was necessary to provide safety and security for your family. You worked to ease the burden of your loved ones. This was no different. For his woman, his wife, he would take the world off of Atlas' shoulders and smile while doing it if it brought her the slightest bit of relief.

Besides, how bad could it really be having her cousins follow him around for a couple of days?

~

Kenneth read the same line of the report he was working on for the fifth time. He closed the file with a hard click of his mouse. His concentration was for shit today and trying to force his brain to work wasn't happening.

He stood up quickly and walked from around his desk only to be impeded by the two men that had been shadowing him for weeks now.

"Hey cousin, where're you going?" Free asked.

God, if he heard them ask him that damn question again he was going to throw something.

The last time he'd had to report his whereabouts he was still living on his father's dime. He was a grown man now with a son of his own. This shit had to stop now.

Yeah, Heart was trying to protect him. Kenneth would admit that she'd had a reason to want to, but there hadn't been a single threat against him since the mall incident that happened weeks ago. This shit was a nuisance, and his nerves couldn't deal with constantly being in the company of two other people, never having a moment of time to himself to think.

"Free, I need five minutes to myself, back off."

Free shook his head. "You know it doesn't work like that, Ken. Where are you going?"

Kenneth whipped around, he felt like stomping his foot, but the plush carpeting of the floor wouldn't give him that gratifying sound that came when the heel of a shoe met wood.

"If you must know I'm going to the fucking john. Would you like to hold it for me while I piss?"

The two men shared a look between one another and then turned to Kenneth. Law, usually the more silent one of the two brothers stepped inside of Kenneth's personal space.

"If that's what it takes to keep you safe, then we'll shake it when you're done too."

~

*L*aw stayed behind as Free escorted Kenneth to the restroom. He pulled his phone from his pocket and swiped his finger once across the number he needed to dial. The phone rang once and the call connected.

"Searlington," the voice called out.

"Cousin, I don't think this protective detail thing is going to work with your husband. He feels caged. He might just bolt if we don't give him a little breathing room. What do you want us to do?"

"What do you suggest we do?" Heart asked.

"I think it might just be time to make him walk the gauntlet."

"Law, Kenneth has a background in martial arts, but I don't know if he's prepared for what you have in mind."

"Really? Pretty boy can throw down?"

His cousin's voice filled the line with laughter. "Don't sleep on my man, he's pretty, but he actually has some defensive skills. But even with all the training he's had over the years, it wasn't for combat, Law. Especially not *that* kind of combat," she replied.

Law agreed with his cousin, a background in defensive arts wasn't the same as combat training. Especially if you were trained by someone whose goal was to fleece people's money and just make them think they could handle any physical threat that came at them. He shook off the doubt, it didn't matter whether Kenneth was ready or not, this was their reality and it had to be done.

"Heart, you can't cripple him. That's exactly what you're doing by not involving him in his own protection. He's family, don't you think it's time we start treating him like he is?"

There was a pause on the other end of the line and he could hear her thoughts turning over in her head. It was a dicey thing involving Kenneth in something like this, but the truth was. They didn't have much choice.

"All right," she answered. "Call Hunter and set it up. I'll bring him tonight." "Copy that," was all he said before he ended the call.

~

*K*enneth watched the buildings pass by on Linden Blvd in a blurry haze. His wife was a lead foot when it came to driving. She blamed it on her academy training, he blamed it on the fact that her crazy uncle who drove tanks for a living taught her how to drive.

Kenneth felt the car shift to the left as his wife turned on to Crescent Street. He turned questioning eyes to her, but her eyes were conveniently glued to the windshield. Kenneth was tired; he'd spent the day dealing with problematic contracts and clients coupled with being shadowed by his very own protective detail every moment of the day.

The only reason he was free of them now was due to Heart's impromptu call for him to meet her at the precinct for a late dinner. He'd walked into her office to find food from their favorite pizzeria spread across her desk and her waiting for him with open arms, a smile, and an apology about their recent blow up. The drain of the day had easily melted off of him and he welcomed the relaxing calm his wife had created. But, sitting next to her as she detoured from their usual route, his senses heightened causing some of the calm he'd donned to slowly dissipate.

"Is there a reason we're headed down Crescent instead of going home. Forgot something at the pizzeria?"

Still silent, she shook her head. He heard the click of her indicator and watched as she pulled into a recognizable spot on the street.

"Why are we in front of Hunter's house?"

She shut the ignition off with a quick flick of her wrist and removed the keys before turning in her seat to face him. "Kenneth, I know that you and I have been butting heads about this protection thing. I know my cousins following you everywhere has made you feel trapped. I also know you think I'm babying you, stepping on your masculinity."

He couldn't deny any of the things she'd stated. The recent events in their lives had him sitting on edge. If his temperament didn't get better, Abby was probably going to quit. And since she pretty much ran his business life, there was no way in hell he could allow that.

"Yes to all of that," he replied. "But what does that have to do with us stopping by
Hunter's?"

She wrapped her hand around his and instantly some of the tension building inside of him seemed to bleed out. It had always been like this for them. Touch was always such a powerful tool in their relationship. They were always at their best, at their strongest when they were touching each other. Kenneth relaxed back into his bucket seat and waited for her to speak.

"It would really make me feel better if you would cooperate with the protection detail," she began. "Those two will lay down their lives to protect you, Kenneth. They'll stop any threat."

He shook his head quickly. "But that's not what I want."

"You don't want to be protected?"

"I don't want another person I care about to have to nearly sacrifice their lives for my safety.

Bryan almost died because he jumped in front of a bullet that was meant for me. He's awake, and

I'm so grateful for that, but none of us knows what kind of impact his injuries are going to have on him in the long run. What if he can't work again? He loves that job; I will have taken that away from him. I don't want that on my conscience."

She sat back watching him silently. He could feel her gaze trace every inch of his face calculating what she saw inside of him.

"Is that what this is about? You feeling guilty about Bryan?"

"You act as if I shouldn't."

"Kenneth, he was doing his job. He would have done the same for anyone who was in your position. He is a Marine first and a cop pretty close to that, you don't get more dedicated than him. Not to mention, I would never have him watching my back as my second if he wasn't that dedicated."

"You can say that all you want. It doesn't assuage my guilt. I won't put another person I love at risk to protect me from this maniac that's after me. If he's still after me," he added.

The stiffening of her body screamed her displeasure. She wanted to protect him, she loved him, he understood that. But having something like this happen to someone else on his behalf, he couldn't live with that.

"Well if you won't let me protect you the best way I know how, then I'm going to make sure you can protect yourself...at least until help can arrive." She reached for her door and stepped out of the car signaling for him to follow her.

Once past the fence in the front yard, he headed for the porch but she shook her head and motioned for him to follow her along the perimeter of the house until they were in the back yard and she was reaching for cellar doors.

He followed her into the darkness, barely making out the familiar outline of her body in their murky surroundings. She pulled out the small utility flashlight that she carried for work and shone the single light toward a side panel. It looked like smooth concrete, the same as the rest of the walls, but she pressed down on different places along that particular section until he heard the cranking sound of gears unlocking.

Like something out of a movie he watched the wall slide to the left until there was just enough room for one body at a time to pass through it. When she stepped forward the space was flooded with light and she beckoned him to continue to follow her lead.

They reached a solid metal door with a hand shaped pad over its handle. She placed her hand flat against the empty palm print, leaned in front of the door, and spoke a single phrase,

"This is my house." As soon as she spoke the last syllable a red light scanned the eye she held in front it.

What the fuck is this?

She stepped back and a pop of pressure released as the door slowly opened to them. She stepped inside and he stood there in the hall wondering if following her was the best option available to him.

"You want Law and Free off your ass?" she asked.

He stood there trying to see into the brightly lit room behind her. It wasn't that he didn't trust her, but everything about this place made invisible hairs on his body stand up. She held up her hand and he took it out of instinct. Whatever they were going through, she was always a safe place to him. He might not like the way this cloak and dagger routine was playing out, but he knew his wife would never allow harm to come to him.

He grabbed her hand and let her lead him down another tight hall that finally let into a large open room. The floors were padded. Not like when you went to a gym, no this was different, the mats looked like cushions, like you might find in a fighting arena.

"What is this place, Heart?"

"As far as everyone outside my family is concerned it's Hunter's basement. For those of us that are in the know, it's a highly classified military training installation. We call it the Gauntlet." "It doesn't look like much," he replied.

"To the naked eye, no it doesn't. But we believe in hiding in plain sight, and this is part of how we do that. There are two floors beneath this one. On this first level this is where we have hand to hand combat training. Below is a soundproof gun range, below that is a supplies bunker, food, weapons, medical supplies. This is where we go to prepare for battle."

It certainly felt like war was coming. The room was quiet and empty. The lack of sound and inhabitants making it seem more daunting as they took subsequent steps inside of the room. From the other end of the room he saw her uncle appear from behind a wall. They all walked until they met in the exact middle of the room.

"Son," Hunter said, the vibration of the rich bass in his voice shaking the very foundation they were standing on. "I'm assuming if my niece brought you here, then she'd already explained just what it is that my children and I do."

Did Kenneth really know what they did; judging from all the secrecy he was certain it was intense and serious. But to actually believe he truly understood what the Amares were really doing in this underground bunker...that would be stretching the truth.

"I know my niece hasn't given you specifics, and that's because she can't. Just know that if you're going to be a part of this family, you've got to know how to survive in the worst of situations."

As far as Kenneth was concerned, the worst had already arrived. Someone had tried to kill him in broad daylight and as a result his wife was treating him like a captive.

"Remember that program I told you Hunter developed for the armed forces?" his wife interrupted. "It was titled Project Gauntlet."

Kenneth's eyes widened as the pieces began to fit together. "You don't mean..."

"Yes she does," Hunter answered. "I'm going to train you like one of my soldiers. The same way I trained my children and my niece. So every night after work you're going to head over here and we're going to bend you until we break you, and then rebuild you again."

Kenneth pinched the sharp bridge of his nose hard. Hell if he could apply just a little more pressure he was certain he'd hear the fracture in the cartilage and bone.

"And if I don't agree to this?" the question was directed at Hunter, but he held his wife's gaze as he spoke.

"Kenneth, please." Her voice was filled with a mixture of exhaustion, frustration, and...fear. She was scared, scared for him. That sound was the same sound he'd heard her make when she'd woken up in a hospital bed with a bullet wound in her shoulder four and half years ago. She'd saved him and his niece from his mother's terror. She'd nearly died protecting them. He'd never seen anyone as strong and courageous as she was that night, but just a few hours later she looked so fragile and broken, most of all afraid. Afraid she wouldn't live, afraid that if she did she'd never function again, afraid she would lose the thing she loved the most, her ability to do her job, be a cop.

That voice she was using to plead with him now was the same shaken voice she'd used to ask him to stay with her and comfort her. It had owned him then, and now was no different. He wasn't exactly thrilled about this new arrangement, but if it kept that heartbreaking sound of fear out of her voice he would, he'd agree to whatever plans Hunter and his clan had in mind.

He nodded his head in agreement and followed Hunter into the back. Apparently training began at this very moment.

CHAPTER 17

*H*eart sat at the conference table slowly sipping the scalding liquid from the Styrofoam cup in her hands. To anyone looking in it might seem like she wasn't paying much attention to the conversation going on around her, but she had complete focus on this sit-rep, slowly cataloguing each detail presented.

Bryan's investigative team of detectives and Agent Weaver were each going over the case findings for both Bryan and Kenneth's attempted murder cases. Her mind hung on the word *attempted*. Without it, her team, her family would be dealing with a totally different scenario.

She said a silent prayer of thanks for the lives of the two men she loved, and focused on trying to track their shooter down.

"We were actually able to track the gun back to a bust the ATF made about two years ago," Agent Weaver added. "These were guns that were smuggled into the country through Mexico. At first we thought the cartel was behind them, but we found out they were just couriers for someone else."

Weaver placed a picture of a dark-haired man with angular features on the table. Heart stared at the photo, there was recognition in those eyes, green with flecks of hazel, but she couldn't quite place it.

"Who is he," she asked.

"We only know him as Reign. He's from a small country in Europe that's just off the shores of Sicily called Azuria," Weaver replied. "We think he has some ties to the royal family there, but we can't be certain. What we do know is that he's become a major player in the political scene in Azuria. He is fighting to overturn the current regime there by way of his terror cell. They call themselves Forza di Liberazione."

"The Liberation Force?" Sage Santini's voice drew her gaze.

"You know something about these people, Santini?"

"I still have family back in Sicily. One of my uncles works on the docks. He said these guys are becoming a problem. Moving whatever products they have in and out through customs.

They're actually pretty lethal, got many of the crooked politicians in their pocket." "Why are they after the royal family? They crooked?" Heart asked.

Weaver shook his head. "No, they're actually pretty decent. The people love them and they love the people. From what we can gather, Reign isn't a fan of the U.S. and he's doesn't like the fact that the King has a strong relationship with us. He became a major weapons dealer in order to finance his campaign against the monarchy."

He slid another photo onto the table. This man she recognized, the gray-eyed monster that shot Bryan and Kenneth looked back at her with cool confidence.

"We finally got a hit on the shooter," Weaver added. This is Giacomino Conti. He's from Azuria and has known ties with Reign. He's actually a high-ranking member of Forza di Liberazione. Wet work is his specialty. He handles high-profile targets, so if he's after someone, you can bet they're significant to their cause."

Heart stood up from the table and walked to the window. Although her fixed gaze pierced the glass, she wasn't really staring at anything in particular. She just needed to move in order to get her mind working. She crossed her arms across herself and moved her weight from one foot to the other.

"I don't know why a terrorist cell would be after Kenneth. He doesn't align himself with any major political associations. As far as I know he only does business in a handful of major cities in Europe and Asia, a small country like Azuria wouldn't really register on his radar."

She turned around to face the team; a new thought crossed her mind. "Is there any way we could contact the royal family of Azuria, or their representatives to find out more about this

Reign?"

"That might be problematic," Weaver responded. "Reign has been gunning for the royal family for some time now. So much so they don't actually stay in Azuria. They go back to be seen for public events in order to maintain power, but they're actually in hiding here in America."

"So where are they?"

"I don't know. I don't have that kind of clearance," Weaver answered. "They're in some international form of Wit-Sec for high-value assets. Finding them isn't going to be all that easy."

Heart smiled as she headed for the door. "Maybe for you," she laughed. "But I know someone that might be able to get us the intel we need."

Weaver sat back in his seat giving her a wary stare. "Do I want to know just who this contact is?"

She shook her head. "No you don't, but even if you did, I'd never tell anyway."

"Is this something that's going to land us in federal prison?"

"Maybe, but for now you can just sit back and let me do all the work. Plausible deniability and all that jazz," she answered.

She gave him a wink and headed for her car. This was a conversation she needed to have in person.

~

*H*eart dropped her car off to Mac's Place and walked around the corner to the local gas station. She walked up to her waiting party and sat down in the blacked out SUV.

"You know I got shit to do," the relaxed voice said. "What's all this about?"

Heart looked at her waiting companion stretched out in the vehicle with the driver's seat reclined all the way back. Anyone looking in would have mistakenly taken the relaxed position coupled with the dark sunglasses covering most of the occupant's face for a sign of rested oblivion. It would have been a deadly assumption. Heart knew the woman sitting next to her was aware of everything in their surroundings. More importantly, she was ready for all seen and unforeseen situations that might bring them trouble.

"I need some intel on something my local FBI connect can't get me," Heart stated.

"And so just because you need, I'm supposed to go find it? It's not like I know everything about everything in the world."

"You might not know directly, but I'm sure you have a connection somewhere that can find something out for you. We both know if I go through the usual channels I'm never going to get anything useful from the government."

"What do you need to know?"

Heart pulled her phone out of her pocket and swiped through her gallery until she found the photos she'd had Weaver send to her. She handed the phone over to her companion and pointed to the first photo.

"That's the shooter in Bryan and Kenneth's case. His name is—"

"Giacomino Conti," her contact answered. "He's the hired gun for some freak show named

Reign. Why would he be coming for Kenneth? This dude is bad news."

Heart put her phone back into her pocket before speaking. "My detectives are calling Kenneth in to ask him that question now. As far as I know, he doesn't have a direct connection to these two or their terror ring."

"Then what do you need to know?"

"I need to know where and why the Azurian royal family is hiding. Finding them could be the key to shutting this guy down."

"No."

Heart turned to the woman sitting next to her with disbelief in her eyes. "What the hell do you mean 'no'? No you don't know who they are or how to find them?"

"I know who and where they are," she answered. "If I wanted to I could lay hands on them right now. But I'm not going to risk their safety or an international incident to help you solve a case."

"This isn't just any case," Heart countered. "This is the attempted murder of my husband and your brother-in-law. I would think you would be interested in catching this son of a bitch, True?"

True pulled the sunglasses from her face, the picture of leisurely relaxation was gone and it was replaced by sharp eyes filled with danger. "Some things are beyond familial connection. I can't help you with this, Heart."

Heart popped the door open and turned to step out of the SUV. She gave a quick glance back over her shoulder to her cousin. "Can't or won't?" Heart asked.

"Doesn't matter which, the result is the same," True replied.

Frustrated and pissed, Heart slammed the door closed and made her way back to Mac's Place to get her car. Once inside her own vehicle she slammed the heel of her hand against the steering wheel repeatedly.

"Fuck Kenneth, what the hell have you gotten yourself into?"

~

"*M*aybe you need to look at the photos again? Maybe you didn't get a good enough look the first time we showed them to you, Mr. Searlington?"

Kenneth rolled his eyes. He'd been sitting in this interrogation room for the last hour and quite frankly his wife's detectives were beginning to piss him off.

"Sage, can you cut the Mr. Searlington crap?" Kenneth snarled. Being the boss' husband sometimes awarded you special favors like getting out of a speeding ticket when one of her officers pulled you over for doing seventy on the Brooklyn side of the conduit. But then there were moments like these where her detectives were determined to follow every letter of department protocol just to make certain there was no apparent impropriety because of his connection to their captain.

"Mr. Searlington…"

"Detective Santini," Kenneth countered.

The detective sat back in his chair and threw his palms up in a show of his seeming exasperation.

"Sage," Kenneth groaned as he placed an elbow on the table while he tried to rub some of the tension and frustration of the day away from his forehead. "You ate dinner at my house the month before all of this craziness started, I think we're acquainted enough to use each other's first names."

Santini seemed to be weighing Kenneth's words, but he didn't seem to be completely sold on the idea. "I get what you're trying to do, but I've spent all day dealing with irritable, unreasonable clients, and you made me come over here just as I was leaving a grueling personal training session. I'm tired, and I'm really not up for the bullshit today. Can we just be straight with each other? I promise this will go a great deal faster if we do."

Detective Santini finally nodded his head and pulled at the knot in his tie. "All right,

Kenneth. Have you ever seen either of these men before?"

"No," he answered. "I don't know either of them."

"Have you ever done business with a company by the name of Forza di Liberazione?"

"No, not that I know of anyway?"

Santini sat up in his chair and leaned across the table. "What does that mean exactly?"

"Not all businesses do business under the formal name of the business. My company is called Searlington Realty. That's the name I use for business. But the actual name of the company is K&K Searlington Incorporated. I've never heard of this name, but that doesn't mean I've never done business with a parent company or a subsidiary of this entity. There really would be no way for me to know."

Santini opened another file and Kenneth slunk back in his chair groaning audibly. If only he could lead them to the nutcase that took a shot at him. At least then all of this madness he'd been living in would be done and he could go back to his regularly scheduled life.

If he could just roll back to the day before this mess happened his life would be perfect.

He'd roll over in the morning, make love to his wife, and wallow in the aftermath of their lovemaking until their son demanded their attention. He'd play with his boy, give him his first bottle of the day while his wife showered, and they'd play and giggle until Heart came to dress the little man.

Kenneth would shower, go through his grooming routine, and then dress himself in whichever suit caught his eye in his walk-in closet. Elvia would come in and take the little man, and he and Heart would head out the door to begin their respective work days.

He'd work, make a shit load of money by signing his name to multiple sheets of paper, and try to beat rush hour traffic back to Long Island. He'd shower then relieve Elvia and he and Amare would have father-son alone time until Heart walked through the door. They'd greet each other, fawn over their son while they ate dinner, give him a bath, and play again until the little guy just fell into slumber.

One of them would take the baby to his nursery, and they'd either watch the tube or find some other way to entertain themselves until their bed called to them. They'd make love again;

because that was the one thing he never got tired of in his life. Didn't matter if he'd already had it fifteen minutes before, sex with his wife was always worth repeating. Once they were sated, they'd falling asleep in each other's arms and start the cycle all over again with the rising sun.

It was simple, it was boring, it was repetitive, and it was what he ached for more than anything right now. Monotony was a blessing that few appreciated when they possessed it, but if he were ever able to grab hold of it again, he'd clutch it with his whole being and never let it escape him again.

Kenneth allowed the simple scene of his usual life to play over and over again on a loop in his mind. His mental motion picture was a distraction, he knew it, but he'd do anything at this point to keep from facing his present reality. A reality where he didn't know what to expect from one moment to the next, a reality that might destroy him and the people he loved without warning.

"Kenneth?" he heard Santini's voice breaking through his vision and tightened his lids to protect it, protect him. "Kenneth, I need for you—"

"Sage, I can't do this anymore, I'm tired and I need to go home," Kenneth answered quietly

"But—"

Kenneth was drawn from his daydream by the loud sound of a door slamming and the familiar click of tiny little heels clicking against the industrial tiles on the floor.

"Detective Santini, I believe my client said he's not up for any more of your questions."

Relief bloomed in his chest as soon as A.J.'s voice reached his ears. When Kenneth opened his eyes he saw the detective looking slightly uncomfortable under his attorney's scrutiny. He couldn't help the smile that tugged at the edges of his mouth. Standing barely above five feet, A.J. could stare down a giant and have him ready to apologize to her for the sky being blue in a matter of seconds. The fact that Sage

Santini was only mildly fidgeting in his chair spoke volumes of the man's resolve.

There weren't many men that could stand up to A.J., himself included. The only man he could actually remember going toe to toe with her and managed to keep his balls in tact at the same time was Alan. He'd have to remember to ask Alan just how he'd managed that feat. That was definitely a skill-set he needed to have in his arsenal for dealing with her.

"Come on, Kenneth, if the police have any more questions for you they can set up a meeting at a more convenient time."

He nodded his head and slowly moved his aching muscles until he was standing, barely, on his feet. He shuffled his feet one in front of the other until he was in the buzzing squad room.

The brighter lights forcing his lids into slits as his eyes adjusted.

"You look like shit," A.J. said as they made it to the front door of the precinct.

"Thank you, Alexis-Jeovonni," he smirked. "That's exactly what I needed to hear after being locked in an interrogation room for the last hour or two with a detective."

"I got you out, didn't I?" She shrugged her shoulders. "You should be thanking me, not giving me grief."

"Giving you grief's what I live for," he responded. "And I pay you to get me out of jams like that. How did you know I was here anyway?"

"I was going over the Denver contracts with Quillen when you called him to ask him about any possible deals with that business the cops were asking about. I rushed right over."

"'Cause you love me," he preened.

"'Cause I love the paychecks you write for me."

CHAPTER 18

Kenneth dragged his ass into the house and flopped down onto the couch. He really wanted to stretch out and lay across it, but every muscle he possessed screamed at him for even thinking to do something so foolish.

Everything hurt, his toenails, the porcelain fillings in his teeth, everything. His body kept asking him why and to date he'd not been able to manufacture a reasonable explanation for the torture he was putting himself through.

Every night after work he reported to Hunter's home for a training session. In the beginning he'd assumed Hunter was just going to be conditioning his body, and he did. He worked Kenneth through physical paces he'd never experienced even with the most renowned martial arts instructor. What Hunter was doing was sculpting him, molding him into something that Kenneth hardly recognized.

Yes, his body was getting stronger. He was able to lift more weight, his body was becoming more defined and cut, and he was actually putting on mass, something no other trainer had been able to do for him in all the years he'd been working out. But there was something else there beyond the new physique that Kenneth couldn't quite yet put into words.

He noticed things, things that didn't catch his attention before were so obvious to him now.

He saw things in his surroundings that just didn't seem to be there before like his ability to anticipate another person's movement.

There was a woman on the train yesterday whose bag had fallen open. Prior to working with

Hunter, Kenneth would've been reading some sort of business report as he traveled to work. But lately, he'd put away idle distractions like that and watched what was going on around him. He'd noticed the young twenty-something man staring at the wallet sitting proud at the top of the bag.

Just from watching the young man's eyes, before he made even the slightest move, Kenneth had known he was going to slip his right hand into that woman's bag and take her wallet. Before he could move, Kenneth stepped in front of him as if he were just trying to move from one spot on the train to another and accidently on purpose bumped into the woman. Once he had her attention he apologized and informed her that her bag was open.

He'd watched the would-be assailant scurry out of the cars and felt relief that he'd helped a fellow passenger. He stepped off the train a few stops later headed toward his office. When he'd placed his foot on the steps to the street he sensed a presence behind him. Before he could exactly explain how, Kenneth turned around, his fingers closing around a neck and his arm was pressing the person into the hard tile of the wall.

The motion had been fluid, and Kenneth's heart rate hadn't even risen, not until he looked up and saw the same man who'd tried to steal that woman's wallet.

"I'm thinking after today you might want to change your line of work," Kenneth whispered to the man. Kenneth stepped back just far enough to let the man escape. He gratefully took it and Kenneth stood there with his hands shaking as his thoughts raced through his head.

How the hell did I know he was there? How did I do that?

When he arrived at work that day, he'd wondered how many time scenes like that had unfolded before his eyes and he'd been completely oblivious to them. How many times had he been as close to danger as he was when the thief decided to make Kenneth his mark instead?

His senses weren't the only thing about him that seemed to be working more efficiently either. He remembered details about people and things that as a native New Yorker, one just didn't notice about others. He noted things like eye color and shape, hair color and texture, clothing, distinguishing marks. It was all very strange to him, strange but still somehow felt natural, like he should have been noticing these things all along.

But right now his head and his body were tired and the only thing he wanted to do was lay down somewhere and not be moved until daybreak.

He felt that cozy prickling sensation that always signaled his wife's proximity. Usually it was a welcomed phenomenon that always warmed his blood with desire and anticipation. But right now, when his muscles were on fire and his mind was exhausted, even this was too much for his senses to process.

He opened his mouth to call her name, but all that spilled from his lips was an achy groan.

He felt the shift in the air when she actually entered the living room.

God, I'm actually thinking like these people too. Who the fuck notices shifts in the air?

He thought about trying to open his eyes to look at her, but decided it was just too much effort and that his eyelids hurt too much to try to make the slightest movement with them.

"Hunter is kicking your ass," she gloated. "Isn't he?"

She was taking pleasure in his pain. Hell, she wasn't even attempting to hide it. He was probably injured for life and she thought this shit was funny.

"You know, I used to think you loved me," he drawled, his tongue and lips lazy, too tired and pain-ridden to actually make a real effort to speak. "I really did believe you loved me. But there's just no way you could really love me and ask me to allow this madness."

He could hear the sound of her muted chuckle, the harsh way she tried to suck in air quickly without the benefit of noise. It wasn't working; he could still hear her laughing at him, even if she was barely making a sound.

"I do love you, and I tried to warn you that this would be the hardest thing you'd ever been through. This would have been much easier if you'd just let Law and Free tail you every day."

If he could have commanded his muscles to actually roll his eyes he would have. Instead he saved what little energy he had to take in needed air.

"I swear if you let 'I told you so,' slip past your lips I am going to make you sleep on this damn couch for a month."

"I wasn't going to say I told you so, I was going to ask you if I could offer you a massage."

Hearts hands on him, on any part of his body always equaled pleasure. And if he could move, he'd be all over that idea. But damn if this couch didn't have him shackled to the damn cushions, because his ass wasn't moving from this spot. Not even to get his wife's hands all over him.

"Babe…can't move."

He could still hear her laughing at him under her breath, but again, with the pain he was suffering through, he couldn't really give a damn.

"You don't have to move. Just let me take care of you."

Fuck if he was going to argue with that offer. He heard her moving behind the couch. He didn't know what she was doing exactly, but he could hear her opening something up. His mind drifted off somewhere between the soreness and exhaustion hoping to find that theoretical Nirvana you're supposed to tumble into after pushing your body beyond its physical limits.

Apparently that shit was some delusional bastard's daydream, because all Kenneth saw was the black nothingness behind his eyes and all he felt was pain.

The soft touch of his wife's hand gently placed at the back of his ankle brought him back to the present. She slipped off his sneakers and socks, and walked her hands up his legs until her fingers were digging into the waistband of his gym pants. He sucked in a breath and held it as he attempted to help her by shifting from one hip to the other. He wasn't really sure how effective he'd been at helping, but eventually he felt the slide of his gym pants and underwear down his legs and over his feet.

By some miracle she got him standing. Once upright he cracked one eye open enough to keep from walking into to something. The slit of his eye caught sight of a massage table behind the couch. He couldn't even bring himself to wonder how it had ended up in their house, he was only grateful he wouldn't have to climb the stairs to get this massage.

She helped him sit on it, then pulled his t-shirt over his head before he started to recline on it. "On your stomach," she whispered and he obliged, partly because he wanted to cooperate, but mostly because he was too tired to do anything else but fall on his face. Fortunate for him there was a hole cut out for his face to rest inside of, so there was no damage to be had when he fell the rest of the way from his upright position.

She left him for a moment and returned resting something on a nearby table. Soon he felt warm oil dripping over his shoulders and back. She sat the container down and laid flat palms against his skin.

He couldn't really tell if it was the warmth of the oil or just the heat of her touch, but balminess began to permeate the layers of his skin and slowly seeped into the rigid tendons and muscles beneath.

She slid from one shoulder to the next; replenishing the oil several times as her hands traveled the length of his back, down to the hard globes of his ass. She let her hands linger there for a while.

If he could have smiled, he would have. Staying in shape was something he'd always worked toward, but once Heart had walked into his life, he'd had a reason beyond his own vanity to make certain his body stayed as close to perfection as he and time would allow. Hunter may have been trying to kill him, but the end result was that his wife was enjoying his body more than ever, so it wasn't a total loss.

Heart's hands worked their way down the backs of his legs manipulating the large muscles until they gave under her fingers. God, was she always this strong? Or had she somehow taken up studying massage therapy and he'd somehow missed that?

Her hands stopped for just a moment and just as he was about to question why he felt something hot and smooth press against his skin. It was warmer than the oil, a degree or two below uncomfortable, but when she pressed it into hard muscles relief bled through him.

A slow moan escaped his throat and his eyes closed to the ecstasy his battered ligaments and tendons were experiencing.

What seemed all too soon, her skillful hands stilled and he immediately missed the bliss they'd wrought.

"Turn over so I can do your front," she whispered and he obliged.

"I hope Elvia went home," he murmured. "Otherwise this could get really awkward really quickly."

"I actually sent her home early. Considering all of the overtime she's been putting in as a result of this case, I didn't want to burn her out. She's earned some time off."

Before he could respond, her hands began their magic again first warming the front of his body with the oil and then using what he could now see were hot stones to break down his stiffened muscles.

When she was done, she let oil-covered fingers glide back up his torso and rest over his heart, allowing them to swirl in a matching rhythm against his skin.

"You feel better?" Her eyes were filled with the warmth and concern that only one spouse could have for another.

"Yeah, where'd you learn to do that?"

"When Hunter put me through the Gauntlet these massages were the only thing to get me through."

"If this story doesn't involve one of your cousins or a professional masseuse doing this to you, then I don't want to hear about it," he growled trying not to lose the mellow calm her massage had brought.

"True and I are about five years younger than Justice. By the time we started the Gauntlet, her brothers were already in the military. True's mom would rub us down. And when she became too ill to do it, Ida Mae took over."

He rubbed his fingertips lightly over the hand that was still pressed to his heart. He took that moment to look at his wife; really see her through the new lenses this time in training with her uncle had given him.

She'd been doing this since she was twelve years old. As a grown man in his late thirties his body felt broken and crippled after each of these sessions with Hunter. How had such a young child been able to endure this kind of torture and survive?

"You've been doing this for such a long time. How have you handled it all this time?" he asked.

"The Gauntlet?" she queried.

"No," he answered. "Being battle-ready. Hyper-vigilant. I've only been doing this with Hunter for a few weeks and I sometimes feel like I might go crazy trying to always be prepared for the worst. How do you do it without managing to go crazy or becoming paranoid?"

The muscles of her face relaxed and she took on a more thoughtful expression. "I was raised in this. It seems like Hunter was always preparing us for the worst. I never understood why. I didn't know that he did the kind of things in the military that could gain him enemies and cost him the people he loved."

Her eyes softened as she looked down at him, there in their depths he saw so much emotion it made his chest tighten in response.

"I didn't understand then that Hunter was just trying to give himself a measure of peace. He knew he couldn't be with us at all times, so he decided to prepare us for the world he lived in just in case it ever came knocking at our doors. He was just trying to protect the people he loved."

As was she, he could see that now. She'd gone about it the wrong way, had made him feel like a child in the process, but he could see now this wasn't a control issue. Heart was just as afraid as Hunter must have been, must still be.

"Kenneth, I never wanted you to walk this path, not because I didn't think you were capable, I just didn't want you to experience this reality. There's a difference in knowing there's ugliness in the world and actually experiencing it. I never wanted you to be touched by this. Training you would have done that."

He stilled her moving fingers making her focus all of her energy on him. "And now?"

"Now I find myself in the same position my uncle must have been in all those years ago.

Wanting to protect the person I love the most, but knowing I can't realistically protect him from all threats. So I'm doing the only thing that will give me just enough peace of mind that I don't go crazy. I'm giving him the tools he needs to be able to protect himself."

He pulled her lips down until they met his. He intended a chaste kiss, but the touch of her skin against him made his skin burn. When he sought to deepen the kiss, demanded she allow his tongue beyond the borders of her mouth she pulled out of the embrace.

"All right there, mister, I didn't do any of this to turn this into that kind of party."

He looked down at his sleeping dick. Usually a kiss was all it took to get him to thicken up.

He chuckled; he knew it really didn't take all that much effort. Usually just the thought of his wife in the most benign ways made him rock hard. The fact that he could barely see a visible twitch in the flaccid flesh supported her theory that this shouldn't be that kind of a party.

"You're tired."

"I'm never that tired."

"You need to relax and if we start doing other things, all my hard work will be for naught. If you're too sore to move tomorrow the kids will be disappointed."

Kenneth's mind skimmed over his mental calendar and he realized what Heart was referring to. The kids at Mac's Place were having their spring concert. LaQuisha had even called him at work and made him promise he'd show up.

His chest rose and fell in quiet movement and he resigned to his wife's recommendation. "Them damn kids had better give the performance of their lives if I'm giving up making love to my wife."

She giggled as she grabbed his outstretched hand and helped him sit up. He sat for a moment bracing for the stiffness that had nearly rendered him immobile a short while ago. It was barely there any longer, just a dull, achy memory. Amazing what the touch of someone who loved you could do.

⁓

*K*enneth was pulled from sleep by the sound of his beeping phone. He rooted around until his hand finally made contact and pulled himself up on an elbow to check the incoming notification. He glanced quickly at the time and saw the missed text message from his wife.

*H*ad to go to Mac's Place early.
    Took Lil' Man with me.
Expecting a delivery near ten.
Biscuits eggs and bacon warming in the oven.
Coffee brewing.
Luv ♥

*H*e took a long drag of air in through his nose and he could make out the inviting scents of buttermilk and honey filling the air. Damn, he usually had to do something really special to wake up to Heart's biscuits.

The first time she'd blessed him with them had been during her rehab. The kneading motion was actually a really good exercise to help her regain strength in her wounded arm. He'd come home from a grueling day of work, pissed because a deal had fallen through, and as soon as he'd walked into the house, that intoxicating smell made him forget all about why he was so upset in the first place. By the time he'd actually wrapped his lips around the first one; his entire shitfest of a day had been completely erased from his memory.

Then there was a time after a night of making love so sweet he woke to this aroma, except then they were resting on the nightstand waiting for him to reach over and grab one. The most recent account had been about six weeks after Amare was born. The boy had his nights confused with his days and poor Heart was exhausted trying to stay up with him all night and still function during the day. He'd decided to take a few days off of work to help bear his share of the burden so his wife could recuperate. He let her sleep well until the early afternoon while he'd taken over the baby and household duties as she slept. She came downstairs smiling and refreshed. She kissed both him and the baby and headed straight for the kitchen and whipped up a batch of those famous biscuits.

Those things were damn good, and well worth whatever he had to do to get her to make them. Hell, even the Gauntlet seemed a reasonable trade for the buttery soft pieces of heaven. If he could just get her to tell him the recipe, he'd market that shit and triple his fortune. But after all their time together she still wouldn't tell him what was in them.

The time read fifteen minutes until ten. He shuffled out of bed and into the bathroom to relieve himself, wash his face, and brush his teeth. No need scaring the delivery man half to death. He pulled his long locks into a messy man bun and headed down the stairs.

His hand had just touched the full coffee carafe when the doorbell rang. A quick glance at the bright green digital display on the microwave read ten on the dot. Damn the one time he would have been all right with a delivery service being behind schedule, they show up on time.

He gave the carafe handle a loving stroke with his thumb, a promise of an anticipated reunion he'd spend their moments apart longing for.

He heard the doorbell ring again and gave a quick jog to the door. "Hold on, I'm coming."

He gave the knob a quick turn and opened the door for the delivery.

"Shit."

The tall frame of his wife's cousin Justice stood with a smiling Bryan next to him.

"Delivery," Bryan laughed through his wide grin. He was standing on his own power, well mostly on his own power except for the cane in his right hand and the other wrapped securely around Justice's bicep.

"If I wasn't so happy to see you out of that damn bed I'd tell you to return it to sender. I see you and my wife are conspiring to set me up again."

He stepped back and watched Justice help Bryan through the door, he thought they would stop at the couch, but they continued on toward the kitchen.

"I guess my woman told you she made biscuits, huh?"

Justice stopped and flashed Kenneth with a charming smile that only a practiced enchanter could pull off sincerely.

"Even if she hadn't, I'd be able to smell my grandmother's biscuits anywhere."

Kenneth couldn't lie; he would have noticed them even without Heart's message. His two visitors pulled up at the table and he went to the cabinet pulling down mugs and plates. It was obvious his wife had expected his company, so he wasn't very surprised when he found a large rectangular dish filled with bacon and eggs on one rack, and a full baking sheet of biscuits on the other.

He pulled the food out and began plating it up. He knew from his time with both men that black coffee was all they drank. It must be a law enforcement/military thing because his wife preferred it that way too. He handed them two full cups of the black brew and went to the fridge for cream for his.

When he was done, he sat down and they all tucked into their plates simultaneously coming to some a silent agreement that no conversation should be had on empty stomachs. After four of those biscuits he was about as mellow as one could be when you knew a serious conversation was about to happen.

He figured there was no sense postponing the inevitable, so he took one final sip of his coffee and asked one question of them.

"Why?"

They each stared at one another and then returned their gazes to him. "What do you mean?" Justice asked.

"I mean, why didn't you tell me you two were together? Why was this such a big deal that I couldn't know?" he asked. "Am I not family, or am I just you know, the play-play kind of family that on the surface you treat like your own, but when they leave the gathering you talk about how much they really aren't part of the crew?"

"Kenneth," Justice muttered. "You're family; there is no question of that."

"Oh, so my marriage to your cousin validates my place in the Amare clan, or is it just because we had a child together?"

Justice shook his head. "It's neither of those, it's because my cousin loves you more than life and you love her the same. It's because my grandmother claimed you as her own before she left this world, and it's because my father lets you eat at his table that makes you one of us."

"If that's true then why was I kept out of the loop?"

He watched the two share a passing look speaking without ever uttering a word. He was familiar with that ability. Well-practiced in the ability to convey an entire conversation with only shared looks with the person he loved.

"It was my fault, Kenneth," Bryan interrupted, turning slowly toward Kenneth as he spoke. "I didn't want you to know, I didn't want you to think less of me. We'd built a friendship and I

didn't know if you could handle the truth about me being gay."

Kenneth waited a bit; the foodgasm he'd been enjoying after savoring his wife's last biscuit was beginning to wear off. In its place a sharp spike of anger shot up and Kenneth stood so fast his chair fell behind him, hitting the floor with a loud thud.

"All this time you've sat in my house, eaten my food, drank my goddamn beer, you thought I was some homophobic asshole that was secretly holding 'hang all fag parties' in my office? How long have you fucking known me that you should have known better? Have you seen my wife and son, how the fuck did you believe I could harbor that kind of hatred in my heart?"

He righted the chair and walked over to the island needing the small distance it put between himself and the two men sitting at the table.

"Bryan, didn't you hear what I asked you? I didn't ask anything about you being gay; I

asked why you hadn't told me the two of you were married. I could give a fuck who you play hide the sausage with Bryan, what I care about is that I am treated like a member of this family. Like I can trust and be trusted in return. What I give a fuck about is that the man I call brother, the man I entrust to take care of my wife when I'm not there is honest with me. Man I trusted you with the most precious thing in the world to me, my woman's life, and you can't even be honest about whom you love?

"I'm a lot of fucking things, Smyth; arrogant, cocky, a little too domineering when it comes to my wife sometimes," he added.

"Yeah, I still remember you dinging me in my damn mouth about putting my hands on your woman."

Justice's brows came to a sharp point, apparently he wasn't apprised of the dust up between Bryan and Kenneth when Kenneth had accidently walked into an undercover sting Bryan and his wife were involved in.

"Don't worry about it, Jussy, I'll tell you later."

"Yes," Kenneth interrupted. "Tell him that later, but explain to me right now how you lied to me so many times over the years," he directed at Bryan and then turned to Justice. "And tell me how you allowed him to."

"It's not Justice's fault, Kenneth. It's mine. I've just lost so many people I've loved by coming out with my truth. I just really didn't want to lose anyone else. Jussy's family was never a gamble. He'd told me from the beginning how supportive they were. It wasn't until you and Heart got together that I worried about your reaction."

God his head hurt, he just couldn't understand this shit. Yes, he could understand the trepidation that many people in the LGBTQ community harbored when it came to revealing their true selves to the world, especially when they were met with rejection from their own families.

But Bryan had known him too well; this shouldn't have been an issue.

"Why were you so worried about me, Bryan?"

"Because you had the ability to take it all away from me,' Bryan breathed on a heavy sigh.

"How, what?" Kenneth asked his head still muddled with confusion.

"You don't even know how much power you have over MacKenzie. I watched you change her; bring her out of her shell, help her function in the real world. We both hid in the darkness before you came, but after…after she wanted to stand in the light. If you couldn't deal with who I was, she might reject me too. MacKenzie and I have built our careers together; losing her could very well have meant losing the only thing I had to keep me sane after Justice and I fell apart."

"You thought she'd fire you?"

Bryan shook his head and dropped his eyes from Kenneth's gaze. There was something he was missing here and he couldn't really identify what it was. Heart would never have fired a man she already knew was gay. This conversation wasn't making any sense. Why did Kenneth's appearance on the scene pose a threat to Bryan and his relationship with Heart?

"She was your beard?" Kenneth said softly. "She helped you perpetuate the lie that you were straight on the job."

Bryan didn't have to admit it, the truth was floating there between them, a solid tangible thing they could each feel.

"We never told anyone we were a couple. We just didn't disabuse people of that notion when they jumped to the wrong conclusion.

Our friendship, our familial ties looked like romance to the average person looking in. I didn't have to explain anything to those that might have been watching too closely. Being black and on the force is hard. Being black and gay, is a cocktail for disaster."

Kenneth folded his arms across his chest trying to piece all of this together. Heart had explained to Kenneth she'd kept quiet to protect Bryan, but she'd never told him just how far she'd gone to protect him from the possible dangers of the outside world.

"You were afraid that my marrying her would eventually out you to the squad who'd assumed you two were together all along."

Bryan nodded his head in response, the wet eyes and ticking jaw told Kenneth he was too chocked up to verbalize his thoughts.

Part of him was so fucking angry with Bryan. Insulted that he would just lump Kenneth in the same category with every other garden variety bigot without once giving Kenneth the opportunity to show himself for who he really was. But then he watched the strong man he had spent nearly five years befriending and sadness rippled through him like a crashing wave. Beneath that ever-present smile and laughing demeanor was so much pain and fear and Kenneth had never even noticed it. He'd never once looked beneath that contagious smile to see if there was anything more than the picture of happiness Bryan displayed so readily.

He could be angry, but if he chose that route he'd have to shove some of the blame in his own backyard. Yeah Bryan had lied, and the entire Amare family had covered for him, but

Kenneth had committed the worst crime by far, he'd been so wrapped up in his own life that he hadn't seen the pain his friend must have been wearing like a cloak.

"I'm sorry," Kenneth huffed as he dropped himself back into his chair. The tight coils of anger that had only moments ago felt like a bone-crushing snake wrapped around him were slowly loosening from his chest and limbs, making it easier to breath...to think...to feel.

"I'm sorry I wasn't more of a friend that I didn't see your pain and do something to help you. You know that's kinda my thing, right? Figuring out the problems of those I love and fixing them. And yet somehow, somehow I missed all the signs that were screaming your pain in dayglo neon orange letters."

"It's not your fault that I'm still in the closet at work, Kenneth. It's not your fault that I'm afraid. Just because every other person in this family covers up my infirmities doesn't mean you should have to as well."

"No one can force you to come out, Bryan, that's your decision alone to make. But eventually, everything that's hidden in the dark comes to light, and often in ways we don't want it to. Don't let someone else tell your truth, be proud enough to tell it yourself."

"Pride is not my issue," Bryan answered. "I'm not ashamed of being gay, I've always known it, always accepted it. I'm just afraid that everything I love will be taken away from me because of it."

CHAPTER 19

$\mathcal{K}$enneth walked into the auditorium of Mac's Place waiting for the show to begin. There were sparks of excitement buzzing throughout the room. Kids, counselors, parents, and benefactors were filling the seats row by row. It was a good thing he knew the woman that built this place with her blood, sweat, and tears intimately. Sleeping with the most important V.I.P. in the room gave him perks like a reserved seat in the front row center of the room.

He was about to take his first step down the aisle when he heard his name being called. He turned to find his godfather, retired NYPD captain, David Porter.

He pulled his godfather into a manly hug in greeting. "Hey, Uncle David," he beamed.

"Glad you made it down to see the kids."

"You know I wouldn't miss this. Not to mention, your wife has already told me, retired or not, she expects me to keep making my annual pledges to the foundation."

Kenneth shrugged a shoulder. "I swear that woman is the best damn negotiator I have ever met."

"I don't know that I would call what she does negotiation as much as extortion."

"Better not let her hear you say that," Kenneth countered and let his eyes sweep the room looking for the woman in question.

The lights began dimming in the auditorium, signally the beginning of the show. Kenneth and Porter, along with the other attendants still milling around quickly found their seats just before the master of ceremonies was introduced and the curtains slid open to reveal the face of his friend John Tenetti.

At the first glimpse of the onyx waves of his tapered hair, coal black eyes, and European features, the crowd went wild. John had spent the last ten years dominating the pop music charts and by the deafening screams filling the tiny auditorium, he was still just as relevant as he was when he first began in the music industry.

As far as Kenneth knew, John was supposed to be overseas on a world tour. How the hell had he ended up in Brooklyn tonight? Kenneth saw the cocky grin of John's little sister A.J. from the side of the stage and he instantly knew. She'd arranged this, gotten this megastar here to perform for these kids.

Heart might not have seen through A.J. yet, but Kenneth had a long time ago. These kids were working their magic on her, just like they did any adult with half a heart beating in their chest.

He nodded his recognition to her, his thanks really and continued on watching the show.

John might have been a trust fund baby, but his family's wealth had nothing to do with his success. The man was talented in a way few in his business were. He didn't just perform, but he anticipated trends in the industry, created them really, always keeping him relevant and in a class that few in his industry could lay claim to.

Getting the audience to quiet down at that point was hopeless, so John gave his band their cue to begin and the first notes of his current chart-topper blared through the speakers. The crowd sang and danced along with him, and Kenneth felt a sense of pride and gratitude that his friends would chip in and help with the fundraising for this place.

In his circle, few of the people like him that grew up wealthy, ever understood what it was to go without the bare necessities in life, they just didn't understand a place like East New York, Brooklyn. They didn't understand that no matter how much you saw in the news, the truth was if you never lived it, you just truly didn't understand.

The greatest gift Kenneth's father could have given to him was exposing him to his godparents. Allowing him to experience the world they came from so that he would always count the blessings of his wealth instead of allowing it to define him.

Seeing so many people from all walks of life coming out to help Mac's Place made a seed of hope bloom in his chest for the world these kids were going to create. If he were lucky enough, he'd live to see it and take pride in the fact that he'd fostered a place where these kids could create, grow, and thrive despite their circumstances.

Kenneth felt his skin hum with excitement and he looked around for the source. Heart was at the top of the aisle carrying their son. When she was standing next to him, she met him with a knowing smile that promised something more.

He wasn't quite certain what that more was, but there was something dancing around in her bright eyes.

He took the baby from her, cradling him in his arms. He looked down at the boy, in the middle of all the surrounding noise who slept so soundly, unaware and apparently unconcerned with the fuss being made about daddy's friend.

The kids put on an amazing show, each act better than the last, each exhibition proving how vital Mac's Place was to the children of this community.

The spotlight illuminated the dim room and drew the audience's attention the center of the stage. Standing there in a red and black ballerina costume was LaQuisha. She was graduating this year, on her way to college on a full scholarship. Kenneth didn't know if this was how he would feel when it was Amare's turn, but the pride and love he felt for this young woman and her accomplishments helped him to understand that he was father to more than just the sleeping babe in his arms.

He used his free hand to cradle Heart's, overwhelmed with the knowledge that the simple act of falling in love with this woman had given him so much love in return.

"Ladies and gentleman, my name is LaQuisha and I am one of the many students here at Mac's Place. When I arrived here a few years ago I was loud, combative, and mistrustful of the world. I didn't believe that anything positive could come from Brooklyn, including me."

Kenneth's heart tightened. He hadn't known LaQuisha when she'd first arrived, but Heart had told him stories. She'd lost her parents to the drug trade, her father murdered on the streets by a rival drug dealer, her mother serving multiple sentences for drug-related crimes. The child was left to be raised by her ailing grandmother who hadn't the resources or the health to properly raise the girl.

Crossing paths with Heart and Mac's Place had literally snatched her from the streets that were waiting to lay claim to her life. To remember the details Heart had given him about this young woman, and to see her standing here now proud, strong, able…he was witnessing a miracle.

"But with the help of our Cop Lady," she bowed her head slightly and gave Heart a little smile, "I mean, Captain Searlington. I learned that good things do indeed come out of Brooklyn, and I was one of them. Being in this place with Captain Searlington and Mr. Seyah kept me off the streets, taught me how to survive, and taught me most of all that I didn't have to be a casualty of my circumstances.

"Not too long ago Captain Searlington brought us a new member of this family. He didn't look like the rest of us, and he had a nice car and loads of money and he got them all legally, at least that's the story he tells us.

"We were really afraid when Kenneth Searlington came in, because we thought somehow he was going to take our Cop Lady away. He didn't really seem the type to be hanging out in East New York, Brooklyn just for kicks. But we were wrong, because week after week he kept coming back, to see about us and to help us in whatever way he could.

"One of those ways has been his motto of share and share alike. He shared his money with us, provided us with educational technology to help us stay on top of our studies. He gets many of his rich friends to donate money so that kids like me who can't afford the hefty application fees for college can still apply. And just because he loves getting people to give us money, he also created a scholarship fund to alleviate undergraduate debt for those of us who are a part of this program. I live in the projects, but because of all the help Kenneth Searlington has offered me and kids like me, I'll be living on campus at UCLA come this fall."

The crowd stood applauding LaQuisha's accomplishments; at least he hoped that's what they were applauding. LaQuisha was correct; he had started a fund to help give their kids a chance to attend college. He'd personally called the wealthiest people on his rolodex and had A.J. handle all the legal details to make his dream a reality. But what LaQuisha didn't know is that none of that money would be available until next year.

When A.J. informed him of this, he didn't so much as hesitate for a second. He picked up the phone, called the bursar's office at the school and found out the exact dollar amount of a

Bachelor's degree. Before the call was over he'd paid the full tuition, lodging, and meal plan bills and left enough disposable cash for the girl, she probably could have paid for four more years of school.

Yes, he'd spent a ridiculous amount of money on the young woman standing before him, but this moment was proof that it was all worth it, that it would all be worth it.

"Mr. Searlington you keep this place, us, running and we're thankful. Not just because you have money in the bank, but you've got more soul than most people we know, and you share it with us freely. So

Mr. Searlington, AKA Mr. Money, we wanted to show you just how much we appreciate you and all you do for us."

LaQuisha gently laid the microphone on the ground and stepped back behind the curtain.

Soon the room was filled with the heavy bass sounds of "All I Do is Win," by DJ Kaled. The lights on the stage flickered with the bass line and the dancers all began to move in sync. The dance moves were a mix of classic ballet and hip hop and although on opposite sides of the dance spectrum, the movements seemed to blend seamlessly together.

These kids had the right idea, taking from all things to create their own chaotic beauty.

That's what this place was all about, blending the worlds of the haves and have nots, blending differences and showing each how to learn from and lean on each other to balance out life.

Before the last verse was sung, the kids came off the stage and pulled Kenneth from his seat. He handed his still sleeping son over to his wife and allowed himself to be moved along to the stage.

Some of the kids demonstrated the dance steps to him and he quickly fell in line with them, matching their swaying movements. Yeah, he could dance, a fact he was more than grateful for as he moved up on that stage with those children with an audience full of people watching them.

But even if he couldn't, even if every last bone in his body was rhythmless, he would still have gone up on that stage and danced with those babies because that minor blip of embarrassment would have been worth the feeling of absolute adoration he felt at that moment.

∾

"*A*J, can't your brother take you?" Kenneth said as he shook the last hand of the last person that stopped him on his way to the door.

"No, John had to get back on a plane; he has a show in two days in Asia. He only dropped by to do this favor for me and the kids."

He looked around the room attempting to find his target. "Let me check with Heart first. We came in separate cars. She may need me to take the baby home if she has to stay behind and finish up some administrative things."

Just as his eyes passed over the throng of people again he was able to see his wife standing next to his godfather. He made his way over there stopping to play with his son whose eyes were wide open now that all the noise had stopped.

"Hey, babe," he greeted her. "You need me to take Amare home so you can stay?"

She shook her head. "No, Willie already left to put tonight's donations in the bank. I had a few of my officers escort him. I'm actually free to go anytime you are."

"All right. A.J. needs to borrow my truck for props she needs to get back home. A delivery service was supposed to pick them up, but the arrangements were screwed up somehow."

"You gonna ride home with me?"

"No," he answered. "She drove the two-seater sports car; she can't leave it in the lot overnight. I'll take her car home and she'll drop by tomorrow sometime to swap vehicles with me."

Kenneth made his goodbyes and swapped keys with A.J. before heading out to the parking lot. He looked at the time on his watch; he didn't see his wife come downstairs yet. He pulled out his phone to call her when a message from her appeared across the screen.

*S*omeone I've been looking for just popped in Go head, we'll be a few minutes behind you.

*K*enneth hesitated for a moment, he never liked them splitting up, especially with the current circumstances in their lives. He went to respond that he'd wait when he received another text.

*S*top stalling, go ahead, I'll be right behind you.

*K*enneth opened the door and sat down in the driver's seat of the sleek looking car. His knees were bent in an uncomfortable strange twist, the bottom of the steering wheel cutting into the skin of his lap.

"God this woman is short." He searched the console for the button that would allow normal blood flow to return to his limbs. At over six feet tall, Kenneth felt like someone had pressed and folded him into a tight piece of luggage. Once he found it, he kept that blessed button depressed until his legs were straight and his torso no longer felt like it was bound in a straitjacket.

He looked up to the rearview mirror and saw his chest in its reflection. A.J. really was a tiny thing. After making all the necessary adjustments in his pre-driver check, he snapped his seatbelt in place and let the engine roar to life. He revved it a few times just to feel the power rumble through the black leather interior.

The boy in him that loved fast cars was doing back flips. A car this pretty and powerful was enough to make his dick hard in his teens and twenties. Now as a husband and father, the only thing it did was raise a familiar smile in homage to the days of his misspent youth. They were fun, but hardly compared to everything he held in his possession now.

He pulled out of the lot and onto the street. The eastbound Conduit was clear; he hoped the Belt Parkway would offer the same. Getting stuck in traffic tonight was not on his list of things to do.

He made it about a block away from Mac's Place when he noticed
three dark vehicles, large

American made SUV's, accelerating behind him, one in each lane
of the highway. As he merged left onto the Belt, he saw the three vehicles fall in line behind him. Inching closer than Kenneth was comfortable with.

He merged into the middle lane, hoping to give the three trucks
space, but they still continued to tailgate, riding the ass of the car too
close for safety's comfort.

His foot pressed lightly on the accelerator while he contemplated
his next move. The egotistical bastard in him wanted to let A.J.'s car
out of its stable and rip down the highway. A few years ago, he would
have done just that, but with a wife and a child that depended on him,
taking unnecessary risks with his life or health wasn't something he
was willing to do.

He put on his indicator and began to slowly ease to the right lane
so they could pass. Just as before, when he moved, so did they.

A cold chill spilled down his spine. Not long ago he would have
categorized it as fear, but that wasn't it. This wasn't fear. He didn't feel
the need to hide; he felt the need to assess. He began looking in his
rearview mirror again. The cars were still there trailing behind him
and suddenly he knew pulling over was not an option.

He changed gears and peeled out of the right lane just before they
reached him. Just as anticipated the trucks sped up too. He weaved in
and out of the light traffic to keep them at a distance. He pressed a
button on the steering wheel to engage the Bluetooth calling system.

"Nine-one-one. What is your emergency?"

"My name is Kenneth Searlington and I'm being chased by three
black SUVs on the Belt Parkway East. We just passed the one hundred
and fiftieth street exit. There is an open case of my attempted murder
at the seventy-fourth precinct in Brooklyn where my wife is the
Captain.

I'm afraid this might just be the third attempt the unknown
suspects intend to make on my life."

~

*H*eart stood with Agent Weaver catching up on some details she needed to follow up on when both their phones went off. They looked at one another, both knowing that scenario couldn't be good. She turned from him and pulled her phone from her pocket in one motion while heading toward Porter. By the time she spoke her name into the mouthpiece she was handing her son and his diaper bag off to Porter.

"Call Elvia, get him home." She walked away, focusing on the words being spewed at her through the phone.

She catalogued the info and headed toward the door, noting Weaver was headed in the same direction. She didn't turn around; simply spoke over the casual hum of voices filling the room.

"I need three squad cars with me now!" She was in the parking lot headed for her car when she heard Weaver call her name.

"Captain, get in."

Changing direction in one smooth motion, she was sitting beside Weaver in his car and they were on the highway before she could fasten her seatbelt.

She put her phone to her ear and barked orders into it. "This is Captain Searlington of the seven-four en-route. Get me ESU, I suspect these vehicles are heavily armed. Have uniforms block off the Belt Parkway from the Rockaway Parkway entrance down. I don't want anyone on that stretch of road that isn't one of us. Get us an assist from the State and Nassau County police to set up at thirteen on the Southern State and Twenty-six on the Cross Island. I don't want the suspects to be able to exit anywhere."

She ended the call and quickly began another. "Are you still in Brooklyn?"

"In Valley Stream," True responded. "I was on my way to your house to hang with Lil' man," True answered.

"Change of plans. Three SUVs are in pursuit of Kenneth on the Eastbound Belt."

"Is Kenneth in his truck or his car?"

"Neither, he's driving his lawyer's sports car." She gave True the specifics on the make and model of A.J.'s car before asking, "Are you armed?"

"Always."

"License to carry?" Heart questioned.

"Intact and up to date."

"If you get there before I do, go to work."

Heart ended the call and took a breath before making the next call. It rang twice, leaving just enough time for Heart's fear to claw at her heart before she heard his voice. Throwing up a silent prayer of relief her shaking fingers tapped the speaker icon.

"So I guess you know I'm a little busy at the moment." He was in a life-threatening situation and he had the nerve to be cavalier.

She closed her eyes tightly and tried to remember that she could knock him upside his head later when he safe, right now she needed to focus.

"Not really the time, Searlington. Tell me what you see."

Kenneth ran off the details of his encounter and the current situation and she made strategic notes according to those details.

"Kenneth, listen to me very carefully, whatever you do, don't slow down, don't stop that car until you see the State Police, Nassau County Police, or NYPD."

He started to speak when Heart heard loud popping sounds coming through the phone filling the car. She looked at Weaver for confirmation of what she already knew.

"Kenneth?" she shouted receiving only the sound of squealing tires as a response.

"Searlington, fucking answer me. What the hell is going on?"

"Oh shit, they're shooting at me!" Except for the brief ripple in his tone, he kept his voice quiet and steady.

"Kenneth, just drive. Don't look back, just drive," she implored. "I'm on my way."

They were nearing Kenneth's position; she could see uniform squad cars in the rear lining the local streets running parallel to the highway. The road was mostly clear, whatever citizens remaining on the road pulled over to the side at the sight and sounds of the lights and sirens. Soon she could see the three SUVs in question. Three identical vehicles, each hogging a lane, moving fast. Too fast.

She could see Kenneth dodging from lane to lane trying to stay ahead of them, away from their line of fire. The wife in her wanted to scream and cover her eyes. If this went wrong she would never recover from watching him... No, she wouldn't even go there, no way was she giving in to her fear. She grabbed the bullhorn speaker and spoke clearly into the microphone.

"This is the police, drop your weapons and pull over."

She didn't have to wait long for a response. The SUV in the middle lane opened up its liftgate. She saw the muzzle of the gun first, reflex pulled her weapon from her hip and had it trained out her window.

"Pull back!" she yelled to Weaver leaning out of her window and fired shots at its rear tire. The tire gave a loud pop and the vehicle swerved to the side slamming the suspect into the wall of the cargo space, his gun falling out the back of the truck.

Weaver's skillful driving allowed them to out maneuver the vehicle as it spun and ended up on the shoulder slammed into an underpass wall. As soon as there was a break in the road, Weaver moved around the wreck while two of the following squad cars fell back and surrounded the disabled SUV.

"Kenneth, I need you to move. Floor the damn gas and put as much distance between you them as possible."

His response was the throaty sound of the car's engine cycling faster. She watched Kenneth pull away a head of them, providing a little more space. God she hoped it was enough to keep him out of harm's way. She looked over to Weaver, his face still focused on the road, both hands locked on the steering wheel.

"You got anything stronger than my snub-nose," she asked.

"Bag on the floor in the back."

She turned in her seat and reached for the long duffle. It was already open, within seconds her hand was touching the buttstock of a semi-automatic rifle. She pulled it out, checked that the magazine was full and returned her gaze to the driver.

She needed to finish this. When she took aim, the SUV in the right lane peeled off toward a closed off exit. She waved at the remaining squad car for them to follow the errant vehicle while she and Weaver kept chasing the lone vehicle that was trapped between her and the fleeing sports car in front of them.

She leaned out of the vehicle again the buttstock pressed against her shoulder, one hand tight on the pistol grip, the other on the hand-guard. The SUV driver must have anticipated what she was going to do because he began swerving back and forth between the lanes making it almost impossible for her to lock on to her target…almost. She let her eyes sway back and forth with the rhythm of the vehicle, and when her sights crossed over the tire, she gave the trigger a tight squeeze and the firearm came to life, spitting several bullets out with almost no pause between each ejection and within seconds the tire exploded and the vehicle veered out of control and into the concrete median separating one side of the highway from the other.

"Searlington!" Weaver yelled. She jumped back into her seat and braced herself for either a hard brake or impact. Squeezing the "oh shit" bar at the top of her window with her right hand and grabbing the center arm rest with her left, she closed her eyes and waited for whichever was their fate. Inertia pulled her forward in the car and then snapped her hard to the right as Weaver cut the wheel left and stopped the car. When she opened her eyes, they were horizontal across the middle and left lanes and had just enough time to duck down when the demolished SUV burst into flames.

Weaver got his door open and pulled her across the console and free of the car. They ran into brush on the shoulder hiding behind a tree while the SUV, its driver, and any possible evidence they could use to catch these killers exploded.

She reached for her phone, but found an empty pocket instead. Realizing it was probably still in the car somewhere, she borrowed Weaver's and dialed the number she knew as well as her own name.

"Hello," the voice was hesitant, filled with uncertainty, confirming her fear that he'd been close enough to see the explosion from his rearview.

"Are you all right?" she asked carefully.

There was a beat of silence and then a loud rush of air. "I was afraid…"

"I know…I was afraid of the same thing. Turn off at the next exit. There should be an officer waiting. Tell them who you are and they will bring you back to the seventy-fourth."

"Heart…"

"No need, Kenneth, we're fine, that's all that matters."

~

True Amare watched the SUV blow right past the parked squad car spilling out on to the local road.

"Looks like the party just came to us, Free." She smiled and braced herself as her older brother fell in line behind the fleeing blacked out SUV. Free followed the car making several tight turns around blind curves. The last curve the driver took too quickly and found himself spinning out on a dead-end block and crashing into a telephone pole.

True was falling instep behind the driver who crawled out through the busted windshield. She took him down low at the knees, but he was able to kick out from her grip. She grappled with him, each of them rolling around on the grimy wet concrete fighting for purchase. The assailant seeming to have a counter for every maneuver True employed.

Something felt odd about this. A tingle of remembrance shook her. Fighting styles were like fingerprints, no two people shared the same. The only problem was this particular fighting style belonged to a dead man. She tried to get a look at her opponent's face, but the darkness surrounding them kept his features blurred.

Damn Long Island for not having street lights. If this shit was Brooklyn I'd be able to see every freckle this motherfucker had.

They both sprinted to their feet and when she went to engage him again she heard the click of a firearm followed by her brother's voice.

"You can either make this easy on yourself or fun for me," Free offered. "Either way I go back to the crib and play a hand of spades like none of this shit ever happened."

The man fell to his knees and put his hands in the air. True pulled a set of zip ties from her pocket and bound the guy's hands behind him. When she was certain he was secured she pulled a small flashlight from her hidden utility belt and turned it on to get a first look at the man in front of her.

All it took was the flash of the emerald fire from his eyes for recognition to take place.

"Teague Maher?" she whispered her reality fighting against the memories of a twelve-yearold nightmare. "Apparently you're not as dead as I believed you to be when I buried you."

CHAPTER 20

*H*eart paced the length of her office. She'd returned to her precinct, written out her reports, triple checking them for accuracy before their submission. The truth was they'd said the same things as the first time she'd sat down to type them, but she was just trying to occupy herself to keep from storming the interrogation room where her husband was now giving his statement.

She wanted to push right in there as soon as she'd set foot inside of the precinct. But she couldn't, she couldn't take his statement, couldn't stand by him as he gave it, couldn't even stand outside of the two-way mirror and watch the interview take place. All for propriety's sake, she had to keep herself as separate from his interview and statement as possible.

Her phone rang and drew a smile from her. After the screen on her last phone had been smashed to pieces by her constant dropping of it, Kenneth insisted she put one of those armoredtank like covers that came with a screen cover, a hard plastic case that surrounded the phone, and a rubber case that surround the hard plastic case.

She'd told him it was bullshit, but had put one on the phone just to shut him up. Now after being dropped in a car during a high-speed chase, and practically stepped on as she quickly crawled out of the car, her phone sat safe and unmarred by any of the night's events. *I hate it when his ass is right.*

"What happened?"

"Nothing happened. We followed the car that barged through the exit. Dude couldn't drive for shit, hit a telephone pole."

"Survivors?"

"Not a one, driver was the only person in the car, he died on impact. We left the scraps for your boys to pick up. Free and I are headed back to Brooklyn."

"Thanks, True."

"Anytime, anyplace, Cousin."

As she ended the call, her door opened. Long dark waves lose and hanging free around his shoulders, Kenneth walked into her office. She met him in the middle of the room and literally climbed him once their bodies made contact. She held on to him, arms locked like vices around his neck intent to keep him tied to her for as long as she could.

With her legs tied around his waist, he walked them over to the couch and flopped down on the cushions with her on top of him.

"Baby, I'm all right," he comforted her with the soothing stroke of his hand up and down her back. "I promise, not a scratch on me."

"I just don't understand what this is about." Her words were rushed, as she tried to get everything out in one breath before the tremble of her voice ushered her tears. "Why are these people after you? What do they want? How would they have even known you were driving

A.J.'s car? It wasn't planned, she just..." *She. A.J.*

Heart pulled away from Kenneth as her mind began to click unknown variables into the equations.

"Is she still here?"

Kenneth watched her with wide eyes. "Who?"

"A.J., one of my officers told me she arrived shortly after they brought you in and was present during your interview. Is she still here?"

Kenneth nodded. She rushed to her desk and pounded numbers on the keypad until she had a voice on the phone.

"Bring the team and Ms. Tenetti in my office now."

A few seconds later a light tap brought her attention to the door and Heart stood in the middle of the room as her detectives, Agent Weaver, and A.J. Tenetti walked into the room.

"Grazo," she barked. "What do we know about this damn case so far?"

Her detective looked at her strangely; he'd just briefed her a little while ago after they'd questioned the two suspects they had in custody from the car chase. Ever the dutiful officers, he answered his superior's question without commentary on her prior briefing.

"We know that these guys work for Reign, an international warlord who is determined to take out the royal family of Azuria. We also have no idea where these people are other than the fact that they're in the U.S. hiding somewhere. We still have no idea how Searlington ended up on Reign's hit list. He doesn't have any known associates or business dealings with anyone or anything remotely relating to Reign. Yet Reign seems determined to get him." "Are we completely certain that Reign is after Kenneth?" she asked.

Everyone in the room allowed wary glances to pass between them.

"Captain, they took a shot at him, sent armed goons after him at the mall, and tonight they tried to run him off the road," Santini offered.

"Did they?" Heart queried.

"I don't follow," Grazo answered.

Heart walked over to where A.J. was now sitting in front of her desk. She sat down on the edge and crossed her legs at the ankles as she looked down at Kenneth's attorney. Her veneer was smooth, no signs of chipping except the brief pass of a shaky hand pushing her curls behind her ear.

"Kenneth wasn't the only person on that podium when he was shot. We know that the shooter took a shot; we've only been assuming that the shot was actually meant for Kenneth. We know that Reign sent two of his associates to the Valley Stream Mall to follow the group of us. We only assumed that Kenneth was the one they were after. We know they followed the car Kenneth was driving, but we only assume it was Kenneth they intended to kill.

"I have an alternate theory; I don't think they were after Kenneth at all." She slid her hands to her thighs and bent down so that she and A.J. were at eye level. "I think they were after you."

Amber eyes that had always held such confidence danced around avoiding Heart's gaze.

Heart wasn't just grasping at straws, there was something to this mess and A.J. was in the middle of it.

"Heart," Kenneth interrupted. "This has nothing to do with A.J."

Heart held up a hand to stop her husband from defending his attorney. "You think not Kenneth?" she asked without moving her gaze from the sitting woman. "She was standing right next to you on that podium when you were shot. The shooter could have been aiming for her but got you and Bryan instead. What about the mall incident? Those thugs didn't start following us until she showed up on the scene. Tonight you were driving her car. You said the SUV didn't start following you until after you left the parking lot of Mac's Place. With the tint on that car there's no way they knew it was you driving instead of her."

Heart heard Kenneth's familiar gait move him closer to her desk where she was bearing down on A.J. "You know they were after you. You've always known they were after you," Heart's voice climbed in volume and tone as she stood to her full height, towering over the sitting woman. "That's why you were so eager to be by Kenneth's side after the shooting. You knew whoever it was that took that shot had been aiming for you. You sat in my husband's hospital room looking all pitiful when you knew damn well it was because of you he was laying in the damn bed in the first place."

Heart felt her husband's restricting hand close around her upper arm as she moved closer to A.J., attempting to pull her back. "How the fuck can you call yourself a friend, a sister to this man when you knew all along who was after him and why and you said nothing to the authorities?"

"Heart," Kenneth screamed her name. "You're out of control. She doesn't know anything, leave her…'"

"Because if I talked, my family could die." Her words were whisper soft, almost impossible to hear in the now silent room.

The hand Kenneth had on her arm relaxed and slipped away as he stared down at his friend.

"How?" he croaked, licking his lips in an effort to moisten their suddenly dry skin. "How are the Tenettis involved, A.J.? Why would someone want to kill them?"

A.J. sat fixed to the chair with her shoulders back, straightening her spine. She was still in a way that only practiced repetition could teach you. She looked calm, unaffected…regal.

"Because her father and mother are the King and Queen of Azuria," Heart uttered as the final pieces to the puzzle all dropped into place. "Kenneth please meet your bestie, Her Royal

Highness, the Princess of Azuria."

~

*K*enneth stepped in front of the girl he'd known for most of his life. *No Kenneth, that's the problem, she isn't a girl any longer. She isn't the little kid that used to follow you and John around.*

"Is it true?" Kenneth questioned.

"God Captain, you couldn't wait to get some dirt on me, could you?"

Kenneth stood in front A.J. blocking her view of Heart, pulling A.J.'s full attention to him. "I asked you a question, Alexis-Jeovonni. Is it true? Are you and your family the royal family of

Azuria? Did you knowingly place my family and friends in danger?"

A myriad of emotions fell down the length of her face. First there was hurt, then defiance, but by the time she opened her mouth there was remorse.

"It's not as calculated as it seems. No, I didn't knowingly put you in danger. When you were shot I really did think it had something to do with the center you were building. But then at the Nassau County Police Department I saw the case file of the man Heart shot. I recognized his

Forza di Liberazione tattoo on his wrist from the crime scene photos."

"So why not say something then?" Heart asked.

The door to the now cramped office opened again and a redheaded man with a tapered haircut walked in. He was a Fed; even Kenneth's civilian eye could tell that. You'd really have to be blind not to see it. The cocksure strut, black tailored suit, and the dark shades indoors were like a waving flag to the federal badge that had to be somewhere on his person. Either that or he was working hard at winning best Men in Black costume ever.

"May I see your invitation to the party?" Heart asked confirming Kenneth's assumption that the ginger was a secret-agent man.

"I'm his boss," the man responded as he pointed to Agent Weaver. He pulled out his badge and presented it to Heart. "S.A.C. Teague Maher."

"Son of a bitch," Heart raged. "Weaver your ass was never here to help me, were you?"

"SSA Weaver had a job to do, that's all you need to know, Captain," Maher's voice dripped with condescension and apparently that didn't go over too well with Heart because she stepped in front of the Agent with her hands on her hips looking as if she were very close to shooting someone.

"If you knew like I did," she replied smoothly. "You would speak with a little more respect when standing in my office talking to me in front of my people. We clear, Special Agent in Charge?"

Kenneth watched the Agent's glasses slide down to the tip of his nose. If Kenneth wasn't so pissed with A.J. he might have laughed at the way the man's eyes dropped just a little making Heart the winner of the let's-see-who-flinches-first game they were playing.

"I'm not here to antagonize you, Captain; my only concern is keeping the Tenetti family safe."

The Agent removed his shades and placed them securely inside his jacket pocket before turning to Kenneth. "And she didn't purposely place you in danger. She's under a federal gag order. If A.J. or any other member of the Tenetti family talks about this, the U.S. government will pull back their support and protection from that homicidal maniac Reign."

All eyes in the room remained on Agent Maher. It was obvious that he was the most knowledgeable person regarding the entire convoluted mess.

"What's your involvement in this Maher?" Heart asked.

"We've had eyes on Reign's movements for a while now. In fact, I was actually able to get inside his operation," Maher replied.

Heart tilted her head and watched the agent closely, as if he were a page she was carefully reading. Kenneth didn't know what this Agent's deal was, but by the way Heart was studying him, Kenneth knew there wouldn't be much left uncovered about man.

"You were there tonight, during this damn car chase, you were there? You watched those bastards chase my fucking husband and you didn't intervene?"

Maher held up defensive hands. "It was a federal operation; we were under no obligation to inform the locals about anything. Not to mention, me intervening would have blown my cover. Trust me, it was safer for your husband to have me in one of those SUVs while he was being chased, than for Reign's men to make me and kill us both."

Kenneth didn't know how he saw it coming, but he anticipated the punch that would have certainly landed the cocky agent on his ass. He jumped in front of Heart and intercepted the punch before she could make contact with Agent Maher's face.

The agent took a small step back after realizing how close he'd come to being coldcocked in the middle of this crowded room.

Heart took a moment to control herself, if the ticking muscles in her jaw were any indication, Kenneth knew it was a herculean effort.

"What do you know about Reign?" she asked through gritted teeth.

"The only thing we've always known, he wants the Tenetti family dead and he'll stop at nothing to make that a reality. As far as we know he's still in Azuria, but as you can tell, his reach extends all the way over here in Brooklyn. Our only concern right now is protecting the royal family and ending this sadistic monster anyway we can."

"How do you plan to do that?" Heart asked.

"Any way we can," Maher replied. Kenneth stood beside his wife as he watched the exchange between the two branches of law enforcement. He watched the emerald fire crackle in the man's green eyes. Reign might be in the wind right now, but if Maher's disposition was any indication, that certainly wouldn't last for long.

"So what happens now?" Kenneth inquired.

"It's our case, Mr. Searlington, it always has been. The FBI will continue to pursue Reign's capture. We are thankful for any and all assistance the NYPD has been able to provide, but now we've got a job to do."

Agent Maher gave his head a brief tilt toward the door and Agent Weaver fell in step behind him. When he reached the door, he turned slightly back toward the room.

"I know you might not agree with our tactics, Mr. Searlington," Agent Maher stated. "I'm sure your perspective on this situation is in line with your wife's. However, it really wasn't our intention to place you in any more danger than necessary, but as I said before, we have a job to do. No hard feelings."

With no more than a crooked smile, the man was gone and his trained lackey, Weaver was following faithfully behind him. This was a crazy fucking mess that Kenneth had found himself in the middle of. His head hurt just thinking about all the entangled details of this current clusterfuck that seemed to be his life. Kenneth pressed pointed fingers to his temple trying to stem the pain that was growing behind his eyes. How the fuck did he end up here? He was standing in a room full of people that were all watching his humiliation and the only thought he could hold on to was that his wife had always known.

Heart might not have known the details, but she'd known from day one that something was off with the Tenetti family. His stomach twisted in on itself and he had to fight to keep the bile down.

"I'm sorry, Kenneth," A.J. whispered pulling his focus away from his churning stomach. "I didn't have a choice."

The hurt in his head somehow morphed into blinding anger, clouding his vision, making it almost impossible for him to see the woman sitting before him as the adored friend she'd always been.

"I'm so sick of the people that I love telling me that they had no other choice but to lie to me. The truth is that you sacrificed my family for yours, A.J., and I can't accept that. And I damn sure can't accept the lame ass excuse that you didn't have a choice, because there's always a choice. You had a choice and you chose wrong."

Kenneth settled the heartbreak sitting in his chest and buried it deep inside him. It wasn't the first time he'd been hurt by someone he loved, but for damn sure it would be the last. He wasn't doing this bullshit anymore.

"I'll be waiting for you in my truck," he stated plainly to Heart. "All this bullshit polluting the air is fucking with my allergies."

CHAPTER 21

*H*eart dropped her car keys on the corner table and stood aside so Kenneth could enter the house behind her.

"Kenneth."

He didn't respond, his long legs strode up the stairs disappearing onto the second floor landing.

"Shit, A.J." That entire blow up at the precinct still had her cringing. She couldn't tell which was worse, being in an almost lethal car chase or dealing with the disappointment festering inside her husband.

Why couldn't it have been anyone else besides this chick and her family? Kenneth held these fucking people on a pedestal that even Jesus wouldn't be able to sit on. He'd gone on and on over the years about how caring and trustworthy the Tenetti family was.

Growing up with Porter as a godfather had taught Kenneth to appreciate his wealth, but to still value people. That simple lesson molded Kenneth into the man she loved. But being around the Tenetti family had given him a model of how to be a rich person who wasn't a douche. He gave to important charities, not the bullshit ones that never placed the money where it was supposed to be, but organizations that were really trying to do some good in the world.

What it must feel like to have all your allusions stripped away when it came to people you idolized.

Heart didn't have to wonder what that felt like, it wasn't too long ago that her family had completely decimated her when the truth of her past was revealed. Her father hadn't tried to kill her, but her uncle and her grandmother had all but perpetuated that lie to keep her in her grandmother's care.

Heart had survived a gunshot wound and childbirth and neither had been as painful as learning the people you loved and trusted with your heart had lied to you.

She tracked up the stairs and found him in their closet pulling on gym shorts. A brief flash of the toned musculature of his ass distracted her for just a brief moment from her task. She shook her head, and forced herself to focus on something other than the fact that she wanted to leave teeth marks there, branding his pale skin.

"Kenneth—"

"Where's the baby?" he asked preempting the conversation he knew she wanted to have.

This was so difficult for her. Seeing him like this, body all tight with tension, cold, uninviting, none of this was him, not the *him* that she knew and loved. This was her, this was how she handled bad shit, this was how she avoided the painful shit in her life. This wasn't him and she wasn't going to let it become him—not permanently anyway.

"He's staying the night with your godparents. Porter took him when the call came in about the car chase."

He remained silent, didn't even look at her as he walked past her. She found herself leaning against the doorway as she listened to him make quick work of the stairs, then a few moments later she heard him opening the door their basement.

"All right, Mr. Searlington, if that's the way you want to play, then let's play."

She removed her weapon and secured it in her gun safe and then rested her utility belt against the top of her vanity. She pulled her clothes off, quickly dressing in a two piece exercise suit. The shorts hugged the deep curve of her hips and stopped just at mid-thigh level. The top was pretty much a sports bra that held her girls in place and left the flat expanse of her toned abdomen exposed.

After tying the laces of her cross trainers, she picked up her utility belt and pulled out the last item she needed.

When she made it to the basement he was hitting the punching bag hard, his skin already glistening with the sheen of perspiration.

"Wanna take on a real partner instead of that bag?" she asked as she watched his form with the bag. These few weeks under Hunter's tutelage had definitely improved his skill. His punches were more direct and precise, muscles tightening all over his shirtless body as he moved quickly on the balls of his feet, bobbing and weaving against his stationary partner.

God he was sexy. In a few more years he'd be forty and the closer he came to that milestone the sexier his body became. Tight, cut, strong, just the thought of letting her hands slide down all that delectable skin made her clit throb.

Not why you're down her, MacKenzie. You're supposed to be helping your husband.

"Heart, I don't feel comfortable sparring with you right now. My head is not in a good place.

I don't want to hurt you."

She crossed her arms and cocked her head. "So because Hunter has taught you a few selfdefense moves you think you can take me?"

He didn't respond, just took off his gloves and headed to the resistance training area. He added plates to each side of the bar. Once he secured them and adjusted his weightlifting gloves—because God forbid he developed a callus on those pretty hands—he tested the grip and went to work.

Damn, Hunter really was working his ass; I know he wasn't lifting that much weight before.

She walked over to the head of the bench unwilling to distract him while he was in the middle of a set. She wanted his attention, but she wasn't trying to kill him to get it—especially after all the hell she'd had to go through to keep him alive tonight.

When his first set was finished and he dropped the weight into its cradle, she straddled him and locked her hands around his.

"Heart, I'm not in the mood. Get up."

"Not until you talk to me," she added.

He went to grab her hips, presumably to move her off of him, but she didn't give him the chance. One metal bracelet of her handcuffs was around his wrist before one of his hands touched her.

She went to restrain the other hand, but he resisted—really resisted.

Shit, this isn't as easy as it was before.

Giving up on getting the other hand under control she snapped the remaining cuff around a leg of the bench that was bolted into the floor.

"Heart, stop playing and let me go now!"

She looked down into the electric blue of his eyes and placed a flat palm on his chest.

"Baby, talk to me. This isn't you, Kenneth; this isn't how you deal with things."

"And exactly how do I handle things, Heart?"

"Directly. I'm the one that avoids emotional bullshit. I'm good at it, and I vote that I keep that position. It doesn't work so well on you."

He closed his eyes and laid his head against the bench. The tightening jaw and heaving chest depicted the very real battle going on in his head. This wasn't right, him suffering like this, struggling to find his center when his world seemed to be blowing up one trusted confidant at a time.

Heart used to wonder if Kenneth had married her out of obligation if he had loved her only because he felt sorry for her. Watching him suffer through this moment she understood that pity could never have entered into the equation for him. She didn't pity him; she hurt for him, as if it were her heart that was being sliced open.

How had he endured her pain for so long without collapsing under its weight? How had he carried her through every single trial and tribulation she experienced, and still managed to drag them both out of the mire with their relationship intact?

She just hurt witnessing his struggle, and that shit had to stop now. If Heart didn't know how to do anything else it was to protect. She was born to do it, and she would provide her man with the safety he needed to get through this mess that was threatening to overpower him.

"Look at me, Kenneth," he refused. Apparently this helping shit wasn't as easy as he'd made it look all these years. Fuck if she was giving up on it though. "All right, you don't want to look at me, then don't. 'Who don't hear will feel,' that's what Ida-Mae used to always tell me. Since you won't listen, I guess you are going to feel today."

She leaned down letting her tongue swipe against his bare nipple and felt a shiver move down the length of him. She leaned down again and gave the same treatment to its partner and added a gentle press of teeth to elicit a moan.

Gotcha.

She felt the length of cock stiffen under her ass and rolled her hips back onto it making him tremble. He might not want to talk to her, but his body was screaming at her, begging for more.

She lifted up a little and freed him of his gym shorts and jock strap in one motion. She sat across his thighs and wrapped warm fingers around his dick, stroking the length in a strong but unhurried manner.

"Kenneth, I know you're mad. I also know you're not blowing up like this just over A.J. I know Jussy, Bryan, the Amares, and me; we're all in that same category as A.J. and her family. We kept things from you that we shouldn't have, all because we were trying to protect the people

we love…"

She continued to stroke him; his hips were rolling to the slow, torturous rhythm she was creating.

He was the picture of masculine beauty. Hard lines creating sharp angles of definition and strength that made her just want to melt against him. Trying to stay focused on the task was testing the limits of her endurance.

"...people we love more than you, right?"

His eyes snapped open, and for the first time since this little dance began he finally let her see his truth.

"This isn't about us keeping things from you, Kenneth. This is about you feeling like we chose them over you because we loved them more than you."

She leaned her torso down again and let her lips cover his. Gently at first, with very little pressure, meant to comfort and console. That's what he needed, consolation, someone to show him that they were thinking of him, that they understood, validating the hurt he'd been harboring all this time. The kiss grew into something more than its original intent. She pressed her mouth harder against his, her teeth nipping at the fullness of his bottom lip, her tongue tasting him.

"It wasn't a matter of loving Justice and Bryan more, Kenneth. With the exception of Amare, there is no human being on this planet that holds my heart hostage the way you do. You are it for me, there is no other, there is nothing better than you. Never doubt that."

His free hand licked up and pulled her mouth back down to his in a punishing kiss. His tongue dueling with hers, teeth clashing, he moved his body under hers, trying to connect flesh with flesh, but meeting the stretchy material of her gym clothes.

"Take these off," he growled between clenched teeth.

"My clothes or the cuffs," she answered.

"Both."

She stood up and stepped out of her shorts. She dipped her pinched thumb and pointer finger in between the cleft of her tits and removed the keys to her cuffs then pulled the sports bra over her head and let it hit the floor.

She straddled him again placing the key in the lock. As soon as the metal click filled the room he snatched his hand free and held the heat of her sex firmly over his cock. He sat up, and the next thing she knew they were moving to the other side of the gym with her legs still locked around his waist.

He placed her on her feet in front of the wooden stretching table and grabbed a handful of her ass, his grip tight, bordering just shy of painful.

It wouldn't have mattered if it did hurt, after nearly five years of marriage to him she learned a little pain mixed in with her pleasure suited her just fine.

He turned her around, pressed her hard and quick against the cool wood and lifted her bent leg onto the table. Without warning or preamble he was pressing into her, filling her. The way he stretched her, the glorious burn of her skin as he forced the walls of her pussy to mold to his cock made an achy moan spill from her lips.

He kept one hand on her elevated leg and the other on her shoulder and thrust hard and dirty into her, riding her. There was no finesse to this, he simply slammed into her over and over pummeling her, raking over that soft knot of nerves ever so perfectly.

She was so open in this position, at his mercy. Her body trying to run from and to him at the same time, the assault almost too much for her senses to bear.

"Touch yourself." His words were chopped by his swift and powerful movement.

She snaked a hand under her stomach and kept sliding lower until her fingers were pressed against her throbbing clit. She shivered, her body racked with tremors, the tentative touch almost too much for the sensitive flesh.

She heard a loud smack and felt the burn of his large hand coming down on her ass cheek. Her pussy tightened in response, starting that familiar clenching motion that signaled the nearness of her release.

"Won't say it again, touch yourself," he barked.

She shoved her hands between the hot folds of flesh, wet and slippery with her juices and his. The pointer, middle, and ring fingers of her hand applying the perfect amount of pressure at the exact speed his rhythm demanded and her body exploded into seizure like spasms as he rode her through the crest of her orgasm. Riding her until it ebbed and she was a whimpering, quivering mess beneath him.

Just as the last shiver of her release passed through her, he drove into her one last time, his balls slapping hard and heavy against sensitive flesh. His howl rent the air and she felt the first spurt of his come splashing inside her.

He collapsed against her back, his tight grip on her leg falling allowing both of her feet to meet the floor. He stayed there, his weight pressing her against the table. When his breathing returned to normal he stood up, took her hand, and guided her down to the cushioned floor where he wrapped his body around hers, placing gentle kisses on her face.

When he finally looked at her again, she could see much of the murky storm disappearing. There were still a few clouds remaining, but the natural brightness of his blue eyes were breaking through the haze.

"I didn't do this because I valued anyone over you, Kenneth. I was just trying to keep my family safe. Can you understand?"

He kissed her again, the smoldering embers of his passion still present, still sending fire through to the core of her. When he pulled back from the kiss her ran a thumb over her lips and bathed her in his cool gaze.

"Yes, I understand it."

"Can you forgive me for it?"

"Yes, I already have," he answered.

"Then can't you find it in your heart to find the same understanding and forgiveness for A.J.

and her family? She was just trying to keep her family safe, Kenneth, that's all. I know you can see that."

Kenneth looked down at her; his love for her was evident. It surrounded her in warmth and cloaked her in security. So many years had passed, so many years she'd spent doubting the healing power of love until she'd met this man. He'd walked into her life unapologetically and demanded her heart. She'd fought him, and damn near pushed him away at every turn, but he'd still demanded her love like it was owed to him, like it belonged to him.

It had taken her a very long time, but she'd finally come to the conclusion that her love did belong to him, that she belonged to him. It had taken her even longer to understand that he belonged to her, that she had a right to demand his love, no matter how unworthy her past told her she was. He was hers and she would never let either of them forget it.

"When did I get to the point in my life when a hard fuck could change my mind about shit?" She burrowed into his arms, feeling the closeness between them repair itself stitch by stitch.

"Does that mean you're going to at least talk to A.J., give her a chance, and listen to her without anger and judgment?"

"Never thought I'd see the day that you'd be A.J. Tenetti's champion," he answered.

"True, neither did I," she chuckled. "And I promise if you ever tell her that shit, I will cut you off indefinitely."

Kenneth let out a loud bark of laughter. "That sweet mouth of yours tells lies," he snickered.

"We both know I'm not the only one that would miss…" he took a brief moment to look down at their naked bodies pressed together before his eyes returned to hers. "…this."

The truth was the truth, she wasn't about to punish herself by cutting off her supply of sweet meat. Pride be damned, there wasn't anything worth the way he made her body sing.

"The truth is Willie told me A.J. and I were a lot alike and I didn't want to see. You know I can't stand her ass, believing we could be anything alike just wasn't happening. But this recent situation just helped me to see how much alike she and I are in several different ways. We both are used to running shit, we both need to be told to relax our crazy asses sometimes, but most of all, we both would do anything to protect the people we love."

She snaked feather-like fingertips over the expanse of his smooth chest. "For that alone, I've got to respect her," she added. "I don't condone her not being straight forward with you, with us, Kenneth. I just feel like if you've given me chance after chance at redemption considering my long list of fuckups, then maybe...maybe she deserves a second chance too."

EPILOGUE

*H*eart watched Reverend Lawrence as he cradled her son in his arms. She felt strong hands squeeze her shoulders and a smiled curved her lips. It was a natural reaction to having her husband near. Kenneth calmed every worry her brain could conjure up, and right now, standing in front of this congregation, introducing her boy to God and the world, she couldn't help but worry—just a little.

The world was huge and vast and she knew first hand that it wasn't very kind. There would be people in the world who would hate him without even knowing him for something as trivial as the color of his skin.

As long as he belonged to just her and Kenneth, he would always be protected, but introducing him to the world was akin to inviting all the horrible things that life could throw at him.

Was her fear irrational, absolutely, she wasn't the slightest bit ashamed of that. She'd come to understand a long time ago that love made her crazy and that she wasn't above stomping someone into the ground to keep the ones she loved safe.

"Would the godparents come forward please?" Reverend Lawrence requested. Heart could see subtle movements in the crowd as the designated individuals rose and made their way down the aisle hand in hand.

Delight and gratitude filled her as she watched her second-in-command walk to the pulpit under his own power. He'd spent months in rehab working toward this goal, to be able to walk without the assistance of a cane and to hold his new godson strong and proud. He'd proven that sheer will was enough to make your own circumstance, your own truth. In a few weeks he would be back on the job with her, helping her keep her city clean.

Just as Bryan took hold of the baby, he stepped aside for the second godparent. The petite woman winked an eye at Heart tugging at the one good nerve that tolerated her.

"You know she only messes with you because she loves you," Kenneth whispered in her ear, and when she still held the slightest bit of tension in her shoulders he added, "We're in church,

Heart, don't show your ass."

Heart heeded her husband's warning and smiled at A.J. through gritted teeth as the minister continued with the ceremony.

By the time the ceremony and service were over, Heart's jaw ached from smiling. If she never did this mess again, it would be too soon.

1. small reception was held at their home in Woodmere for family and close friends and pretty soon the little guy that everyone was making a fuss over was tired and cranky, begging for an afternoon nap.

She'd just closed the door when Heart found A.J. standing in front of her.

"You need something?" Heart questioned.

A.J. shook her head and raised soft eyes to her.

"No, I wanted to catch you for...I just wanted to thank you," she stammered.

"For?" Heart replied.

"For helping me mend things with Kenneth and getting him to give me and my family another chance. I know things still aren't perfect between us, but he's willing to let me earn his trust again. That means a great deal."

"All I did was tell Kenneth the truth, you were trying to protect your family." Heart made to walk away when A.J. held up a hand to stop her.

"I'm curious though, why did you agree to me being Amare's godmother if you had the out you needed to get rid of me for good?"

It was true; Kenneth had stricken her name from a very short list of candidates. Convincing him to rethink his decision hadn't been easy either. It had been fun as hell, sex with her husband was always fun, even when she was using it to coerce him to give in to her demands, but it certainly hadn't been easy.

Heart's lips curved into a wicked smile when she recalled exactly how she'd used her persuasive powers to aid in A.J.'s selection.

"God I don't even want to know what that damn smile was for. My damn eyeballs feel like they need a bleach bath."

"I'm sure whatever it is that has me smiling is no different than some of the things you do with my husband's vice president."

1. J.'s jaw dropped and if Heart had her phone or a camera on her, she would have snapped that picture in a heartbeat.

"I'm a detective, A.J.," Heart bragged. "If anyone was going to figure this out, you should've known it was going to be me."

A.J. opened her mouth to explain, but Heart stopped her. "I don't need to know the details, just be careful with Alan. He's a special one, and he's had a lot of shit to deal with over the years. If you're just playing with him...just don't fuck him over."

"What makes you think I would, Captain?"

"Because you're as afraid of love as I was when I met Kenneth. My fear caused him a great deal of hurt and anguish. Take a page out of my book, if it's real, and you know it's real, don't push him away."

Heart placed her foot on the first step when she heard A.J. call her name again.

"You never did answer my question about why you chose me as Amare's godmother."

Heart smiled, genuinely this time. "Before I answer, answer this question for me. Why did you want to be his godmother so badly?"

A.J.'s eyes fell to the carpet as she appeared to be collecting herself. "I wasn't around a lot when my brother's daughters were born," she murmured. "I was working a lot, set on taking over the world. Then one day I woke up with no love of my own, no family of my own, and no prospects to have any of those things. The night before you and Kenneth announced Amare's conception, I asked God that if he wasn't going to give me a child of my own, to at least give me one I could love and raise as my own from day one. The next day you guys announced you were expecting and I figured God had answered my prayer."

Heart would never have thought A.J. capable of that much emotion. Her husband had been correct in his assessment that A.J. was a great deal deeper than she appeared on the surface.

"You want to know why I selected you?" Heart asked. "That's easy. You proved to me that you'd be willing to sacrifice all for those you love. That's the kind of devotion I need surrounding my son."

Heart left A.J. on the landing and went in search of her husband. After being stopped by every third person on her way to the backyard, she finally found her husband standing at the foot of their deck, looking at the tent that shielded their guests from the mild sun in the sky.

She placed her arms around his neck from behind and snuggled there; inhaling his special mix of spice and man that she loved so much.

"What'cha doing standing here just looking into the tent?" she asked.

He linked his fingers with hers and placed a gentle kiss on the backs of both her hands.

"I'm standing here thinking that this is where it all began, where we started."

She gave him a quizzical squint of her eye, not certain where he was going with his train of thought.

"As far as I remember we met in my office at the seventy-fourth," she replied lowering her voice as her eyes found Kenneth's nearly eleven-year-old niece playing under the tent with her new baby sister. "I was interviewing you about Merri's abduction."

Heart continued to watch the girl. She was happy, laughing loudly, enjoying the festivities and the people. Looking at her, no one would ever guess the trauma she'd experienced at such a young age. That child was living proof that love really did heal all wounds.

"That was the first time we met, and believe me when I say I wanted you then. But life for me didn't really begin until you stepped off the deck and you walked into a tent very much like this one and married me."

He kissed her hand again and pressed it to his cheek as if he were savoring the feel of her touch. "When I came to you, I'd lost everything, Heart. My sister died in my arms, my mother had set a terrible plan in motion that eventually decimated the remaining members of the

Searlington family. With the exception of my godparents, I was alone."

"Speaking of Jacqueline how is she?"

"Fine," he answered. "She sent me a letter asking if I would visit again. I haven't decided if

I'm going yet."

Since that first visit a few months ago, Kenneth periodically checked in on his mother. As far as Heart knew he hadn't physically returned to the prison to visit her, but Heart's law enforcement connections kept him apprised of her disposition on the inside.

She thought back to the beginning of their relationship, her own familial revelations, the emotional hurdles she'd been forced to climb at the beginning of their journey together.

"I was just as alone as you were. The only difference was I had so much fear inside me I thought I was going to choke on it. My heart was breaking and I didn't even know it until you barged into my life and protected my heart, from my fears, from my family, hell...even from me."

He turned in her arms and pressed his lips to hers. No matter how long they were together she would never tire of the taste of him, the feel of his skin against hers.

"Who would have thought a case my captain had to force me to take would lead to the happiest moments of my life? I love you Kenneth Searlington and no one will ever change that." A wide grin lifted his cheeks and laughter filled those perfect lapis flecks dancing in eyes.

"You know you say the corniest shit, Captain?"

"Yeah, I do," she chortled. "But you still love me any way." "Indeed I do, Captain Searlington, indeed I do."

The End

ABOUT THE AUTHOR

LaQuette is an erotic, multicultural romance author of M/F and M/M love stories. Her writing style brings intellect to the drama. She often crafts emotionally epic, fantastical tales that are deeply pigmented by reality's paintbrush. Her novels are filled with a unique mixture of savvy, sarcastic, brazen, and unapologetically sexy characters who are confident in their right to appear on the page.

This bestselling Erotic Romance Author is the 2016 Author of the Year Golden Apple Award Winner, 2016 Write Touch Award Winner for Best Contemporary Mid-length Novel, 2016 Swirl Awards 1st Place Winner in Romantic Suspense, and 2016 Aspen Gold Award Finalist in Erotic Romance. LaQuette—a native of Brooklyn, New York—spends her time catering to her three distinct personalities: Wife, Mother, and Educator.

Writing—her escape from everyday madness—has always been a friend and source of comfort. At the age of sixteen she read her first romance novel and realized the genre was missing something: people that looked and lived like her. As a result, her characters and settings are always designed to provide positive representations of people of color and various marginalized communities.

She loves hearing from readers and discussing the crazy characters that are running around in her head causing so much trouble. Contact her on:

Website: LaQuette.com
Email: LaQuette@LaQuette.com
Amazon: www.amazon.com/author/laquette
Facebook: www.facebook.com/LaQuetteTheAuthor
Twitter: twitter.com/LaQuetteWrites
Instagram: instagram.com/la_quette

OTHER TITLES

Wicked Wager: Texas vs. Brooklyn 1
Bedding The Enemy
Lies You Tell
Heart of the Matter: Queens of Kings: Book 1
Divided Heart: Queens of Kings: Book 2
Protected Heart: Queens of Kings Book 3
Power Privilege & Pleasure: Queens of Kings: Book 4
His True Strength: Queens of Kings: Book 5
My Beginning: Trinity Series: Book 1
Love's Changes

NEWSLETTER

Hello,

If you're interested in staying current with all the happenings with my writing, previews, and giveaways, sign up for my monthly newsletter at www.LaQuette.com.

Keep it sexy,
LaQuette 💋

COMING SOON...

LOADED LONGSHOT

Texas vs. Brooklyn 2

Kandi Adkins, the executive manager of Sweet Sadie's Cosmetics, has her roots planted firmly in Brownsville, Brooklyn. Kandi knows what it's like to have nothing. Education and her friend's late mother, Sadie King, pulled her out of the mire of poverty and enabled her to grab hold to personal and professional security.

Life has taught Aaron Nakai to play his cards close to the vest. Reaching for more than you need only invites trouble into your life. That's what happened to his father, a man who died young attempting to make his mark on the world. He finds comfort and security living in his adoptive brother, Slade's, shadow. Aaron refuses to allow lofty dreams to rob him of the gains he made in life. Being Slade's lawyer and right-hand man suits him just fine.

When Slade needs Aaron to step out of the background and take care of an unexpected problem in New York, Aaron's quiet existence back in Texas is blown to bits by a quick-witted, sassy-mouthed fireball named Kandi. Their attraction is just as palpable as their distaste for one another, making the decision to wager their hearts and their careers a high-stakes game with potentially disastrous outcomes.

Will they fold? Or will they reach for a loaded longshot to win it all?

COMING SOON.

SEDUCTIVE STAKES

Texas vs. Brooklyn 3

Azure Carlisle is simply tired. She's tired of always struggling to do the right thing only to have life slap her down time and time again. She climbed her way out of the projects of Brooklyn by getting an education. Her Ph.D. in Chemistry was her ticket out of the 'hood, but the lingering student loans from both her undergraduate and graduate degrees crush any dreams of personal advancement.

When the financial juggling game she plays every month begins to topple, Azure stumbles upon a way out. With an offer to clear her debts in hand, Azure is nearly burden free. The only thing she must do to escape financial ruin is simple: betray the trust of the woman who offered her a job, and friendship.

Damien Mesías is the former CEO of Logan Industries. He's spent his life paying for the sin of his father's illegitimacy. When your dad is the result of a salacious affair between the respectably married tycoon and his maid, you're not as welcome to the family gatherings as your legitimate cousins.

Determined to prove his worth, and exact his revenge against the remaining Logan heir, his cousin, Slade Hamilton, Damien embarked on a dangerous path that nearly ruined him and the family business. Destroyed, divorced, and wallowing in a pit of despair, Damien aches for peace and forgiveness. But, with so much to atone for, those two things are elusive goals Damien isn't quite sure he can attain.

When an opportunity to get into Slade's good graces appears, Damien rushes to Brooklyn and finds his job is more complicated than he believed. One, the thief is a friend of the family, and two, she's the sexiest thing Damien has seen in a long time. Torn between his desire to do the right thing, and his need to have Azure, Damien is forced to make a decision that could destroy them all.

Will Damien ruin friendships, and Azure's life, by exposing her? Will Azure sell-out the people who have supported her to gain financial freedom? Or, will Damien's wild card play present seductive stakes that neither of them can walk away from?